REAR ENTRANCE

David Barun Kumar Thomas was born in Assam to Tamil parents. He completed his B.Tech. in Mechanical Engineering from IIT Kanpur in 1977, then switched tracks and studied for a Masters in History at JNU, which he did not complete. He started working in 1980, and worked in several roles, mainly in the IT Industry. He spent his last ten corporate years with IBM in India and Belgium. In 2003, he moved to Kodaikanal and started an NGO which works towards women's development in the villages in the Palani Hills. He lives in Kodaikanal. This is his first novel.

REAR ENTRANCE

David Barun Kumar Thomas

First published in 2010 by Hachette India
An Hachette UK company

SRD

ISBN 978-93-5009-055-8

Hachette India
612/614 (6th Floor), Time Tower,
MG Road, Sector 28, Gurgaon-122001, India

Typeset in Georgia 9/10.8

Printed and bound in India by
Manipal Technologies Limited, Manipal

For my mother, Esther Padmini Thomas

God, it was just lunch.

Easy – what a stupid word to use. As morally stupid as Appa's 'decent'. Every day it was 'Behave decently', 'He is a decent person', 'Have some decency.' Eesh.

I'm bad at on-the-spot decision making. One should only be asked out via email. That gives one time to consider and reply. Next time Luc asks me out I am definitely going to accept. Or can I be bold and ask him out this Friday?

Snap out of this childish reverie, Seetha, girl! Start thinking about the visa application. And what to wear today. Has to be a sari. Which sari? I have just two here and both are silk. The violet Banaras silk will be better than the red Kanjeevaram. The Kanjeevaram has too much gold zari and would attract attention even in Chennai. Does it have to be a sari? Yes. Will tell the visa officer that I am a timid Indian, reluctant to change in any way, one who would never dream of immigrating to the West. Downside is, on the way to the embassy I'm going to stand out like a peacock in the crowd of dull winter shades of black and brown on this grey winter morning. Everybody will look with slightly raised eyebrows at 'that Indian girl in a bright sari'. God, I hate standing out. I'm going to wear my long, black overcoat on top of my sari. That way very little of my sari will be seen on the way to the embassy.

I hate the way they make you feel uncomfortable. They can be patronizing with just a raised eyebrow, a pursed lip or a blank look. You're imagining things. They are not patronizing. It's just that they are clear about their place in the world. They don't have existential doubts – at least they didn't. Now maybe they are beginning to. We, though, have been unsure of ourselves for the last one thousand years. Ever since Ghazni – or was it Ghori?

They are just shooting an interested, quick glance at someone different. Don't we stare at whites in India? But the way we stare is different. It is an open-mouthed, wide-eyed, deferential stare. We don't raise eyebrows, purse lips or put on a blank, erasing look when we see a white. Deep down inside we still think they are superior – somehow better put together by God or the Devil or Darwin. Better looking too, we think. Pathetic.

Look at me today. Thinking of what they will think while

deciding what to wear. I'm sure none of them ever spends time agonizing about what the Moroccans, the Senegalese and the Congolese clogging the sidewalks of the Chausee d'Ixelles will think of their choice of clothes. Even when they come to India – our country – the white karma-dharma tourists don't care what we think of their garish glass beads and ill-fitting sweat pants slung low over visible, dirty G-strings. Eesh. It's we who are trying to do the right thing all the time.

Serves you right. Should have stayed in India. Who asked you to come here – and who is now asking you to wheedle a work permit and visa out of the British to stay even longer in the West?

Anyway, up. Time to rise and shine.

Seetha swung out of bed, wrapped a thick woollen housecoat over her pyjamas and began getting ready for the day ahead.

She struggled to tie her sari, standing in the confined space between the bed and the wall. Her flat was small – tiny actually. Her room had a bed, a small sofa, a kitchen counter along one wall and a combination work and dining table built into another wall. Sitting in her bed, which was almost in the middle of the room, she could reach out and touch all the four walls of the room. The real estate agent who'd showed her the flat had described it as 'very cosy.'

Walking briskly along Avenue Louise, Seetha rehearsed her lines. She was a software professional. She had come to Belgium on a six-month business trip. Now, towards the end of this assignment, she wanted to return to her first love – writing. She had written earlier – a taut little thriller with a supernatural twist – and had been published, even if it was only in a short story anthology but there was no need to mention all that. Now she was starting on her first novel, a novel whose 16th-century subject spanned two continents. Needed to work in England – at the British museum – to refer to books and documents on 16th-century England. A period philosophical novel needed to be grounded in fact and she could not possibly write authentically about the 16th century English court sitting far away in steamy Madras. No, she was not planning to look for a software development job in the UK. She might look for a part-time job to meet her living expenses and her publisher may be paying her an advance.

No, she had no intention of overstaying her visa. No, she did not have any immediate family in the UK. Yes, an open work permit and work visa were what she was looking for.

As she walked, she kept an eye on the street signs. She had to find Rue de la Concorde. She was wary of the bizarre language rules in Brussels which insisted that all street signs needed to be in French and Flemish. The names in the two languages were never the same, always being translations, never transliterations. She took out and consulted a large street map of Brussels even though she knew it made her 'the Indian tourist in a sari who seemed to have lost her way'. Just as well she did though, because it turned out that the Rue de la Concorde was the Eendracht Straat in Flemish. Now she had a choice of two street names to look out for.

At each junction she patiently waited for the lights to turn green before crossing the street, even though she could see many others look quickly right and then left and cross through red lights. She had tried that once, soon after coming to Belgium, and unfortunately for her, had failed to see an approaching car. The car had had to brake rather sharply. It had seemed to her then that a hundred Belgian eyes had looked at her censoriously – she could almost hear an onlooker say, 'Look at that stupid foreign girl. I don't think they have many cars where she comes from, or even streets perhaps.' And today, she was in a sari. It was best to play it by the book.

Turning into the Rue de la Concorde she looked for Number 65. Odd numbers on the left of the street, even numbers on the right. She was about to cross when she saw a group of young men and women on the left side of the road, most with shaved heads, some with brightly coloured hair, all grungily dressed. She swerved and kept to her side of the road.

Best not to take any chances. God knows who they are. Maybe just harmless kids or perhaps punks but they could also be skinheads. Don't really know how to tell the difference. Must ask Luc. If they are racist skinheads my sari could be like a red rag. How old are they? Can't tell. Do they age? How do they age? Probably gracelessly.

Luc may not know much about skinheads or their attitude towards foreigners. There are some issues he is oblivious about. He's not the most perceptive person in the world. But his heart is in the right place and if he saw a skinhead bothering me in any way I'm sure he would rush to protect me.

She kept to the right of the road and hurried past the skinheads/punks – who ignored her completely.

At Door Number 57 she crossed the road. 59, 61, 63 and there it was – Number 65, with the Lion and the Unicorn crest on the carved door. She smoothed her hair, adjusted her sari and was about to ring the doorbell when she saw a small sign which read, 'Visa section, please use the rear entrance on Rue du President'.

She snorted and walked towards the rear of the building.

Look at the cheek. Front door only for British citizens. Let all the dirty foreigners trying to get into Britain use the rear entrance. Very appropriate. And look at me. Desperate to get in, never mind the entrance. Truly pathetic.

Don't be dramatic. All embassies are the same. They all have a consular section and a visa section. Remember the long queues every working day outside the Indian Embassy on Rue de Vleurgat of ardent Indophiles – the 'we loath the material West, we love your ancient wisdom and gentle ways' nirvana tourists. The Indian Embassy puts them through so many hoops. Makes them wait for hours. Makes them fill out a sheaf of forms. Often makes them queue on the sidewalk. Wonder why in spite of all this, these misguided souls take the trouble to travel to a country which they mistake for a sylvan paradise peopled exclusively by philosophers, while all it is a seething, heaving, frenetic slice of hell.

The rear entrance was closed and a sign said that the visa section would be open from 9am to 3pm. Another ten minutes to wait. There were already a few people outside. Seetha scanned and quickly slotted them. She loved slotting people. In some way it put her in charge. Two black men in suits talking loudly – must be Nigerian businessmen. There was a short person who Seetha could tell was from somewhere in the Indian subcontinent – probably was a Bihari, Bengali or a Bangladeshi. Too timid to be from anywhere west of the Yamuna. There was a white family – father, mother and two small girls, twins probably. The parents were rummaging in an old travel bag and trying to get their documents all in place and ready. Had to be East Europeans not yet in the EU.

Seetha moved away from this small knot of people and walked over to a small newspaper kiosk across the road. She always did this, almost reflexively and most often unconsciously – moving away from others from the Third world. Moving away from Thirdness. The perpetually tentative look. The cloying desire to win approval – even a smile would do. The unseemly eagerness to be corrected.

Look at that Bangladeshi/Bihari in the queue. Look at the look on his face. He's saying to the Visa officer and to every white person who crosses his path, 'I know you may think I'm an intruder but really, I'm a nice person. I even have a history and a culture. Though if you ask me to, I'm quite prepared to forget them. Please let me stay and please treat me nice. I'm useful too. For loose change, I will do anything from cleaning your windows to working your computers. I've learnt to use a Western toilet and I've stopped picking my nose in public. You may hesitate to ask but let me assure you, I don't wear a suicide belt (if at all I do, it will only be once!).'

Seetha didn't like Thirdness. Wasn't she a professional who was at least as good as her Western colleagues? She was in the West on business; she was proud of being Indian and she had no intentions of settling down in the West. She had to confess that she was a little unsure on that last point, but that did not take away anything from her dislike of Thirdness and her unwillingness to be associated with the millions who were desperate to crawl into any crevice in the Western world and only asked to be allowed to remain there undisturbed.

A short man from the subcontinent with an uncertain smile was walking towards Seetha and she was immediately on guard.

Chapter 2

Harish had not slept at all. He normally went to bed at six in the morning after closing the shop below. But today, since he needed to be at the British Embassy by 9am, he decided to stay awake and do the shop accounts instead till it was time to shower and dress and walk a kilometre to catch the number 23 tram to the Place Stephanie. From there it should be a short walk to the embassy.

Harish and his partner Zulfikar owned the Taj Magazin de Nuit or Night Shop, one of the many that Brussels is peppered with. The Taj stayed open all night and most of the day besides and stocked basic groceries, cigarettes and wine. Night Shops were mostly owned and run by either Indians or Pakistanis. Local Belgians, cosseted by an indulgent welfare state, would not even begin to consider working at night. But they did want to be able to buy liquor and cigarettes at any hour.

The Taj was rather unusual in that it was owned by an Indian and a Pakistani in partnership. The name – Taj – had been chosen carefully. Had to be a name which smelt of the subcontinent but mustn't be too specifically either Indian or Pakistani, Hindu or Muslim. They finally settled on the Taj. Location – Agra, India. Builder – Shah Jahan, Muslim.

Harish and Zulfikar shared the rooms above the shop. There were three rooms. Harish got one and since Zulfikar was married and had a little boy, he got two. They all shared a bathroom and a kitchen. You would have thought that the shared kitchen would be a problem what with the Zulfikars needing to eat red meat (usually beef) every day and poor Harish being a strict vegetarian for whom beef was taboo. But it all worked out nicely. The first shelf in the fridge and the right hand kitchen counter were strictly reserved for vegetarian food. Jemima – Zulfikar's wife – kept a green and white Melmoware set for Harish's food and no one else was allowed to use those dishes or plates. Jemima cooked a lipsmacking vegetarian meal too.

Harish brushed his teeth and showered, soaping and scrubbing himself meticulously. As he showered, he softly sang to himself the old Hindi song, 'Thande thande pani se nahana chahiye'. For the last twenty years he had always sung that song as he showered.

Harish dressed and carefully put all his papers into a little plastic pouch which was a Procter and Gamble giveaway. He took his passport – still Indian and still valid, his Belgian residence card and his Belgian Permit de Travail or work permit. He knocked on Zulfikar's bedroom door and without opening it, shouted, 'I'm leaving for the British Embassy. I'm not sure when I will be back but it can't be later than five in the evening because whites don't work beyond that and the embassy will close.' Through the closed door he heard a Jemima mumble, 'He's still sleeping or pretending to. I'll tell him.'

Harish went downstairs, took off his shoes and stood in front of the framed photo of Lord Hanuman which hung at the bottom of the landing leading into the shop. Harish could see the photograph from his stool near the till but it was hidden from customers. He lit an incense stick and stuck it into a crack in the frame. He folded his hands and stood silently in front of the photograph. The glass in the frame reflected the shelves of liquor across the aisle and hid much of the monkey god. But Harish knew that He was there and that He was listening.

'Bhagwan Hanuman, I need you to help me today. Once again I have to face officialdom. This time I need a visa from the British Embassy. Make them give it to me, preferably quickly, perhaps today. I can't stay away from the shop for long.'

Harish turned, sat on a stool and put on his shoes. Bending, he noticed that the vinyl flooring had frayed to a point where the wooden floorboards were visible at many places.

He really should go to the flea market on Sunday and see if he could get some cheap flooring. He could also ask Zulfikar to go over to the night shop on the Rue de Buyl which closed last week and see if he could pick up some flooring and a glass door freezer on the cheap. There was so much that needed doing. Harish hoped the visa would not take too long. If it threatened to be too time-consuming he decided that he would simply postpone watching cricket at Lord's for a couple of years. The long period of anticipation would be enjoyable.

Harish opened the front door and stepped out. Shutting the door behind him, he tried the door to make sure the newly installed double lock had clicked firmly. Only last week the shop had been burgled. The selective thief had stolen all the cigarettes and most of the liquor in the store. He (or could it actually have been a she?) had left everything else untouched, including the cash in the till.

Harish walked to the tram stop and waited for the tram. Catching sight of a new shop sign, 'Famous Night Shop' across the street, he wondered whose it could be – he had heard that Faroukh, the ambitious Pakistani, might be opening another shop. But no, his shops all bore very Islamic names. This must be some Bangladeshi's. There were so many more of them in Brussels now and they seemed to know how to work the erratic but increasingly restrictive Belgian system and get the required work permits and licences.

Harish had been luckier. He had come to Belgium twelve years ago in the days when Europe had yet to become a guarded fortress. Just eighteen then, he had worked for six years in one of Belgium's last coal mines. That job had got him his permanent resident card. It was at the mines that he had met Zulfikar and they had then put all their savings together, borrowed heavily from friends and started the Taj. The first few years were a grim, monotonous grind. For weeks Harish never left the shop and house.

Now things were a little easier and Harish, normally very careful with his money, had decided that he could afford to indulge a childhood dream – to watch a cricket match at Lord's. He had chosen a county match in May. Always given to preparing in advance, he was going to apply for his British visa today.

Waiting for the tram, quietly excited, Harish thought over all the practical details of getting to Lord's and back. Harish's experience in Europe had been largely restricted to the Taj Magazin de Nuit. He had never travelled outside Belgium and rarely ventured beyond Ixelles, his commune, except to meet suppliers or get his residence card extended. The visit to Lord's would be an expedition and the journey would be as exciting as the destination. Most of all, when he returned, he would have seen a cricket match at Lord's.

The No. 23 arrived. Harish watched, fascinated as usual. Even twelve years in Europe had not made him cease to marvel at the wonder of the orderly ceremony at a tram stop. The doors opened with a whoosh. The few persons waiting to get in stood aside while a young mother took her time to get off the bus with her daughter, her dog and two large bags. Those waiting then boarded the bus showing an automatic courtesy to each other. The doors closed with a whoosh. The tram started but almost immediately stopped again and the doors opened again with a whoosh. An old lady had signalled the tram to stop and she was now approaching the door at a slow shuffle. Stiffly and carefully, she boarded. The driver watched in his mirror until she had edged into a seat, then closed the doors again with a final whoosh and started the tram. For Harish it might all have been the changing of the guard at Buckingham Palace. He ruefully shook his head as he punched his ticket and found a seat by a window. The buses in dusty Hissar – his hometown in Haryana – were on his mind.

There were no trams in Haryana – wonder why – but the buses, baap re baap, always bursting at the seams. Each bus had at least a hundred body parts sticking out through windows and doors. Bus stops were crowded only just a little less than the buses themselves. The bus stop near the Government Hospital – Harish could almost hear the din, feel the searing summer heat and smell the sweet, slowly fermenting, crushed sugarcane waste lying around the stalls of the sugarcane juice vendors. Piercing hoots on an air horn would announce the impending arrival of the bus to Delhi. The crowd at the bus stop would begin to move onto the road, jostling for vantage positions, trying to guess the exact place where the doors of the bus would be when the bus stopped. Harish was usually good at that. He was usually quite good at any kind of anticipation. The bus – it was painted red with green lettering on the bonnet and the rear announcing in English 'No, no, Baby. Nahi, nahi, Meri Jaan. No overtaking' (everybody called it the Baby-wali bus) – would roar towards the stop, scattering waiting passengers, invariably passing the bus stop and coming to a reluctant halt twenty metres away. The waiting passengers would run towards the bus, elbowing their way forward. Invariably a passenger would slip and fall, another would lose a sandal and a third would get her sari pallu caught in another's handbag. Passengers would board and alight from the bus simultaneously in a scene which resembled nothing so much as the departure of the last American helicopter from Saigon in 1968. Harish always got in through the Exit door. Because it was the Exit door, fewer passengers tried to get in through that door. Without warning, the conductor would blow his whistle and the bus would shudder forward, leaving a couple of passengers hanging grimly on to the hand rail or the window near the door and another few still standing on the road, watching sullenly, having been unable to get in. Harish had once lost a book and once a shoe getting into that bus.

After that, to use the trams and buses here in Brussels was very heaven – and you didn't need to be young.

In Hissar, why did everyone risk life and limb to get into a bus? Simple. Because you were never sure when the next bus would arrive or if there would be a next bus at all. Schedules were rarely printed and even more rarely displayed. And then, schedules were merely Haryana Road Transport Corporation statements of intent. At best indicative of average times of arrival. Hence, when one sighted a bus going your way, you were willing to claw your way into it. You never knew if that was going to be the only bus for a long time.

An old Indian habit formed in crowded Indian buses made Harish get up and begin walking towards the door a minute before the tram reached Place Stephanie. Alighting he asked a passerby in fluent French for directions to the Rue de la Concorde. Harish had never read a book in French but standing behind the shop counter at the Taj he had learnt everyday French and now spoke it more naturally than his native Hindi. Of English, he knew only a smattering. He had studied in a Hindi-medium government school in Hissar. They had had one English class a week and the only complete English phrase Harish still remembered from those classes was 'Respected sir, a very good morning to you.'

Harish walked down the Rue de la Concorde looking for Nombre Soixante Cinque. As always, he walked briskly, looking down most of the time. He saw a group of unkempt young people with peculiar hairdos and passed them without any thought, exchanging a cursory Bonjour with one of them. Reaching Nombre Soixante Cinque he stepped up and attempted to open the ornate door. It was closed. He looked around and finding no one, decided to ring the door bell when he saw the small sign in English which said 'Visa section, please use the rear entrance on Rue du President.' He understood the word visa, as also Rue du President. He fished out his worn out pocket map of Brussels and discovered that the Rue du President was the next street. He walked along the wall of the embassy to the Rue du President, found the visa section entrance and seeing others waiting, did the same without bothering to make any further enquiries.

A few minutes later, he saw a young Indian lady in a sari turn the corner, walk briskly to the visa section entrance, read the notice there and then walk over to a newspaper kiosk after a quick glance at the others waiting for visas.

After a moment's hesitation, Harish decided to walk over and meet the Indian lady. With an Indian's fine eye for social levels, Harish could tell from the girl's apparent confidence, her short hair, her skin tone and the way she wore her sari that she or at any rate her parents were either rich or at least part of India's burgeoning middle-class – the thin slice of India that was booming and shining with double-digit growth flowing from exports of Information Technology, low-cost services and contracted manufacturing. In India her family would live in a regular house (as different from a hut or a slum tenement) and probably employ a domestic servant. She would have studied in an English-medium school, probably a 'convent'. Her family would have a car, perhaps a driver too and she would never have had to ride in a Hissar bus! Harish had seen her world from the outside. He was not given to curiosity. The young lady came from within that glass bubble and that was that.

But she could definitely help Harish complete his visa application form which would probably be in English.

Out of the corner of her eye, Seetha saw the short person from the Indian subcontinent walk over towards her. Finding no escape route, she pretended to be buried in a copy of the *Guardian*. The man, taking no notice of her absorption in the news of the day, said, 'Bonjour Mademoiselle, I the Harish, you the who?' and stuck out his hand.

Seetha found herself extending a limp hand and automatically replying, 'I the... I'm Seetha,' but she was unsmiling and after a moment turned back to the Guardian.

'Parlez vous Francais,' he tried.

'No.' What does he want? Why can't he leave me alone? Surely my rudeness is clear enough.

'Aap Indian hain ?' tried Harish in Hindi.

'Yes, but I don't speak Hindi. I'm Tamil,' replied Seetha in English, raising her chin just that fraction and showing her usual resentment of all North Indians who assumed that if you were Indian you would know Hindi. She could understand some Hindi but that was not the point.

Harish didn't know Tamil and only very little English. Quite apart from not having a language in common, it was apparent she would much rather be left alone. Seetha appeared to be like some of Harish's Belgian customers at the Taj who made it obvious that they would prefer to browse the shelves themselves without any assistance, suggestions or small talk from Harish or Zulfikar. This never troubled Harish and he saved the little conversation he sometimes liked to make for Asians, Africans and American tourists all of whom loved to talk and often bought nothing. But now he needed help with the visa. He decide to try again with the little English in his possession.

Thinking hard, selecting, dragging out and arranging the words he said, 'Visa application. I can't. You please filling.'

God, what to do. I want to concentrate on my own form. And this fellow won't even be able to answer my questions. He will be unclear and then blame me for filling the form incorrectly. I'm familiar with his kind. And almost certainly he will want me to write down some real whoppers. Best to stay out of this. I'm sure there will be someone in the embassy to help people like this.

'I'm sorry. I have a complicated application of my own to

fill. I'm applying for a long-stay, visa you see. That will take time. I'm sure you will be able to find someone else to help you. The embassy too may have an officer to help.'

Harish could not understand everything Seetha said but could gather that she was not inclined to help. Oh well. He had to look elsewhere. Harish gave Seetha a quick smile and walked back to the knot of waiting visa seekers.

What a mean bitch I am. Can't I spare ten minutes to complete his form? I pride myself on having a social conscience, I have Gandhian pretensions, I have a signed photo of Mother Teresa on my wall and I can't bring myself to help a poor, unfortunate soul who only wants me to help him fill an application form. Even if I had a complicated form to fill myself, I could have asked him to wait, filled up and submitted my application and then worked on his.

No, don't go and call him back. It's too late. You will simply have to live with this unpardonable bit of callous, uptight behaviour. Shame on you. Horribly hoity terribly toity behaviour!

The knot had grown in the meantime and as 9am approached, they formed into a straggling line, each person seeming to know exactly who all had been waiting before he or she arrived.

Harish was fifth in line and out of the corner of his eye he saw that Seetha too had joined the line a few places behind him.

Behind the glass door of the visa section, signs of life were now apparent. A light had been switched on and a security guard could be seen dusting a desk, opening a drawer and taking out a sheaf of forms which he placed on the desk. He looked up at the queue formed outside and in one glance managed quite remarkably to convey both indifference and superiority.

Harish took out his travel documents from the safe inner pocket of his thick, unfashionable overcoat (bought for a song at Les petits Rien, the Brussels charity store which sold old clothes discarded by the Belgian bourgeoisie) and was checking them when he was tapped on the shoulder. Turning around he saw a wiry Indian, just a little taller than himself, smiling at him and asking in Hindi, 'Is this the queue for the British visa? I think I have managed to reach just in time. Are you also Indian and wanting to travel to England? These bastards have made it so difficult these days. My name is Ratnesh Kumar.'

Harish's first impression was that Ratnesh was another of those recent immigrants who put on an altogether unnecessary swagger which could change to cringing when confronted by a white person in a position of authority.

But at least Ratnesh spoke Hindi. That was a blessing.

Harish replied in Hindi, 'My name is Harish Rawat and I too want to travel to England. I was told that they have a very complicated application form in English that you need to complete. My English is very poor and I think I will need some help to fill it.'

'Not to worry. I will help you,' replied Ratnesh, 'I have my application form with me. It has been completed by one of my well-wishers. You can use that as a guide.'

Harish wondered who Ratnesh was and what made him have well-wishers. Politician? Godman? Ratnesh did not look like either. Ratnesh could simply be one of the many immigrants who invented exotic background stories for themselves. Harish knew a Thiruvengadam from Sri Lanka who claimed to have left behind a flourishing real estate business in that country. Harish later met his brother who told him that Thiruvengadam had frittered away all the money their father had left them. He had then proceeded to sell an acre each year of their twenty acres of paddy fields. When all had been sold, Thiruvengadam had emigrated. The twenty sales transactions had changed in Thiruvengadam's recounting into a flourishing real estate business.

As Ratnesh spoke, he insinuated himself into the queue just behind Harish. Harish noticed but decided that it was none of his business. It was up to people further behind in the queue to object. Harish only hoped that no one would make a loud fuss. This was not India.

Those behind in the queue did look at Ratnesh but no one objected, probably being under the assumption that as Ratnesh and Harish had been speaking familiarly in Hindi, they must be together. In any case most of those waiting for a visa were from the Third World and were familiar with queues that took in newcomers, not just at the end but at various points along their length too.

Seetha though was certainly not planning to meekly look on at any adjustments or insinuations in the queue. She had always been a champion (and beneficiary) of rules, regulations and order. She had been grimly watching Ratnesh for some time and recognized Ratnesh's tactic early. Entering into a lengthy conversation with a person near the head of the queue and then just staying on was an often practised trick to jump a queue back home but Seetha was not having any of that here.

Marching determinedly up to Ratnesh, she tapped him on the shoulder and said. 'Excuse me. This is a queue and we are all waiting in line to get our visas. Please join the end of the queue.'

Startled at this stern admonishment in fluent English with just a touch of an Indian accent, both Ratnesh and Harish turned their heads sharply and saw the upturned nose, flashing black eyes and pursed lips of the young Indian lady Harish had already approached. Harish was at a loss for words but anyway it wasn't Harish she was looking at, it was Ratnesh. Ratnesh recovered quickly and pointing to Harish, replied in English which was just a little better than Harish's.

'We friends. We going to fill our forms together.'

Harish looked on. He was not going to get involved in this argument.

Seetha had heard this before too. 'You may be friends but queues are not ordered according to friendship. They are ordered according to the time when a person arrives. You should go to the back of the queue,' replied Seetha primly, tossing her head and gesturing rather rudely to the back.

Seetha could almost hear Ratnesh weighing the options, considering whether to retort sharply and for a moment Seetha was frightened, wondering whether she had overstepped. She was relieved when Ratnesh slapped Harish on the shoulder and after telling him that he would see him again inside the visa section, ignored Seetha, nonchalantly strolled to the newspaper kiosk, bought a packet of cigarettes, lit one and then joined the end of the queue.

Seetha breathed out slowly with much relief and some triumph. God, that was close.

Why do I need to get these stupid skirmishes when I've come here to fight a different battle? Still haven't learnt to control myself. Lots of maturing still needed. That rascally queue-breaker looked like that Madras cyclist all over again. God, my hands are clammy. Get a grip on yourself, goose, and focus on the work in hand.

In Ratnesh Seetha saw the face of the Madras cyclist who had confronted her years ago. It had been a hot summer afternoon in Madras when the heat stared unblinkingly from every building. She had been driving her little scooterette, sweating profusely, often wiping her face with her sari pallu, yelling at cyclists weaving dangerously into her path. Most cyclists simply ignored her or sullenly moved away but there was this one cyclist who, on receiving Seetha's ire, braked sharply in front of her, causing her to do the same. Seetha remembered that he had been wearing a blue checked lungi and a red shirt. He had a big moustache, dirty hair and a stubbly beard. He must have been around forty. He had then parked his cycle in the middle of the road, walked over to her as she sat on her scooterette, dumbstruck and suddenly frightened. He had come very close to her and proceeded to abuse her in choice Tamil. Apart from various aspersions regarding her parentage and occupation, he had told her that just because her father had dishonestly become rich and bought her up in comfort and privilege, she should not assume that he owned all the roads in Madras and if she did, he would be happy to disabuse both her and her father of that notion. He had brought his face very close to hers, patted her lightly and menacingly on the cheek and left snarling while she sat frozen.

Till that incident Seetha had been given to freely scolding and reprimanding all manner of wrongdoers – litterers, queue-breakers, traffic rule violators. After that incident a shell-shocked Seetha chose her confrontations more carefully. In the tinderbox wrapped in tinsel that was India it was only in the shelter of curtained drawing rooms in south Madras and the indignant columns of the English-language press that righteous middle-class anger could be ventilated freely.

There was a murmur as the security guard unlocked the door and took his position behind the desk. The visa seekers shuffled in, gathering their wits and assuming the gait and demeanour best suited to pleading, arguing for or inveigling a British visa.

Chapter 3

Ratnesh Kumar was thoughtful as he joined the end of the visa queue. He was not overly angry at being ejected by Seetha from near the head of the queue. It was just a minor irritation. He had a sense of perspective. Getting to London was what was important. So far things were proceeding as per plan. Last week he had finally obtained his refugee status attestation from the office of the UN High Commissioner for Refugees. He knew he had to thank Mabel for that. She had filled up all the forms, written all the letters and when the papers just wouldn't move, she had stormed into the office of the Deputy Commissioner, made a scene, accused him of being a racist (he wasn't particularly) and demanded quick action. And it had worked. In Europe, it did help to have a white woman on your side. If he had made such a scene, the Deputy Commissioner would have called the police and by now he would have been back in India, deported by the Belgian authorities who were known to act very swiftly when it concerned aspiring refugees who misbehaved.

Now he needed to get to London. Any kind of visa would do. Once there he would apply for asylum.

He thought about Mabel, her credulity, her determination to redress what she considered wrongs, her world made up of black and white squares, and her ideological need to gloss over the grey, uneven complexities of men like Ratnesh or the lands they came from. In turn, he simplified her. He did not bother to take the trouble to understand her and her passionate sense of right and wrong. As far as he was concerned, she had happened to cross his path; had turned, looked at him and felt she had to be his champion. And that was that. He was rather proud that she had bought his story. He also sometimes wished that she were a little younger.

Ratnesh was hungry and unsettled after a mostly sleepless night. He had been unable to get Mabel to suggest that he could use the guest bedroom in her exquisite Art Nouveau apartment overlooking the Place Chatelaine. She apparently did draw lines but not where or when an Indian would. He had next tried the fat Moroccan, Hamid, who ran the dirtiest cafe in Brussels opposite the Gare du Midi. Hamid had greeted him like an old friend and spent a couple of hours with him, plying him first with sweet, hot tea in chipped, dirty cups and then cheap wine in smudged glasses. They spoke in a polyglot of broken English, Urdu and Arabic. They had discussed Arab and Indian leaders – contrasting Nasser and Nehru, Ataturk and Indira Gandhi. They stayed clear of Bin Laden and avoided mentioning 9/11. Both Hamid and Ratnesh had an eye for an opportunity and they had probed business possibilities – exports and imports. Both had hinted of their connections, their influence with unnamed politicians, goons and administrators in Europe and their own lands. Both enjoyed the evening and the chance to be expansive, but close to 2am, when Ratnesh had asked Hamid for a room or just a bed to spend a night or two, Hamid had turned very Belgian and expressed his complete inability to comply with this extraordinary request. As a special concession to a dear friend however, he had agreed to let Ratnesh leave his bags for safekeeping behind the counter at the cafe.

Ratnesh had no option but to trudge in the cold towards the Gare du Midi. At a street corner two Russian whores accosted him. He declined smilingly – he did not have the money – but only after finding out the going rates in Brussels for assorted services.

He entered the freezing, grey, Soviet-style, perpetually under renovation, Gare du Midi and slept on a bench – the warm overcoat which Mabel had gifted him the previous evening keeping him from freezing solid. The train station announcements in three languages had begun from 4:30am ending Ratnesh's fitful slumber.

Ratnesh had sat up groggily and first checked his pockets. His passport, refugee papers and wallet were safe. He counted the money in his wallet. Eighty-eight euros and forty-three cents. Hopefully he would get his British tourist visa in a day or two and then he'd be in London, safe and supported in Sham's flat in Wembley. He would then apply for asylum – now that he had got the UN High Commissioner for Refugees to attest his case he was very hopeful that his application would be accepted by the British Home Office. Then, oh happy day, he would go legal. He would plan his next few years, he really would. He knew that he had a head for business and he was sure that he would make good.

Ratnesh used the loo at the Gare du Midi. Clearly it had yet to be renovated or even, by the looks and smell of it, cleaned for at least a week. He idly noted that in Europe, the facilities that were primarily used by immigrants and the flotsam and jetsam of society were very comparable to what Indian towns had on offer. He walked over to the coffee stand and asked for a cup of coffee.

'Petite ou grande,' the girl behind the counter asked sullenly.

'No French. Only English please,' said Ratnesh with a hopeful smile.

'Petite ou grande,' she repeated, her eyes just a fraction narrower this time.

Thinking hard, 'Normal, medium, milk – yes, sugar – two,' replied Ratnesh, answering at one go all questions one might be asked at a coffee stand.

The girl relented, even faintly smiled and gave him a grande cup of coffee.

There was a vacant bench some distance away but Ratnesh did not have the Western person's obsessive need for personal space and sat down on the nearest bench next to a thickly bearded man in a dumpy pullover and a ski cap. The man muttered either a curse or a greeting into his beard. Ratnesh would have attempted to strike up a conversation but his complete ignorance of French and Flemish restrained him. This was one of the reasons why he had to get to London. He could not live in a city where he could not converse. Ratnesh conversed with just about anyone he came across – and at length – until he had to leave or the other person did. He was not insensitive to other people's feelings. He knew when the person he was conversing with was bored or irritated or wanted to be left alone. But he would not comply. He did though try and mould his conversation to make it interesting for his listener and more often than not, his listeners grudgingly fell in and began to respond and even expand. Ratnesh listened too.

Warmed by his coffee, Ratnesh began to focus on the day ahead. He wondered what the British embassy might require before they gave him a tourist visa. He did have a letter from his friend Sham in London where Sham had offered to take care of Ratnesh's expenses during his stay in Britain. He hoped Sham's residence permit was in order and he was not in any kind of problem with the law. With Sham one could never be sure.

The tourist visa was not likely to be a problem. The bigger problem would come later: being granted asylum in London. He was not sure how these things worked but the British should really give him asylum now that he had valid UN refugee papers. He had been told they might put him in a detention centre for a while his application was being considered. But that held no terrors for Ratnesh. Once one had done time in Patna's Central Jail, any European detention centre would be like the Ritz. He almost looked forward to seeing what detention and correctional facilities were like in Europe. He would try to get his asylum application processed by himself but would call in Mabel as reinforcement if needed. She was British. She had promised to catch the Eurostar and be in London on a day's notice. But he felt that she would not be necessary. He had practised and used his story so often that he was now sure that he would not be caught out on any point. He had skillfully woven elements of truth into it and to a European it was a plausible, even heart-wrenching tale.

Ratnesh took out his wallet and extracted a slip of paper on which Mabel had written the address of the British Embassy in her clear, round hand. She had also written the name of the nearest Metro station – Louise. He stood up, realized that he was dirty, unshaven and slovenly, but could not think of any way of improving his appearance. Concluding that he was never going to look like the man in the Mercedes Benz ad, he went the other way – slicking his hair back in a very Indian way, letting his shirt hang out and the gold chain with the Om medallion show. He was going to be an ethnic businessman who did not care what the white man thought.

He followed the signs to the Metro station. It was a floor below the train station. He found the correct Metro line and the correct direction making just one wrong turn. The

Metro was full of officegoers, absorbed in their own thoughts,
indifferent to him and all else, most of them using the hour
of travel to plan the day ahead or go over the evening just
passed. Even Ratnesh did not dare disturb this wall of silence
with any attempt at conversation.

Alighting at Louise, Ratnesh walked down to Place
Stephanie and found the Rue de la Concorde without much
difficulty. He saw the knot of punks or skinheads in front and
walked head down through them. He did not particularly
expend much thought on them and would have ignored
any rude taunt, gibe or gesture. And of course, if any one of
them had actually stepped in front of him and stopped him,
he knew he could take care of himself. As it happened, the
skinheads ignored him.

At the embassy, Ratnesh saw the sign indicating that the
visa section was at the rear. He walked around the building
and saw the queue. Ratnesh was not used to joining queues
at the tail end. Seeing an Indian face near the head of the
queue Ratnesh automatically moved towards the face, quite
sure that he would be able to find a way to join the Indian
at that point in the queue. He was not prepared for Seetha's
sudden intervention.

Chapter 4

The queue shuffled in and one by one they were confronted by the baleful eye behind the security desk. If you already had a form and seemed to know what to do, the eye gestured towards a metal detector beyond which was a lift as well as stairs leading to the first floor where the Visa Hall was, with counters and a waiting area for applicants. If you needed a form, the thickly-veined hand beneath the baleful eye pushed one towards you and then pointed you upstairs.

Harish asked in French for a tourist visa application form. The security guard gave him a short-visit application form with a flourish and a 'Voila.' He was probably Wallonian.

Harish negotiated the metal detector. It gave a quick, short beep. The security guard looked up but waved Harish on. Harish waited for the lift although he could see that the Visa Hall was only one flight up and there was a flight of stairs right next to the lift. He had an innate deference towards machines and automation of any kind. Anywhere where a mechanical option was provided Harish felt that it would be almost irreverent not to use it.

On the first floor the lift door opened onto a landing where signs indicated that both smoking and the use of mobile phones were strictly prohibited. Harish switched off his mobile phone. On the left side was a toilet door with signs indicating that men, women and handicapped persons could all use the facility. A notice pasted below informed users that the toilet key was available with embassy staff at the first counter.

On the landing opposite the lift was a large double door which opened into the visa section. Harish walked in, looked around, walked quickly to a seat in the far corner and sat down on the hard, moulded plastic chair. He opened the five-page application form and set himself to trying to understand what information Her Majesty's government required before they could grant him a visa for a three-day visit.

As he had expected, the form was in English and though he

began filling in the easily understandable sections, he knew he would need help with some of the others. He looked up frequently to see if Ratnesh had entered the hall.

Seetha must have been the tenth in the queue but she entered the hall nearly ten minutes after Harish. The East European family in front of her did not seem to have any language in common with the security guard. They had with them a large travel bag which the guard would not allow inside without inspection. He insisted with words in more than one language and many international gestures that they should put the bag on the desk, open it and allow him to check its contents. The gaunt, East European man (Bulgarian, decided Seetha) looked puzzled, then understood and fished in his pocket for the key to the lock on the travel bag. His wife, a short, rather plump woman with a wizened face, urgently whispered into his ear. The man looked undecided, then seemed to make up his mind and slowly and deliberately attempted to tell the guard that the bag contained little more than items of personal clothing. The uncomprehending guard, now a little alarmed, using more energetic gestures, insisted that the man open the bag immediately or take it away, out of the embassy. The man and his wife whispered to each other. The man shrugged and seemed to be telling his wife that they had no choice.

The man opened the bag and Seetha, curious now, leaned a little to the right so as to look around the woman's head into the bag. The woman moved too and seemed almost deliberately to obstruct Seetha's view. Seetha thought she understood why and wanted to tell them not to be silly. It didn't matter. Not in this motley Third World queue anyway. There was no need to be ashamed of one's shabby clothes and tattered underwear. It was par for Third World baggage. Notwithstanding, unobtrusively, Seetha rocked onto her toes and craned to see. There were a few clothes, which probably dated back to the Communist era, a mouth organ, there were a few used and cleaned paper plates, ditto polystyrene cups and a large plastic bag tied with string.

The guard indicated that they should open the plastic bag. The man hesitated; there was more urgent whispering and the man looked up at the guard with a silent plea. The guard, having now placed and sized the family, was no longer alarmed, just officious. He repeated his gesticulated command. The man untied the plastic bag and revealed a striking collection of beautiful Orthodox icons. Almost simultaneously both the man and his wife began to launch into eager explanations in Slav sentences embedded with English and French nouns. The guard looked bewildered but deciding that his job was only to determine that they did not constitute a security risk, shrugged, tied the plastic bag again, zipped up the sports bag, pushed a short-visit application form towards them and pointed towards the metal detector and the lift and staircase. The East European couple seemed undecided, unsure if the last word on the icons had been spoken, there was more whispering and they finally shuffled towards the metal detector, the woman turning back once to look at the guard fearfully.

They must be planning to sell the icons in Britain and not being sure if that would be incompatible with a tourist visa, they don't want the embassy to know. Poor things. The icons are stunning – carved and painted (lovingly?) by hand – and to think that some investment banker in London who worships Mammon will buy them for a song to hang on a wall in an upstairs landing in his Chelsea flat. And what will these poor Bulgarians do when they have sold all the icons? Will they go back to Bulgaria? Will he play the mouth organ in the village tavern? Will that give him a living? Or will he try and get a work visa in the UK (as a master craftsman?) or will they simply go underground in London and wait for the little girls to grow up and become world class gymnasts?

When her turn came, Seetha startled the security officer by wishing him a very good morning in a loud, assertive American businesswoman style. He responded grudgingly and looked up inquiringly at the sari and the determined brown face. She asked him for application forms IM2A and IM2C. He gave them to her and she moved towards the stairs through the metal detector, happy with the controlled transaction.

On the first floor, she entered the visa section. Her eyes took in the visa counters with bulletproof glass and tiny voice windows. The chairs in the waiting hall were plastic – hard and yellow. Three to a single steel frame. Looked like the departure lounge at Madurai airport. She saw Harish

hunched over his form in the far corner. He looked up and
their eyes met. He smiled. Seetha looked away quickly and
took a seat in the near corner, well away from Harish.

He makes me feel guilty. He really does. But I can't help it.
I have work to do. I don't want to be distracted. I'm not Miss
Do Good nor am I a paid social worker. I will help those I can
when I can and if I can. And let me tell you that that's not as
rare as it sounds. Anyway let me complete and submit my
form. If he still has not found anybody to help him, I will.

Seetha was good at filling forms. She had filled college
application forms, scholarship application forms, job
application forms, passport application forms and visa
application forms. To date, none of her applications had ever
been turned down and she was proud of her record.

She knew that one of the secrets of always applying
successfully was to understand as well as possible the
perspective of the person or persons who would review the
application. And today she was very adequately prepared.
Three long conversations on the phone with her uncle (twice
removed) in London (she had called collect) had seen to that.
Mr Mahalinga Iyer had immigrated to London forty years ago
and worked for many years at the Home Office. In his spare
time – and there was lots of it – he had counselled, guided and
shepherded a little troop of other Iyers into Britain. Though
he had worked in the Home Office at an unambitiously junior
level – it seemed that he had exhausted all his ambition simply
in successfully immigrating to the UK – Mr Iyer knew both
the workings of Britain's bureaucracy and the workings of its
bureaucratic minds. He knew the flow of its immigration and
visa laws, he knew the eddies, shallows, currents and reverse
currents too. Seetha and he had hatched this audacious plan
to get her into England, and, what was more daring still
(considering that Seetha had no job offer or appointment
letter in Britain) with a visa which would permit her to work
in any field and for any employer.

Getting Iyers into Britain had become exciting games of
chess for Mr Iyer. And like all chess players, he wanted to win
from more difficult situations with more audacious strategies.
Helping Sanjay Iyer who was brilliant academically and had
been admitted to the LSE to get a student visa though he

had no scholarship and no apparent means of support was a beginner's game of chess. Getting Latha Iyer a work visa once she had been accepted for a job by a firm in the City (never mind that it was a short-term contract) was also a cakewalk. Getting Srinidhi Iyer an immigrant visa even though she had divorced Shivan Iyer as whose dependent she had first come to London had been a little more difficult. Now, Seetha's application would be the real test of his skills.

The British government in its wisdom had laid down that writers and artists were two categories of people who could be granted work visas even if no employer was in sight. And so Seetha was to be a writer and her first creative writing assignment would be the visa application form.

Seetha got down to work.

Chapter 5

Amit Trehan got into the taxi and gave the taxi driver the slip of paper on which he had written down the embassy address. One week in Brussels had shown him the perils of attempting to communicate verbally with taxi drivers in either slow English or broken French. The taxi driver grunted in comprehension and, well, taxied off.

Amit idly looked out of the window. Old European city streets no longer excited him as they had a fortnight ago when he had first arrived in Europe. If you have seen one, you have seen them all, he thought, looking at the sameness of the grey or brownstone facades of the old city blocks, nearly always four or five storeys tall – nearly always merging into a grey sky. The morose, dimly lit shop fronts, the somewhat brighter awnings and the grey cobblestones gleaming dully in the wet morning were in Brussels but could equally well have been in Paris or Amsterdam or Cologne or Rome.

Amit's mind was on business. He knew that if he returned to Delhi without clinching a business deal he would be devastated. He would find it difficult to endure the Chopras and the Bhasins who had established fruitful business relationships in their first business visits to Europe, even though they did not have the political connections and attendant Indian Embassy support that he had. In Punjabi Delhi's wheeling circles of deal-making you had to constantly be proving and growing and showing your manhood – with politicians who would accept your invitations, the Mercedes you drove, the single malt you served (the younger Punjabi, though, had taught himself to say he preferred white wine), the farmhouse near Mehrauli, the children's holidays in Florida or the Gold Coast and the international business associates who called you on your mobile phone when you were at the Oberoi with the Chopras and the Bhasins.

And then there was his other brief – given to him by his father – and he had not even begun to work on that. He did not even have a germ of an idea to work on. If he returned without having found a way to bring back to India as legitimate earnings some of the millions Trehan Senior had stashed abroad in the bad restrictive years of Nehruvian socialism, Amit would be confirmed in his father's eyes as a loser, a wimp, an intellectual, a can't go-won't getter. Someone who did not have a Punjabi businessman's balls and never would.

Perhaps London would be different. Firstly, people spoke English there and Amit knew that he communicated well and could be persuasive – the right school followed by the right B-school had seen to that. Secondly there were more businessmen of Indian origin there and many of them were eager to curry favour with the new right-wing dispensation in Delhi. They would be keen to work with the foreign minister's nephew.

It had perhaps been a harebrained idea to come to Brussels in the first place. But the Ambassador had been so persuasive and had assured his father that the new capital of Europe was the place where the big deals were now being made. Perhaps, but apparently not with Indian businessmen in the food-processing industry. The Ambassador had asked the Embassy Commercial Attaché to help Amit as much as possible but that poor officer knew no French or Flemish, had no personal contacts with any European businessmen and seemed to have gained the little commercial intelligence he had exclusively by visiting the official EU website. And Amit had neither the inclination nor the ability to scout for business on his own.

Amit reached the entrance to the visa section of the British embassy and viewed the queue, the security and the air, thick with deceit and grovelling, with some dismay. An Indian like him with the right business and political pedigree almost never had to queue or in general concern himself with practicalities. You could always get someone in your office or your father's or your uncle's to arrange to have things attended to. He wished he had had the foresight to get his British visa in New Delhi itself.

Amit walked over to the newspaper kiosk. Two English newspapers were on offer. The *Times* and the *Sun*. Amit browsed quickly through the *Sun*, staying with the photographs. He bought the *Times* and joined the queue. One always looked more complete with the *Times* tucked under one's arm.

By defiant manner and faraway look, he distanced himself
from the others. He got his application form for a short-
duration business visa, mounted the flight of stairs and
entered the visa hall. He scanned the hall, his practised Indian
eyes passing over the other Indians and quickly noticing the
Indian girl in the sari who looked like someone who might
be from his kind of background or at least his kind of school.
She had just moved to the visa counter. Amit took the seat she
had vacated and quickly set to filling his form. He was sure he
would find an opportunity to talk to her later.

Chapter 6

Ratnesh Kumar stepped out of the lift and jauntily walked into the Visa Hall. He nearly always walked jauntily. Long ago he had noticed that policemen in small-town Bihar, on the lookout for passersby to intimidate and squeeze a few rupees from, always chose the quiet, the timid and the frightened. They were easy prey. The policemen ignored those who appeared confident and bold, unless one of them happened to specifically attract their attention. Ratnesh could see that the meek were not going to inherit Bihar any time soon. He developed his jaunty, cocky, alley-cat style. It won him few friends but preserved him through fifteen years of lonely poverty in India's most run-down state. For him, it came to embody his will to survive. It seemed to develop a life and will of its own. Sometimes when futility had stared him in the face and he had been ready to give up and just lie down and curl up and die, his jaunty style intervened and kept him going. It was his shield and buckler.

Ratnesh had with him his application form, neatly and thoughtfully completed by Mabel. He went up to the counter, and without exchanging a smile or greeting with the embassy official across the bulletproof glass barrier, thrust his papers in through the little window provided. The embassy officer, who appeared to be Belgian and probably constituted the embassy's first line of investigation and attack took the papers and perused them.

'How long have you been in Europe?' asked the Belgian neutrally, flipping the pages of Ratnesh's passport and looking for his Schengen visa.

'Five months. I am here for business and now want to visit Britain and meet few friends there before returning India.'

'Why did you not apply for your British visa in India itself? That is what you are required to do.'

'I not think I have time to visit Britain. Please read my application. I have explained everything,' replied Ratnesh, trusting Mabel's persuasive and lucid style more than his own.

The Belgian decided that it would be a waste of time to ask more questions at this stage. The new rules were explicit. All visa applicants applying outside their home country had to be interviewed by the head of the visa section. Let the boss, who anyway had little to do and was spending most of his time reading the London papers, do the questioning.

'Please sit down and wait. You will be called later,' said the Belgian and disappeared into the inner recesses of the office.

Ratnesh was guardedly optimistic. The man had accepted his papers and had not suggested that anything was amiss. He turned and surveyed the hall, now crowded with worried visa seekers of all shapes, sizes, hues and odours; all busy completing their forms. He noticed Harish bent low over his form in the far corner and walked towards him. Ratnesh realized that having already submitted his application he could not use it as a guide for Harish. He was almost glad. He wanted to reserve Mabel's clarity for himself.

Ratnesh sat down next to Harish and put an arm around Harish's shoulders. Many years of stay in Europe made Harish instinctively withdraw a little but he quickly checked himself and in a moment moved back and comfortably accepted Ratnesh's supportive gesture.

Harish had found his form less intimidating than it had appeared to be at first sight. Almost all the questions were factual and concerned the length of his stay in Belgium, his source of income, his bank balance and his relatives in Britain if any. For Harish, the most difficult question had been: 'Give reasons why you wish to travel to Britain.' With Ratnesh's help, Harish had answered, 'To see cricket match at Lord's.'

As they completed the application form together, Ratnesh asked Harish a number of questions about himself – not all necessary to fill the form. Ratnesh was naturally curious and was also very keen to get to know some Indians in Brussels. He needed a place to stay and he longed for a hot meal of chapattis, dal and mutter-paneer.

Harish checked his application form one last time and then went up to the counter, Ratnesh accompanying him. They had to wait as the embassy official was attending to another applicant, a slim, dark, African woman who appeared to want to travel to Britain on a Nigerian passport which would expire in just another month. Harish could hear the embassy official explaining that the passport needed to be valid for at least six months from the date of travel as the visa would be valid for that same period of time. He suggested to the woman, gratuitously, thought Harish, that she consider contacting her embassy and getting her passport renewed. The woman only sighed deeply.

Harish understood the sigh. He knew just how difficult it was to get a passport renewed at the Indian Embassy here in Brussels and suspected that the Nigerian Embassy would be no different. The long lines, the cold procedures that mandated that the passport be sent back to India for verification – a process that could take months. Any clerk through whose hands the passport passed in its voyage through babudom could halt the passport dead in its tracks with an adverse comment or a query. Of course it was different if you knew someone in the Foreign Office. Alternatively, late in the evening, you could meet the embassy clerk at L'Amour Fou, and after helping him knock back a couple of Chimays, slip him an envelope containing five crisp hundred-euro notes. You could then collect your renewed passport the next morning – no problem.

The Nigerian woman was silent for a minute and then suggested to the embassy official that they give her a visa for just 15 days for which time her passport would still be valid. The Belgian embassy official solemnly shook his head and said that their procedures did not allow for such short visas.

'But I can't wait. Peter will be gone from London next week and then I'll be alone once again. Please help,' said the woman urgently. She was not loud but she might have been.

'I'm sorry, ma'am. Please ask your embassy to expedite the passport renewal and then come back to us,' replied the official in a flat, sombre voice and deliberately closed the little voice gate in the bulletproof glass barrier. The woman stood undecided for a few seconds and then turned away in blank disappointment, her eyes wet and her face frozen.

The woman having left, the embassy official opened the voice gate again and Harish and Ratnesh stepped up. All of them pretended not to have witnessed the little vignette just concluded. Harish pushed his application form through the little bowl-like window at the bottom of the bullet proof glass. The officer asked Harish if the application form was his. When Harish nodded, the officer turned to Ratnesh and asked him to step back. 'I am his friend. Helping him,' said Ratnesh and Harish nodded in agreement. The officer shook his head, put down Harish's papers and hunched his shoulders confrontationally. Ratnesh shrugged, turned, walked back and took a seat in the first row.

The officer's shoulders slackened with victory. Harish handed over his passport. He recognized the Belgian accent in the official's voice and quickly switched to French. The officer asked him a few questions about the Night Shop – he even seemed to recognize the name. He told Harish that he needed to bring a bank statement establishing his capacity to fund his British visit. He finally gathered up all Harish's papers and grunted a 'Bon'.

'Come back with the bank statement and we will try and give you your visa today,' said the officer.

'Merci beaucoup,' replied Harish. He then turned round slowly, wondering where in the vicinity he would find a branch of his bank, the Fortis Banque.

Chapter 7

Seetha had arrived at the end of her application form. At the bottom she saw that she was required to sign a statement where she swore that all she had stated was the truth and nothing more or less. She snorted softly and without more than a moment's hesitation signed in her neat round hand.

Not the time for moral doubt-mongering now. I'm in the heat of battle. I have to storm the gates of Britain. The combat deepens, On ye brave! Or should it be 'On ye brazen?' Now stop that. It's not very funny and it does not even rhyme. Get on with it, girl.

She collected her papers, read through her answers once again, got up and reached the counter. She furrowed her brows at the sight of the bulletproof glass and the small voice gate. She did not like being intimidated or suspected and here the British embassy was expressing both sentiments in its arrangements.

She intently observed the officer as he perused her application.

'So you are a writer,' remarked the officer, savouring the noun.

'Yes,' replied Seetha, her tone even and guarded.

'You have not mentioned what you have published so far,' asked the officer, looking for the chink.

'In the form I was not explicitly asked to do so,' shot back Seetha in her instinctive, combative style.

What's wrong with you, stupid girl? This is not the time to score debating points or to show how smart you are. Reply to his question politely.

'I have been published by Vivek, India in their latest collection titled *Stories Which Bend Belief*.'

'*Stories Which Bend Belief*,' the officer repeated as he wrote this down on Seetha's form in the section marked 'For Official Use Only'. He wondered if he should ask her why she needed to live and work in Britain but then decided to leave the questioning to his boss. Three years in the visa section had drained him of curiosity, sympathy or dislike. Nowadays he concentrated on the paperwork – the application form, the passport, the letters of invitation or sponsorship. At a glance he could spot inaccuracies, missing information or contradictions. He rarely looked up at applicants' faces.

'Please sit down, Miss Seetha Subramanium. You will be interviewed by the Visa Officer later,' said the Belgian evenly.

'Thank you,' relied Seetha

Round One over. Points even. I guess it all now depends on the interview.

She turned to go back to her seat, only to find that it had been taken by an Indian she had not noticed before – a businessman – no, a businessman's son, decided Seetha.

Seetha's love of categorization came perhaps from her professional life where she was trained to analyze business systems. She found categorizing people challenging and it was thrilling when she got it right. She knew that categorization went against the grain of the Indian philosophy she loved and had decided to live by some day, but for the moment it was good clean fun.

The businessman or businessman's son had seen Seetha turning back from the counter and glaring at him and he got up immediately and offered Seetha the seat with a chivalrous flourish. Seetha disliked ever being in the position of receiving a favour, especially from businessmen's sons but she could hardly walk away. She took the proffered seat with a faint 'Thank you'. To her horror, the man sat down in the next seat and began a conversation.

'I'm Amit and I'm here because I need a British visa. I plan to visit London next week. I presume you're here for the same reason.'

Businessman's son, living in Bombay, visiting Europe, Daddy must have bought him his tickets – Seetha was busy slotting him. But the English was fluent and Seetha could not immediately find anything in his manner or tone to dislike.

'My name's Seetha. Yes, I'm planning to move to London next month.' The word 'move' immediately established her superiority. She lived here – and would live next in London – she was a Non-Resident Indian, an NRI, while he who lived somewhere in the Indian jungle was just visiting.

Amit noted the positioning and presented his own credentials.

'I live in Delhi and we have an organic fruit pulp processing and canning unit there. I'm touring Europe to explore export opportunities in the food processing sector. The Indian Ambassador here was keen that I look at Belgium as a gateway to Europe. He and the Commercial Attaché have helped me meet a few Belgian importers. I think though that London will present better business opportunities and that's why I plan to travel there as soon as I can.'

Ooh, we're well connected, aren't we? And we don't mind flaunting it, do we? Delhi. So we must be Punjabi. But sophisticated, rich-for-four-generations Punjabi. Not the kind who lives in Shahadra and who's idea of an evening in paradise is a plate of butter chicken, a bottle of cheap whiskey, and a buxom Punjabi kudi.

Seetha accepted the presented credentials with a smile and a nod.

'And what field do you work in?' asked Amit.

Seetha decided to be consistent with her visa application. 'I'm a writer,' she replied simply.

'Wow, this is probably the first time I'm meeting a writer in flesh and blood,' said Amit. 'What kind of books do you write? Fiction?'

Great. Let me treat this as a rehearsal for my interview with the visa officer.

'I write stories and essays around philosophical themes — by philosophy I mean Indian philosophy.'

Amit leaned forward. Anything to do with the world of the intellect and the creative arts thrilled him. In college, everything in him had inclined to a life — a successful life — in academia or the arts — but his father had made it clear that Trehans could do better than be academics. They were successful Punjabi businessmen and industrialists. They might employ academics occasionally. A Madrasi might aspire to be a professor. Trehans did not. In time, Amit had reconciled to his father's world view. It was true that Delhi's cocktail circuit received business tycoons far more reverentially than it did professors at Delhi University. Nowadays Amit saw himself as the successful scion of a successful Punjabi business dynasty, but a scion who was more than just a businessman – an intellectual too, well read in the social sciences and a connoisseur of the arts. And here he was talking to a writer of stories with supernatural and philosophical themes. He was in his element – one of them at least.

'I've spent a lot of time probing the mysteries, but without much success or conclusion I must say. You must tell me something about your own understanding of Indian philosophy. But first let me go over and submit my visa application form. I'll be right back,' said Amit, getting up and walking over to the counter after receiving Seetha's confirmatory smile.

Seetha was thoughtful, her right hand stroking back her shoulder-length, black hair slowly and repeatedly. It was not easy to change personas. It was difficult to live a lie. But it wasn't entirely a lie. She had published a short story and she had read philosophy but she had never thought of herself as a writer, particularly a philosophical writer – except for the visa of course.

Wonder what it will be like to be a professional writer. I'll be successful of course. Salman Rushdie, Arundhati Roy, Kiran Desai and then Seetha Subramanium. But I'm writing on philosophical themes so perhaps critics will bracket me with Jostein Gaarder. *Seetha's World* – hmm.

She looked forward to playing her new role with Amit and looked up impatiently to see if he had completed his transaction at the DMZ surrounding the bullet-proof glass barrier.

Chapter 8

Amit reached the counter and pushed forward his application with a smile and a 'Good morning'. There was a style he adopted when dealing with government officers in India and he quickly slipped into that.

The Belgian officer scanned the form and said ponderously, 'Why did you not apply for your British visa before you left India? You are supposed to apply for your visa only in your home country.'

'I'm sorry sir. I had not planned to visit Britain when I left India but in talking to the Indian Ambassador here, we saw some business opportunities in Britain and that is why I would like to travel to London. Along with my form there is a letter from the Indian commercial attaché here endorsing my request.'

'What business opportunities? Do you have any correspondence with any British firms or any letter of invitation from them,' asked the officer, still concentrating on the form and not yet having looked up at Amit.

Amit thought quickly. He could get the commercial attaché or the Ambassador to ask their counterparts in London to ask one or more British firms – probably run by Britons of Indian origin – to invite him for a meeting.

'I'm afraid I did not realize that such letters would be necessary. We have mostly been communicating on the phone. I can certainly ask my British business associates to fax me letters of invitation. I can bring them with me tomorrow. Will that be okay?'

'Please bring the fax or faxes tomorrow and we will see what we can do,' said the officer, pushing Amit's application form and passport back towards him.

Amit thanked the officer and turned around and walked back towards Seetha. The faxes were no problem. He would anyway be seeing both the Deputy Chief of Mission and the Commercial Attaché at the dinner tonight at the DCM's home. They would see to the faxes.

That was quick. And he's bringing his papers back. Quick and immediate rejection of the Ambassador's friend. Surely not.

Seetha smiled at Amit, removed her shoulder bag from the seat next to her and asked questioningly. 'Smooth sailing?'

Amit sat down and smiled. 'It wasn't too bad. They wanted me to show them some correspondence with firms in Britain. I'll give them that tomorrow. The Brits tend to play by the book – their book of course – and its best to simply play along. If they want a fax, they'll have three with them tomorrow.'

Seetha smiled and nodded vaguely, eager to resume her role.

'Now tell me what your personal understanding of Indian philosophy is,' asked Amit, eyes bright, crossing his legs and settling into a comfortable position for a long discussion.

Seetha smiled. 'Now, if we're to have a serious conversation and hold the world, as it were, in the palm of our hands, then we must first see if the day and time are right. Indian sages have always maintained that objective thought about first principles, the basics beyond cabbages and kings, is impossible if the day is too hot – I guess here it's more likely to be too cold – or the road too dusty or you have an itch or your clothes are ill-fitting. Your body must be comfortable and your mind must be at peace. If today you have fought with your brother or taken your neighbour to court or wooed and lost the king's daughter, it is not the day for philosophy, for your view of eternity will be shaped by your cares of the moment and that won't do.'

Amit smiled, excited at this heady beginning, 'If my application for a British visa is rejected I suppose it would be quite the wrong time for dispassionate philosophy but at this time I'm quite composed. No cares or worries – at least nothing that's gnawing at me – and I'm wearing comfortable clothes.'

'Okay,' said Seetha, 'So be it. The next thing to do before we begin is to locate ourselves securely both in space and in time. Here we are – speaking for myself – two unremarkable persons, in the capital of a not very significant country called Belgium. We're waiting along with many others in the visa section of the embassy of a no-longer-very-significant country called Great Britain. We are two among ten billion on the face of the earth and our earth is a little dot in the universe.

'We are in a morning in December and there have been more than five thousand Decembers since civilization began and more than a million Decembers since the sun formed itself and allowed us to count our Decembers. And you must remember that scientists say that the sun arrived only recently in the calendar of the universe.

'So do you now feel completely dwarfed and insignificant? And do you still dare to question the universe as though it owed you an explanation for its and your existence?' asked Seetha, arching her eyebrows.

I don't know if he is following my words or just playing interested student. If it's a role he is playing, he is playing it well. Look at his interested, puzzled, hand-on-cheek, straining-to-follow look.

Amit did not want to reply to Seetha's question with some inanity. He had been watching the flow of ideas, the way spectators at an air show watch different planes flying past. He was not concentrating on any particular plane. He was just thrilled to be at such an air show. He nodded thoughtfully and Seetha continued, happy to answer her questions herself.

'I'd answer yes to both those questions. And almost all of us would do the same. I don't think that my insignificance temporally and spatially makes me any less qualified to ask questions. I might be just a tiny point in space and time, but to me I am the still point in a turning universe. I view the world, I oppose myself to it, and, speaking for myself, if I did not exist, the world wouldn't be there either.

'That's the astonishing arrogance of man's mind. Our minds are outsize philosophically. They should simply have been instruments of logic and coordination for our daily lives. Their realm should have been exclusively physics, not metaphysics. But instead, we seek for a raison d'etre, we look for something beyond and sometimes we receive intimations of immortality, or so we think...'

'Miz Seetha Subramanium,' boomed the intercom. Seetha looked up with a start. At the counter she saw the Belgian officer holding a mike. He had been responsible for the in-flight announcement which had so rudely interrupted

Seetha's philosophical ascent.

'Please come to the counter,' the officer now added into the mike.

With a quick 'Excuse me, I guess bureaucracy takes precedence over philosophy,' she left Amit and walked towards the counter.

'I'll wait for you,' Amit called out but Seetha did not hear him. She was already focused on the work at hand.

She reached the counter. 'Yes, I'm Seetha.'

Chapter 9

'You will now be interviewed by our Visa Officer. Please sit down in Interview Cabin Number Two,' said the Junior Officer to Seetha, pointing with his eyes to a row of three interview cabins to the right.

Seetha nodded briskly and went up to Interview Cabin Number Two. She knocked on the door and getting no response, tried the handle gently. The door opened and she entered. She found herself in an empty room quite unlike anything she had ever seen. It appeared to be a cross between a padded cell and a Stalin-era KGB interrogation chamber. That she had seen neither did not really matter. She had read enough about both. The walls were actually padded – soundproofed anyway. Why? So that other waiting applicants outside would not hear the sounds of rage, anguish and frustration that were likely to emanate from the hapless applicant within? The room had a bulletproof glass partition right across the middle with a chair, a small, round table and a door on either side. The partition was perforated with angular holes designed cleverly to prevent bullets, arrows (Third Worlders were the applicants) or poisoned knitting needles reaching the Visa Officer but permitting truth and lies, screams and sighs, to do so.

High on a wall, on the Visa Officer's side of the room, there was a framed portrait of the Queen circa 1960. Applicants wishing to enter her realm could study her calm countenance and compose themselves before the Visa Officer entered. That was what Seetha did, wondering idly how much the Queen's appearance would change if she sported an Indian bindi on her forehead.

Doug Evans entered the room with a little cough. Once upon a time he had thought that it was a nice touch to let the applicant know that the British Visa Officer was just another bloke. Now he didn't care what applicants thought but the habit had formed.

Doug looked across the glass at Seetha. She looked gorgeous in her sari.

'Good morning, Miss Subramanium,' said Doug cheerily.

'Good morning, sir,' replied Seetha warily.

Now concentrate, girl. Steady. Think before you answer. Curb that evil tongue of yours. Don't retort, don't spar, don't preach. This is an important interview.

Doug sat down and arranged Seetha's papers neatly in front of him. He had been through them but nonetheless pretended to read from them as he spoke to Seetha.

He had noticed that Seetha's career so far had been in Systems Analysis and the sudden desire to be a writer in England had caught his eye. He remembered that Stewart – Sour Stewart as he had been known at Winchester – had made much the same shift and successfully too – but what might not be too remarkable in a British collegian may well conceal ulterior motives in an Indian visa applicant.

'Writing. Difficult profession. You've not exactly been a prolific writer so far.'

'No, sir. Only one of my stories has been published – but it has been well received – and I have now decided to take up writing as a full-time career,' replied Seetha, her whole mind and body focused on the task in hand.

Take it easy, girl. Don't rush to answer. Take your time. Choose your words. Don't trip. God, my left foot is itching. Don't bend and scratch, you yokeli.

'You have been a Systems Analyst so far. You have probably written more C++ code – or is it Java now – than prose...' said Doug, trailing off intentionally.

'It is Java now, sir, but I'm a Systems Analyst, not a programmer. I do have some familiarity with Java but we in Applications are mostly concerned with systems design and process flow charts and logic diagrams. I have not written too much code.'

Doug was warming to his task. It was always more interesting dealing with an intelligent applicant who spoke English fluently even if you knew that he or she was lying through his or her pearly teeth – and this girl was pretty too in a very Indian way.

'Thank you for explaining so lucidly the difference between

programming and Systems Analysis. Now you say here that you plan to write on philosophical themes. Do you philosophize yourself?' asked Doug, probing.

'Yes, I do. I would not be a philosophical writer if I didn't,' replied Seetha. She was settling down now. The interview was evolving into civilized exchange of views and Seetha knew she had to thank Doug for that. He had sheathed his standard issue British embassy broadsword and had chosen to use a Cambridge University debating club practice foil instead. And he was allowing her to use one too.

'Why do men philosophize?' mused Doug aloud, teasing Seetha into continuing.

Where to begin? Show your understanding of the subject. You don't have to be sequential. Don't argue. Don't orate, just muse aloud.

'Sometimes it can be pain. The Buddhists feel that all philosophy is an attempt to understand suffering and alleviate it. Suffering takes many forms. It can range from specific grief to angst to weltschmerz.

'Sorrow makes one think. Unhappiness makes one ponder in a way happiness rarely does. The hour of thought which follows many hours of tears is often philosophical. In thinking about the immediate cause of pain, we also wonder at the nature of pain itself. From that it is a small step to pondering about the nature of a world in which pain exists. Many religions have taught us that suffering was introduced by God to force men to think beyond the material world.'

Today was a relatively light day and there did not seem to be too many people Doug needed to interview. He moved the table to his right and stretched his legs. Elbow on table, cheek in hand, he silently asked Seetha to continue.

She did willingly.

'Sometimes, men begin to philosophize when they are awed or frightened by the strength of their desires. We often find that our desires shape and mould our minds like putty. Our minds are reduced to being instruments of desire. They then reel back with fear to study this beast within.'

Doug breathed a silent Amen to that. He was very familiar with the beast within.

'Some of us grope at philosophy hoping that it will show

us some door to escape from the grim fact of our mortality. That I must go the way of all flesh is something I accept academically but not in truth. So I ponder over death, call it merely the death of the body, consider it a prelude to another life or call it merely an event in the indelible canvas of time. In any case I seek out philosophy to support my claim and preserve my sanity.'

I think I'm doing fine but how long does he want me to go on. I can go on for a long time but surely, all he wants is to know if I really know a little about philosophy. Should I continue? I can give a couple more reasons for philosophizing. Mustn't sound too rehearsed.

Seetha paused to give Doug a chance to interject but he did not. Seetha continued.

'Others turn to philosophy because they have a strong intuitive belief that something lies beyond, behind or above the reality they see around them. They feel that the world is more than the sum of the parts they see. We all have moments when we are certain that we are guided by some kind of destiny. There are days when we seem to be able to transcend ourselves and swallow the stars. There are times when it seems to us irrefutable that there are forces in this world which we do not understand. Then there are a few of us, just a few of us, who turn to philosophy out of intellectual curiosity. We use the tools of science and logic, which have helped us so much in understanding the material world, to try and understand all else. The Indian scriptures come out strongly against such doctors of logic and the intellectually curious because their tools and methods are thought to be wrong. The Upanishads feel that such men will never arrive at the truth.'

'So you see, sir,' said Seetha smilingly in peroration, 'it is a motley but large crowd which comes knocking at Philosophy's gate.'

'Are you talking about India specifically?' asked Doug slowly, thinking that this conversation would have been so much more pleasant, had it been taking place on a punt drifting down the Wye on a lazy, sunny July afternoon.

'I think all of us, human beings, do philosophize but I was talking more specifically about the India of old. Not the India of today unfortunately. In the India of old, philosophical speculation was the number one spectator sport. Sages argued in front of kings, scholars and astonishingly large crowds of lay people. They found the cut and thrust of debate, the tumbling deductions, the soaring inductions, all infinitely more satisfying than a bending free kick or a crunching shoulder charge.

'In ancient India, sages were honoured far more than kings, warriors or merchants. That is why, so many Indian religious chronologies and genealogical tables are a listing of who taught whom, and not, as in certain scriptures, who begat whom.

'But all that is in the dim past. In today's India, philosophical discussions attract only a few, sad grey heads. The young don't care who teaches whom. Come to think of it, they don't care who begets whom.'

Seetha became bolder.

'When was the last time you were engaged in a deep philosophical discussion?' she asked Doug, unconsciously sensing that the discussion could now be made to transcend its context.

Startled by suddenly being at the receiving end of a question, Doug blurted out a reply, forming his thoughts as he spoke, 'Come to think of it, not any time in the recent past – I guess these days our minds are so busy handling the tricky business of living, there is little time and even less inclination to muse.'

'Exactly – and in time to come, as we muse less and less, darwinevitably we will gradually lose the ability to do so. Man's mind will become an efficient functional coordinator and its reach will not exceed its objective grasp,' pronounced Seetha.

You're doing well, Seetha girl, a touch cheeky and a touch preachy but I think you've got him where you want him.

Doug found the Indian girl becoming a little overwhelming. He wanted to re-establish context. He paused, then bent forward and picked up Seetha's application form again. He put away the practice foils and unsheathed his broadsword.

'Miss Subramanium, in Belgium you are on assignment to Expobel. What remuneration are you paid?' asked Doug.

Seetha had been leaning forward, eyes bright, mind keen and ready for more musing. Now, suddenly hauled back to the visa interview, she slumped back in her chair and replied a little numbly, 'I receive a living allowance of a thousand euros in Belgium apart from my salary in India which is the equivalent of another thousand euros.'

'Monthly?' asked Doug.

'Yes, sir,' replied Seetha.

Context had been re-established. Doug was a little sorry for Seetha but was relieved that he was back in control.

Once more the Visa Officer, he felt he needed more convincing before he could give this bright penny a work visa. The girl knew something about philosophy and probably could write. He was not sure that she could make a career from philosophical writing. Or that she really intended to. Or that she needed to make that career in Britain. Or that she really intended to abandon her current career in Systems Analysis.

'Why do you need to live and write in Britain?' asked Doug, 'Would India not be the best place for a writer on Indian philosophy'?

Seetha and Mr Iyer had gone over this.

'My next novel is set in the sixteenth century – a century of much religious upheaval both in India and Europe. Let me briefly give you the storyline. A young cleric, attached to Thomas More, is forced to flee England soon after More's execution in 1535 as he too is suspected of conspiring with the Nun of Kent. The cleric travels East, through Catholic France, Calvinist Switzerland, Lutheran Germany, Orthodox Russia, Islamic Turkmenistan and eventually, thirty years later, reaches the Moghul court at Delhi just in time to be invited by the liberal emperor Akbar to participate in an exciting project – the creation of a new syncretic religion by royal decree – the Din-i-Illahi. The cleric shares with Indian scholars More's *Utopia* and Erasmus's *Colloquies* and espouses their tolerant, humanist philosophy. He influences the king and helps shape the new religion in softer lines. The cleric also meets and falls in love with the daughter of Abul Fazl, one of the King's courtiers and a profound thinker, scholar and writer. He then... well, I won't bore you with the rest of the story.

'While I am reasonably familiar with Indian philosophy and the Moghul era I'm much less familiar with Christian theology and the intellectual milieu in which More thought and wrote and Henry the Eighth lived and loved. I don't know much either about English history, English courtly life, manners and mores. In order to write about that period and those questions I need to be in England, visit English palaces, the Tower, Chelsea where More lived, the great Cathedrals and some of the old monasteries. I need to soak in England. I must speak to English scholars. I also need to refer to several books and documents of that period and the British Museum will be a good place to work in. Besides, I intend to publish this book in Britain and not in India. I need to find a publisher and then I'll have to work quite closely with them,' replied Seetha evenly and matter of fact.

She has it all pat, thought Doug, and it may all be true – it's certainly plausible and he could believe that she could write that book. Unable to decide and uncertain how to proceed he picked up Seetha's application form again.

'*Stories Which Bend Belief* – who edited that?' asked Doug hoping to find some clue in facts.

'Raghunath Singh. He teaches at Delhi's Jawaharlal Nehru University. He is a writer himself. He has been asked to deliver the Brotherton Memorial lecture at Cambridge this year.'

'Miss Subramanium, can we speak to him on the phone and refer to your application?' asked Doug.

'Certainly. I think I have his number with me,' answered Seetha fumbling in her bag for her diary. She would give the Visa Officer Singh's work number. It would be four in the afternoon in India and Singh would be in the library. She knew that he was never available in his room after two. The Visa Officer would only be able to speak to Singh the next morning and in the meantime, tonight, she would call Raghunath at his home and speak to him, making sure he would support her application. It would not be difficult. Raghunath thought well of her. He thought well of the few pretty young women who wrote.

'I have his work number. It is 91-11-26783722,' Seetha called out from her diary.

'Someone from our office will speak to Mr Singh today.

If you can come back tomorrow at 11am, we should be able to process your application further. Depending on what Mr Singh says and our further perusal of your application, you may need to be interviewed again tomorrow,' said Doug.

'Sure,' replied Seetha, 'I will be here at 11 tomorrow.'

Reasonably happy that he now had a plan of action, Doug sheathed his broadsword and brought out the practice foils again.

Doug bent forward and gathered his papers, 'It has been interesting talking to you. Tell me something. Why or how is it that Indians – from the ancient sages to today's new-age gurus – have been so prolifically philosophical? A chosen people?' he asked, leaning back once again and smiling quizzically at Seetha.

Seetha had risen and turned to leave but she now turned back again. She rocked on her heels, at ease, considering an answer.

'Probably not. You're more likely to find the answer in India's history, geography and social structure. India's always been an ethnic and cultural melting pot. In the two millennia before the birth of Christ, the Indo-Aryans, or at the very least, Indo-Aryan culture, spread further and further into India from the North-West. As it spread, it came into contact with other ethnic groups and cultures. The Indo-Aryans never annihilated or totally displaced existing cultures, some of which were remarkably advanced. Hence we had very different cultures and value systems existing in close proximity. That is a sure thing to make men think. There is stimulation and the excitement of looking at new ways of thinking.'

Doug nodded thoughtfully. He too had risen.

'India's geography and climate played their part too. They allowed simple living and high thinking. To put things in sequence, high thinking was possible because simple living was possible. The climate was mild, the elements were friendly and all a family needed was a simple thatched hut and the shade of a banyan tree. The land was easy to till and the forests were full of trees heavy with low-hanging fruit. Since living was easy, men turned their minds to the mysteries – the bright stars, the wheel of life and the door of death.

'Another reason for the fecundity of ancient Indian thought

was the prodding of Nature. In the India of those days the forests were deep, the rivers were broad, the mountains were high and mighty oceans surrounded us on three sides. Nature was always around with its orb, sceptre and diadem. It drew from ancient Indians awe, homage and, most importantly, thought,' concluded Seetha in presto.

Chapter 10

Harish having left to get his bank statement, Ratnesh found himself at a loose end, waiting to be interviewed. He looked around and more from want of anything to do than real need he decided to use the toilet. He found the toilet locked, read the notice on the door and went up to the counter to ask for the key. A large white man was at the counter, vigorously remonstrating in broken English with the Belgian officer. The Belgian officer had his head buried in some papers – presumably the white man's application.

Ratnesh went up to the counter and standing next to the large white man he said to the Belgian officer, 'Excuse me, please. Toilet key, please.'

The Belgian officer looked up for once and calmly told Ratnesh to wait until he had finished with the other gentleman.

'Urgent need, please,' replied Ratnesh, always relishing a little challenge.

The Belgian officer looked Ratnesh over and seemed to be visually evaluating Ratnesh's urgency. Unconvinced, he turned back to the large white man.

'Pressing need, sir, forced soiling trousers here otherwise,' hissed Ratnesh, now committed to winning the exchange.

The large white man moved back a step sharply. The Belgian officer looked at Ratnesh with deep loathing, then turning around, he took a key from a tray and handed it to him.

'Thank you, sir, thank you, weak bladder, weak bowels, sir,' said Ratnesh, his voice combining urgency and triumph.

He went over to the toilet and opened the door. The toilet was quite elaborate, equipped, as the sign on the door had said, for men, women and the disabled. Ratnesh elaborately washed his face and wiped it dry. He took a cheap plastic comb from his hip pocket and combed his hair – slowly, meticulously – parting it down the middle and slicking it back with practised dexterity. This toilet smelled a little but was certainly cleaner than those in the Gare du Midi. Perhaps it was because they kept it locked.

Ratnesh suddenly wondered if the Nigerian woman had used the toilet before leaving. If she had, she might have sat down on the toilet seat and cried and then pulled out a tissue from the tissue dispenser to wipe her swollen red eyes. So might have many before her. Ratnesh had only one piece of advice for all of them. Be tough. Don't cry. This world gives no quarter to the weak.

Reluctant to leave the neutral emptiness of the toilet so soon, he studied himself in the mirror, vigorously twisting his index finger in his ear by way of cleaning it, rubbing the stubble on his chin and wondering, as he often did, if Western women found him attractive. Today he came to the conclusion that he was not unattractive. They would find him exotic – a mysterious Eastern mystic – no, that was not him. A mysterious Eastern rebel, fighting against oppression – yes that was him and that was what his UN refugee status application said too.

He left the toilet and entered the waiting hall. The large white man was still at the counter. Ratnesh interrupted him once again and slipped the key through the slot in the bullet proof glass barrier, thanking the Belgian officer profusely. He thought that he noticed both the officer and the white man cast a quick glance at his trousers.

The hall was now quite crowded. But it was not noisy. Some of the applicants had submitted their applications and were waiting to be called to be interviewed or to be given their visas. They sat back in the hard plastic seats with low backs and no cushioning, expressionless, hands folded in front. Others were struggling to complete their forms. Applicants who knew a little English were helping others who knew none. The applicants were mostly black or brown. There were a smattering of Chinese and a few white Eastern Europeans. If some researcher at the University Libre in Brussels, working on the connection between skin colour and milieu were to use a colourometer here, then on a scale of one to ten where one was Dahomey black and ten was Scandinavian blond, the instrument would probably have recorded a three. The score at the Palais des Beaux Arts on an evening when the Brussels Symphony Orchestra was playing would be a perfect ten. The

Gare du Midi would normally have recorded a five.

Ratnesh looked around. He saw a person who looked South Asian sitting at ease some distance away also looking around. Ratnesh had earlier noticed this person speaking to the prim, uptight Indian girl who had so rudely ejected him from the head of the queue. Ratnesh decided to give the gentleman the benefit of his company.

He went up to the gentleman, sat down next to him, and asked without any unnecessary preamble, 'Are you Indian?'

Amit straightened himself in his chair and replied, 'Yes, and you?'

'Yes. Myself Ratnesh. Yourself?' asked Ratnesh putting out his hand.

'Myself Amit,' replied Amit in spite of himself, shaking the proffered hand with just a little reluctance.

'Glad to meet another Indian in this strange country,' said Ratnesh, switching to Hindi.

'It does feel strange to be in a country where you can't understand any of their three official languages,' replied Amit, staying with English.

'I'm leaving soon. As soon as these motherfuckers give me my visa,' said Ratnesh, gesturing with a bent thumb towards the area behind the counter.

There was a moment's silence in which each of them consolidated what they had learnt of the other. They sized each other up easily and accurately from a hundred small clues as fellow countrymen do.

A crude, small-town, fighting cock, thought Amit.

A lucky, rich, English-speaking bastard – perhaps worth cultivating, thought Ratnesh.

'Do you live here? Do you have a Belgian passport?' asked Ratnesh in the information gathering style of conversation favoured most commonly in the second-class compartments of long-distance trains in India.

'No, I don't live here. I live in Delhi. I run a couple of food processing industries there. I met the Indian Ambassador to Belgium in Delhi last year and he suggested that I come here on a business trip. The Indian embassy is trying to help me establish a relationship with some European food product importing firms,' replied Amit. He was one of those who wanted to impress everyone, a small-town fighting cock included.

'The best people to deal with are Indians settled here in Europe. They understand us and at the same time, being citizens of European countries, know how to work the system here. I have been in Europe for the last six months and have many contacts with Indians here,' said Ratnesh.

'And what is your line of business?' asked Amit.

'I make deals. I have made deals in leather, in tea, in diamonds – you name it – both imports and exports from India. I've decided not to touch drugs or arms but everything else I have done or can do,' replied Ratnesh.

Ratnesh regaled Amit with stories of Europe and business seen through Indian eyes. Of Russians who were the Punjabis of Europe, of the British who were its Banias and Greeks who were the continent's Sindhis. Ratnesh dropped names of people and companies. As always he mixed a little fact and a lot of considered imagination. The fat Moroccan, Hamid, who ran the dirtiest cafe in Brussels metamorphosed into an Arab sheikh in the hospitality business, and the wealthy heiress who was Ratnesh's business associate was inspired by Mabel.

Amit recognized the exaggeration and the bravado. The small-town fighting cock must have been alternately strutting and fluttering across Europe desperately trying to make a deal, any deal – and probably may have stitched together one or two – undoubtedly likely to dissolve in recrimination and law suits sooner or later.

In Delhi, people like Ratnesh were unlikely to ever cross his path. The circles that Ratnesh probably wheeled in would never intersect the elevated circles that Amit dealt in. Amit would not find a need for Ratnesh in India. If his father was ever to meet Ratnesh, he would have dismissed him as a petty Paharganj broker with an eye for the main chance.

Amit weighed the pros and cons of exploring business opportunities with Ratnesh. Amit knew that any business transaction with Ratnesh would be fraught with danger. There would be every likelihood that he would be double-crossed, sold short or at least let down. But then Ratnesh and his ilk were street-smart. They could make deals – dubious deals, yes, but deals nonetheless. In business acumen, Ratnesh contrasted favourably with the smooth, balding, bland, free-of-initiative Promod Khera, the Commercial Attaché who had been assigned to help Amit. Khera spent his days visiting websites – his three favourite sites were those of the European Union, the WTO, and Round and Brown – and his evenings escorting his wife to shopping malls. He had not yet facilitated business worth a single euro to or from India since he took on this job role three years ago.

Ratnesh might just enable Amit to make that critical first business foray into Europe. Later on, he could always jettison Ratnesh, the way a space rocket would jettison its first stage booster. And there was the whole problem of Dad's dirty laundry in the form of a couple of million black dollars. They needed to be dyed and siphoned back to India – lily-white. Ratnesh may be just the kind of person to understand the situation and find a solution.

Another reason which inclined Amit towards dealing with Ratnesh was Amit's image of himself. He thought of himself as a compleat man who was equally at home discussing Advaita philosophy in rarefied intellectual circles one day and fighting bare knuckled business brawls the next. Associating with Ratnesh would be a challenging experience but Amit had no doubts that he was clearly the superior man and would be able to handle this farmyard rooster.

'We have a problem that you must be familiar with. We have some funds in Europe – in dollars – and we need to bring that money back to India to help finance some new projects that we are planning. We need to bring it back as export earnings – which will be tax-free and white,' said Amit as one man of the world to another – they were equals now.

Ratnesh leaned back apparently in mature thought, but more in satisfaction. So Mr I-know-the-Ambassador did have need of Ratnesh Kumar. He let Amit wait for a few more seconds.

'It can be arranged of course and there are many ways to do this. What we need to choose is a method which meshes well with your line of business and makes the transfer of funds completely invisible,' said Ratnesh sagely.

'Obviously,' said Amit, irritated at having to listen patiently to a pontificating Ratnesh.

'How much money are we talking about?' asked Ratnesh.

'Two million US dollars – in a bank account in Zurich that I am authorized to operate.'

'Saffron. That could be the solution,' said Ratnesh, pointing his finger dramatically at Amit.

Amit wondered how saffron could be the answer. In his mind – and in the mind of most Indians, saffron was associated with the ruling right-wing party. It brought to mind violent movements to destroy mosques, to build temples, to save the cow. 'Saffronize' had come to be accepted as a verb by the English-language press.

Amit was puzzled. Was Ratnesh implying that he use his political connections – but no – he had not told Ratnesh about them.

'You could take back twenty dollars for every hundred grams. So you can have your two million back in India over a hundred thousand packets – ten months – ten thousand packets a month will not attract any attention,' continued Ratnesh.

So Ratnesh was referring to the spice and not the colour. But Amit could still not figure out how money could be laundered through hundred-gram packets of an expensive spice. His face showed his bewilderment.

Ratnesh sighed deeply, surprised at the naiveté of the Ambassador's friend. He leaned forward and explained gently, as to a child.

'Arrey bhai, there are so many varieties of saffron. There is a common variety of saffron which costs less than two dollars for a hundred grams. Then there are exclusive Kashmiri saffron varieties that cost as much as twenty dollars for the same quantity. You are going to buy common saffron in India at two dollars and send it to Belgium, invoicing your buyer in Europe for Kashmiri saffron at twenty dollars a packet. Most European customs officers have no idea what saffron is, much less what Kashmiri saffron is. They will only want to make sure that you are not smuggling in drugs and that you are not. Your problem will be to find a helpful importer in Europe. A good Indo-European – Indian blood and European passport, even a permanent resident will do – who runs a business that

allows him to import saffron without suspicion. He will buy
your saffron at twenty dollars a packet. And sell it to me at
twenty-one dollars a packet. Of course I will be paying him
the money from that bank account that you are authorized
to operate. I will be withdrawing twenty-three dollars a
packet. The importer need not know that you are both the
buyer and the seller. He will send twenty snow-white dollars
to your exporting company in India and will keep a dollar to
help with the education of his children – educating children
well is always important. I will keep two dollars a packet – to
meet my frugal expenses. I will take the cheap saffron from
him and arrange to have it delivered to anyone you name in
Europe. If you don't need it I will sell it or give it away free as
a promotion.'

'Currying favour by flavouring curries across Europe,'
murmured Amit automatically. He could never resist a pun.
Ratnesh ignored him.

'So I will be spending twenty-three black dollars to get
twenty white dollars – expensive,' said Amit aloud, showing
he was keeping up and following the dollars between the
lines.'

'Think of a cheaper way, then,' retorted Ratnesh evenly. He
knew when he had his man.

Amit could not think of a cheaper way. For the last week
he had not been able to think of any way at all. He left the
question of cost and moved tangentially – as advised by
business school textbooks on negotiation.

'We need to find a helpful importer. I suppose Promod, the
Commercial Attaché here should be able to find one who is
trustworthy.'

'I'm sure he will,' said Ratnesh.

Amit was sure he would not. He regretted having introduced
Promod Khera into the discussion. He waited for a minute
hoping that Ratnesh would suggest an importer himself but
negotiators who have cut their teeth negotiating bribes with
municipal officers in towns like Arrah are merciless and know
when to wait silently.

'Can you suggest an importer' asked Amit. 'Come to think of
it, Promod may not want to be seen helping Indian business
men change the colour of their money.'

'A couple of options come to mind. There is a German I know who is the president of a chain of food stores in the area around Hamburg. I have helped him in the past and he will be willing to return a favour. Then there is an Indo-European I know very well – he is a small-time businessman right here in Brussels – runs a single retail food outlet. Although he is a much smaller player, he is Indian and will be accommodating and understanding. The German, like most North Europeans, will take ages to understand what we want him to do and when he finally understands he may put on a constipated look and call it unethical. I would recommend the Indian retailer,' finished Ratnesh strongly – and with very good reason. The German existed only in his imagination while Harish was flesh and blood – and even though he had not been spoken to, Ratnesh was absolutely confident he could get Harish to play his part.

Amit was silent for a moment. Ratnesh seemed to be calling all the shots and taking all the decisions. But then textbooks on negotiation urged one to put aside questions of ego. In fact they encouraged you to make the person you were negotiating with feel that he or she was in command. Just as long as you met your objectives. And what were his objectives? To find a way to launder and repatriate the wretched two million dollars and by doing so earn the approbation of Trehan Senior. He was meeting those objectives, wasn't he? Wasn't this what they called a win-win – the holy grail of textbook negotiation?

Reassured, Amit replied, 'I agree. I think it should be the Indian. Well, I think we have a plan. When can we meet the Indian retailer?'

'As a matter of fact, he's right here today. He had to apply for a visa too. He wants to go to London to watch a cricket match at Lord's,' replied Ratnesh, his smile showing his amusement at the thought that grown-up businessmen might have such distractions.

'Cricket? It's winter now. What cricket does he think he is going to watch?'

'Oh, he's planning to watch a county match in May. But he's one of those who must do everything as much in advance as humanly possible. He's booked his match tickets, his train

tickets and now he's here to get his visa too. He lives a very
ordered life. He's the kind who will have his hair cut on the
fifth of every month without fail and will trim his nails every
alternate Monday morning exactly at seven. Must have a
printed schedule for his sex life too. Not a very busy schedule, I
suspect. Just a couple of entries for the year. Shouldn't bother
us. As far as we are concerned, he is a safe and dependable
person to do business with. At the moment he has gone to his
bank. The clerks behind the counter here wanted him to bring
proof of his means. I will speak to him when he returns, and if
he seems amenable – which I am sure he will for my sake – I
will bring him over to meet you.'

'Thanks,' said Amit, a little reluctantly.

Both were silent – Ratnesh tried to calculate how much
would be his slice from the two million dollars. Two for
every twenty-three. Roughly a tenth. Roughly two hundred
thousand dollars. Multiply that by forty. That made eighty
lakh Indian rupees. Now that was decent money.

Amit thought about his nightly call to his father – today
he would have something to report. Trehan Senior would
not hint that he thought that Amit was doing little more
than spending his time sampling the bubbling fleshpots of
Europe.

'You must also be applying for a business visa. They asked
me to produce some proof that I had some meetings lined
up in London. Did they ask you for the same?' asked Amit
conversationally.

'I'm not applying for a business visa. I'm applying for a
tourist visa – I'm travelling to London to meet an old friend.
Ah, there comes Harish, the Indian retailer I told you about.
Let me go and speak to him,' said Ratnesh, rising and hurrying
to intercept Harish as he entered the visa hall.

Chapter 11

Harish was sure that there would be a branch of his bank, the Fortis Banque, somewhere on Avenue Louise. He left the visa hall and as he passed the security desk he told the officer there that the visa process seemed to be less cumbersome than he had anticipated. The security officer shrugged, pursed his lips, rolled his eyes and muttered a non committal 'Ah oui'.

Harish walked towards Avenue Louise. He walked slowly but purposefully. He had been so apprehensive about the process of obtaining a British visa. Perhaps he should not have been. These whites normally had systems that worked reasonably well most all the time. They were justified in asking to see his bank balance. They did need to be sure that he was solvent and could fund his stay in Britain. Given the fact that half the Third World was trying to emigrate, he did not blame European governments for being paranoid. He did not blame that half of the Third World either. It was just the way it was.

As he turned into Avenue Louise he thought about the cricket match he was going to watch. Here in Belgium there was no cricket and even if there had been he would not have found the time to follow any of it. He hoped everything at Lord's would be as traditional as possible – as close to the image of English cricket he had built from looking at the pictures in *Sportsweek* and listening to commentaries of Test matches on the radio in India more than fifteen years ago. The last time he had visited India was a year ago and he had watched some matches on television and had been disappointed. Everything had seemed more frenetic now. The players seemed to be trying to do in one day what earlier they had done in five. Not surprisingly they appeared to be in a bad temper all the time. Even when a player scored a century or when a bowler got a batsman out, they celebrated angrily. Harish had been told that English county cricket was different – still very genteel – the players still wearing white, the spectators still good-natured. That is why he had chosen to watch a county cricket match at Lord's. Lord's, the Mecca of cricket, the hallowed home of the gentleman's game as the radio commentator called it. The thought of watching a match there gave Harish goosebumps.

A friend had told him about an Indian sweet and snack shop in Wembley. Harish guessed that there would be enough time for him to visit the shop, buy some samosas and take them with him to Lord's. And he should also buy a couple of cans of Pepsi too. It was likely to be so much more expensive if he bought them at Lord's. In May, the sun could be quite fierce sometimes so he should take a cap along with him – the Stella Artois baseball cap which he had received a long while back as part of some promotional campaign and never used so far would do just fine. Since he had quite a few things to carry and would be alone, perhaps he needed to take along a small rucksack.

Harish was so full of his own pleasant thoughts that he almost forgot to look for the bank. He finally found a branch of the Fortis Banque near the intersection with Rue Blanche. He and an old lady reached the door of the bank at almost exactly the same time. Harish stopped to let the lady enter. She saw him and seeing him standing still near her, looked at him suspiciously and entered the bank, clutching her handbag tightly and casting backward glances at the coloured man.

Harish entered after her and chose to print out his bank statements at an automatic teller machine. He went to the nearest one and after placing the folder with his visa papers on the ledge next to the ATM, he stood himself square in front of the machine and interacted with it slowly and deliberately. He obtained the printouts and studied them. He realized that his balances were not exactly large – the Visa Officer might not be satisfied. Harish would need to explain to him how Night Shops operated – cash in the bank was cash wasted – every cent was put into inventory or sent to the subcontinent to support a gaggle of relatives and causes.

On his way back to the British embassy Harish's thoughts returned to his trip to London. He planned to take the 3pm Eurostar on the day before the match. That would get him into London around six in the evening. Enough time for him to find the Tube station, buy his ticket, find the right line and the right direction to take him to Kentish Town which was where Mukesh lived. Mukesh was from Hissar too and had immigrated to Britain ten years ago. Harish did not know him too well but you did not need to know an Indian very well to ask him to put you up for a couple of nights. That was the nice thing about Indians, especially poorer Indians. They accepted without question the need to help each other, particularly with food and shelter. Nodding acquaintance was enough to ask for and be given a hot Indian meal and a place to sleep. And that was all Harish wanted of Mukesh. There was no need for Mukesh to like him.

He wondered what he should wear to the match. He wondered what the other spectators would be wearing. It was only the players who wore white, although he was not absolutely sure. It would be May so it would not be cold. The spectators would probably all be wearing casual clothes – jeans, bermudas, shorts, t-shirts, sneakers and sports shoes. Harish did not possess any shorts or t-shirts. All Harish had were shirts and trousers. Four shirts and three pairs of trousers to be precise. All tailored in Hissar during his vacations there. They were cheap and they were what he was used to. He wore shirts and trousers everywhere and on every occasion. At work in the Taj, he rolled up his shirt sleeves to mid forearm and left the top couple of shirt buttons unbuttoned. On the rare occasions when he had to visit people or attend social functions he wore full sleeves, neatly buttoned at the wrist and his shirt would also be all buttoned up too. On his feet, at home and sometimes even in the shop in summer, he wore slippers. After all he was behind the counter most of the time and no one could see his feet. He did have a nondescript pair of scuffed leather shoes bought in Hissar. He wore his shoes whenever he had to leave the shop. He did shine them frequently but their age and origin showed.

Harish decided to wear his white shirt which had a pattern of small yellow flowers along with his dark green trousers. They were the newest he owned and the shirt would lend an air of appropriate casualness and good cheer. He was worried about his footwear. Maybe he should use this occasion to invest in sports shoes. Zulfikar owned a pair and said that they were most comfortable. He decided he would. He had noticed that the local supermarket chain, Carrefour, stocked their own brand of sports shoes which were likely to be much cheaper than the Nikes and the Pumas that he saw advertised everywhere. He would buy a pair soon. He wondered if he should also buy white sports socks. No. Not really necessary. That would be trying to buy too many new things at the same time. The black nylon socks he used with his leather shoes should be okay. Socks were hidden most of the time.

Smiling contentedly to himself, Harish reached the British embassy and re-entered the visa section. He exchanged bonjours with the security officer and took the lift again. Entering the hall, he saw Ratnesh bearing down towards him.

Harish stopped, smiled at Ratnesh and waited for him. Harish rarely formed opinions about people. People were just people, each person with his or her angularities.

'I have good news for you. You should buy me beer tonight,' said Ratnesh, loud enough for the Belgian officer to look up. He quickly looked down again though.

'No problem,' replied Harish smiling like Mona Lisa with the mildest of anticipation. 'Just give me a couple of minutes. Let me go and submit my application. It is now complete. I have obtained the bank statements they wanted.'

Ratnesh sent Harish on his way with an avuncular pat on his shoulder, then turned and sat down in the nearest empty seat, fidgeting, eager to keep a good thing moving along.

The counter was fortunately free and Harish stepped up to it.

'Bonjour, I have got bank statements of both my accounts. Here is my completed application. Now I'm sure you won't have a problem sending me to London,' said Harish in French, with the familiarity a shared language brings.

'Non, non,' said the officer, taking the application form and the bank statements. He studied the bank statements.

'You have a total of 634 euros in your accounts. That's not much for a businessman who has been in business for eight years – your London cricket splash will drain the little that's there,' said the Belgian combining grievance and dismay in the gruff tone that comes naturally to most Belgians, particularly in winter.

'All the cash we have we use to increase the stock we have in our shop – and each year I send to India any surplus that I have. In our country we have a saying: If your money is idle, you can't be. If your money is busy, you can be idle,' explained Harish.

'I'm afraid that an Indian proverb cannot be cited in a visa application as supporting evidence. I need to have proof that you have the means to pay for your expenses during your visit and that you have sufficient reason to come back to Belgium,' said the Belgian officer, his tone hardening just a little.

'I have a Permanent Residence Permit which I have shown you, I have attached the registration papers of our shop. What else can I produce to convince you?' said Harish, trying to think aloud and see if there was any other document that might help.

'Well, I can't think of anything obvious. The onus is on you to convince us. I don't think I can approve the visa at my level as I earlier thought I could. I'll have to put up your papers to the Visa Officer – my boss. He may want to interview you and be satisfied,' said the Belgian officer, deciding to play it safe.

'Don't worry. It will probably work out all right,' he added, seeing the look of dismay slowly darkening Harish's face.

'When will I be interviewed?' asked Harish

'It's already lunch time now. You will probably be called tomorrow morning. Come around ten. Just be yourself in the interview. You have an honest voice,' said the Belgian officer by way of farewell. He was a little surprised at the way he had taken to Harish. It happened very, very rarely.

Harish turned, sighing. Everything was always more difficult than it appeared to be. He would have to tell Zulfikar to mind the shop tonight. Harish wanted to sleep well and be ready for the interview the next day. Tomorrow would be Friday and that would be the day the wine and liquor wholesaler would come to the shop for the weekly replenishing. It was Harish's duty to fill out the weekly liquor order form. He must check the stock in the shop tonight and fill out the form and give it to Zulfikar and ask him to deal with the liquor wholesaler.

Harish also decided that he needed to take more care with his clothes and appearance tomorrow.

He saw Ratnesh waiting for him. Harish would have preferred to go back home straight away, using the time on the Number 23 tram to think of arguments he could give the English officer the next day, but Ratnesh had been helpful and now seemed to have some news to share. He walked towards Ratnesh.

Ratnesh put out his hand and helped Harish into the seat next to him.

'What would you say if I showed you a way to make around ten thousand euros a month, sitting on your haunches?' asked Ratnesh, full of bonhomie and good cheer.

'I would say that you have had too much wine,' said Harish smiling. Such miracles did not occur in his world.

'Listen, have you imported any food products from India for your shop?' asked Ratnesh.

'I have imported mangoes quite often. Indian mangoes sell well here,' said Harish.

'Listen, last month I made a deal with a French food store chain to supply them with saffron. I don't have an organization here in Europe though and cannot import directly. You can. Today I met an Indian businessman who markets good Kashmiri saffron. He is willing to sell at twenty euros a hundred-gram packet. You will import the saffron and I will buy it from you at twenty-one euros a packet. You make a euro a packet. We will import ten thousand packets a month. You make ten thousand sweet euros a month. No sweat. No risk. You will be rich. You can travel first-class to London every week. Watch a cricket match. Watch a whole test. Or better still, you can call at a particular address in Southall that my friend Sham will give you. The girls there – oh hohoho – they will uproot your middle stump – and what's best, they speak to you in Hindi while they are doing it. Now how are you going to thank me?' asked Ratnesh, driving to a conclusion in great good humour.

'I don't know. It all sounds so unreal. Zulfikar and I, together we earn ten thousand euros in around two months of the daily grind – and here you are with a way to earn ten thousand a month doing nothing,' said Harish slowly, his soft smile still present. 'I never knew that the French would buy ten thousand packets of saffron a month,' he added, expressing just one of the many aspects of the deal which puzzled him.

'Oh, the French. Fusion cooking is now the rage in France. French traditional recipes modified to include Asian spices. I personally can't understand why anybody would want to mangle food. Can you imagine what Indian fusion food would probably be? Samosas stuffed with diced asparagus or biriyani cooked not in ghee but in olive oil! Toba toba! But this is a business opportunity and I'm a businessman. So if they want saffron, I'll give them saffron. Let them corrode their insides,' replied Ratnesh, his imagination straining to keep ahead of his tongue.

'I take time to understand things. That's why I have Zulfikar. Let me discuss this with him tonight. I will be back here tomorrow and we can talk about this again then,' said Harish gently but with finality, unwilling to be steamrolled.

No steamroller in full momentum likes to be told by the macadam that it will not be steamrolled. Ratnesh had assumed that Harish would be a walkover.

'You should decide. I will be dealing with you, not with Zulfikar. Why do you need to involve a circumcised motherfucker in this?' said Ratnesh a little angrily.

'He is my partner. I will discuss this with him and let you know tomorrow,' repeated Harish, his smile now a little strained.

Ratnesh quickly realized his misjudgment. He changed tack.

'Arrey bhai, discuss with Zulfikar or Iftikar or whoever else you want to discuss this with. I know only you. I am making you this incredible offer because I like you. God only knows why though,' said Ratnesh, putting an arm around Harish.

Harish smiled again. 'You are being kind. May God be good to you.'

'Come, I want you to meet the Indian exporter of saffron,' said Ratnesh, rising. 'He too is here applying for a visa. He is one of India's top exporters. Very well connected. The entire Indian embassy here in Belgium is virtually in attendance on him – to make sure that his visit to Europe is a success. It pays to do business with such people. You get much collateral benefit.'

Chapter 12

Seetha emerged from the interview room with a whole slew of feelings which she wanted to mull over. She saw Amit sitting alone in the Thinker's pose. Ratnesh had given him much reason to be uneasy. He looked up, saw her, straightened, smiled expectantly and gestured towards the empty seat next to him. She went up to Amit thinking though that she needed some time with herself to go over all that had transpired in the interview.

'Did you tie the Visa Officer in all kinds of philosophical knots?' asked Amit, calling out to her as she approached him.

'Not really. I need to use the Ladies. I'll tell you about it when I'm back,' replied Seetha quickly.

'There's no Ladies. There's just one toilet – a Visa Seekers' toilet, for Ladies and Gents, both able and disabled. It's just outside, off the landing,' said Amit helpfully.

Seetha nodded quickly and hurried towards the landing. She tried the toilet door, saw that it was locked and then read the notice about the key. She turned and walked back towards the counter but had to wait as the officer was busy with another applicant – a person of Middle Eastern appearance. Seetha took in the Swiss gold watch and his fluent French and decided that he was a Lebanese trader with a daughter in London. The Lebanese trader, if that was who he was, had handed over a whole sheaf of documents to the officer and was in the process of extracting one more from the smart briefcase he was carrying.

Seetha waited, her thoughts returning to the interview. She thought she had acquitted herself fairly well. But she was still uneasy. Doug had asked too many questions about her present career. He seemed to be unconvinced about her dramatic career change. But he seemed to like her. That was important. He would probably give her the benefit of doubt...

I guess if I were him I would have rejected my visa application. I would have seen through me.

The Lebanese trader clicked his briefcase shut and left the counter seemingly pleased with himself. Seetha went up the counter and asked for the toilet key. The Belgian gave it to her wordlessly.

She went back to the toilet, unlocked it and entered. She thought it smelt a little. Did the embassy expect the first visa seeker who used it each morning to clean it? You never know. She stood in front of the mirror, mechanically arranging her hair and continuing to think about the interview. She should remember to call Raghunath later. She hoped he would be at home. Often he wasn't. He and his neatly trimmed beard were a fixture in most of Delhi's happening soirees. Hostesses sought him. He was erudite, witty and did not get drunk. And he did not repeat jokes and anecdotes even though he had reached the age when most people did.

She would tell him the official story – the one in her visa application, the one she had told Doug – about wanting to change her career, live in London and write that philosophical novel. Raghunath would believe her because she would then have become an interesting person, not just another computer nerd – and he was the kind of person who believed (sometimes a little desperately) in a world full of interesting people. Besides she was young and a woman and Raghunath found it difficult to resist young women. No, he would not be a problem. If Doug were to go by Raghunath's report, she would certainly get her visa. But she had a feeling that Doug would need more convincing.

She sat on the toilet seat and continued to think. She was a little surprised at the ease with which she had grown into her visa application persona – both with Amit and with Doug. It had not taken much effort for her to be consistent, fluent and convincing. She was pleased and Iyer would be too. Come to think of it, she liked her new persona. She might actually live it.

She looked around and idly noticed the large space and railings to accommodate disabled people in wheelchairs. She tried to trace the path a wheelchair would take inside the toilet. It came to her mind that she had never seen a toilet for the disabled in India. She had seen plenty of the disabled though.

Seetha wondered what she should do next. Perhaps she should return to Expobel and work for the rest of the day. She would be able to meet Luc.

Luc, Luc. Handsome Luc. Big Luc, Slow Luc – no, Deliberate Luc. If I took him to India how would he view the dirt and the noise? The squalor and the desperate poverty. The Indian honour guard of defecating backsides lining village roadsides and suburban railway tracks early in the morning. The stench of open sewers – with pigs rummaging, crows pecking and street children foraging. The hypocrisy, transactional dishonesty and cunning that want had spawned. Eesh.

Luc thinks of Indians as otherworldly. Full of deep, inner meaning and a peace that passeth all understanding. India as being a land of green fields, majestic rivers and mysterious forests. Happy, contented, simple people living in spotlessly clean huts of mud-baked walls and thatched roofs. All huts ensuite of course. Evenings spent under the banyan tree debating the finer points of the Upanishads. This idyllic landscape would of course be broken every few miles by a towering HP Software Development Hub or a Barclay's Customer Call Centre.

I'll have to prepare him for India.

Luc's nice but he's so different. I can't get into his mind and I'm sure he does not understand how mine works either. There are whole acres in my mind that he will never enter. Can one have a meaningful, intense relationship with a wonderful person while keeping the keys to a distinct, large, unshared personal world? Not sure.

Luc's got blue eyes. Blue, not like the Chennai sky but like the Chennai sea.

Enough about Luc. I'm getting obsessed with him. Get a grip on yourself, girl. I'm not obsessed with him. He is the only male I meet on a regular basis. I discuss Expobel's financial system with him for around two hours every day, sitting across a table, face to face. Naturally I have to look at his eyes. I'm not an Indian bahu whose sari pallu covers her head and most of her face and who will never look directly at any man save her husband. Husband. Luc will make a good husband. I don't just mean for me but for any woman. He's husband material. What do you know about him? Precious little and still you make these statements.

In the mirror, Seetha examined the tiny birthmark she had on the side of her neck.

Amit's waiting for me. Does he really want to listen to my philosophical rambling or is it just his way of making a pass? Don't know, but he seems interested and is polite, so why should I probe any deeper? He is going to be my acquaintance for a day, no more. Philosophy is okay with his kind. Far removed. I won't ever trust him with even a tiny sliver of my feelings.

With a last look in the mirror, Seetha left the toilet and went back to the counter to return the key. This time a large African woman with a little girl beside her was at the counter. The woman was very dark, the little girl much lighter skinned. Her brunette hair was braided the African way. Zimbabweans. White father. Can't go back to Zimbabwe was Seetha's surmise.

Seetha was prepared to wait but the Belgian officer noticed her – miraculously, because he had never looked up – and motioned to her to step up and return the key. Seetha did so and then walked towards Amit, smiling a working smile.

Amit had become the Thinker again. It seemed to be a favourite, much practised posture. He held the pose till she was very close and then looked up and smiled. She sat down next to him.

'Did Her Majesty's government welcome with open arms this highbrow writer from India? They should have. Indian writers are in fashion,' said Amit with a laugh.

'I did not see any open arms. I only saw a suspicious mind. But to be fair to the Visa Officer, he was pleasant and reasonable. I need to be back tomorrow for another interview,' said Seetha, unwilling to elaborate further.

'The Deputy Chief of Mission in the Indian Embassy here is hosting a party at his house tonight. It's likely to be an all Indian party – mainly ambitious embassy officers and their pretty wives. I suspect that I'm what you might call the guest of honour so I think I have the right to bring a friend along. Would you like to come? They are a bright lot, these foreign service officers. Good conversation, great food and the best of liquor.'

Only one of the three – good food, good Indian food – appealed to Seetha. She was starved of it. But she was also curious about the diplomatic world. Its glamour and glitz. She had often passed the sedate brick Indian Embassy building in the Chausee de Vleugart and had wondered about the Indian Foreign Service officers who worked behind its heavily curtained windows. Weren't they the brightest in the civil services? It would be nice to peek into their world. She decided to accept.

'Sounds interesting. Are you sure I can gatecrash? Won't there be some official bouncers? What time is the party and where is it?' asked Seetha.

'This is an Indian party. There won't be any bouncers. Haven't you received invitations to traditional Indian weddings, birthday parties and just about anything else? They always have a line: Please bring your family and friends along. It's at the home of the Deputy Chief of Mission – somewhere in an area called Sint Genesius Rode, or is it Genesius Sint Rode? Anyway I will be picked up from my hotel by someone from the embassy. I'm staying at the Hilton. We can pick you up if you don't live too far away. I don't think any place in Brussels is too far away. Probably around eight in the evening.'

I haven't had a single social evening since I arrived in Brussels. This should be exciting and it will also be fun telling Amma about it on the phone.

Seetha lived in an apartment block on the Avenue de la Couronne. The Hilton wasn't too far. She would take a bus up the Rue du Trone and then walk to the Hilton. She enjoyed walking and would burn some calories and feel less guilty being a glutton at dinner time. And Amit did not need to know where she lived.

'I'll meet you at the Hilton lobby at eight. I hope that's okay,' Seetha said and as Amit nodded, she continued: 'I'm curious. From all accounts the Indian Embassy here is not known for its hospitality or often even courtesy to visiting countrymen. Why are you being treated like royalty?'

Amit loved the question. He laughed modestly. He played it out. 'Maybe they are just doing what they are supposed to do – which is to be nice and helpful to visiting Indian businessmen

– or maybe it's the Amit charm at work.'

'I think there's more to it but I don't know what it is,' said Seetha, playing along and smiling expectantly.

'Well, my uncle is our foreign minister – that may have helped,' said Amit, waiting for the new respect he anticipated seeing in Seetha.

'Well, well, I'm honoured to be speaking to one who walks the corridors of power,' said Seetha laughing a strained laugh, hiding for the moment her dislike of the political class as a whole, particularly the new saffron regime in New Delhi.

'I don't. My uncle does. And I don't take advantage of that fact. He would not let any of his relatives do that in any case. But if bureaucrats and others give me a certain importance simply because I am my uncle's nephew, there's little I can do, can I?' asked Amit in an aggrieved tone.

Oh yes, there is plenty you can do. For starters you can stop advertising your exalted relations to people you meet in passing in foreign embassies, thought Seetha, wondering if she should reconsider the party tonight. Curiosity won. She decided against reconsidering. As a small sign of protest she changed the topic.

'Have you ever seen a toilet for the disabled in India?' asked Seetha.

Amit was still taking in the sudden change of topic and the unexpectedness of the question itself when they were interrupted by Ratnesh with Harish in tow.

'I'm sorry to interrupt you but I wanted to introduce my friend and business associate,' said Ratnesh to Amit in Hindi, completely ignoring Seetha.

Chapter 13

With a quick 'Excuse me' to Seetha, Amit stood up and shook hands with Harish.

'This is Harish, Amit,' said Ratnesh.

'I am very glad to meet you. Ratnesh has told me so much about you,' said Amit in English.

'Amit is very close to the Indian ambassador here. He is one of India's leaders in the food processing industry. His father is a well known business tycoon,' said Ratnesh to Harish, intending equally that both Amit and Harish should hear.

'Very pleased to meet you,' responded Harish in measured Hindi. 'And you too, madam,' added Harish, turning to Seetha and joining his hands in a namaste.

'Harish is one of the pillars of the Indian community here in Brussels. He is well known in the European retail trade,' said Ratnesh, even handed in the extravagance of his introductions.

'I am a partner in one of the small grocery stores here – a Night Shop,' said Harish, unable to stop himself downsizing a whopper.

'Harish is very modest. Like all great businessmen. Like Jamshedji Tata, like G.D. Birla.'

'Here is my business card. It has my office, mobile phone and home numbers. All in Delhi, I'm afraid. Here I'm staying at the Hilton,' said Amit. Seetha watched an expensive, gold embossed business card change hands.

'Thank you,' said Harish, 'I'm sorry but I don't have a business card. I have not printed any. I need one so rarely. Let me write down our address and phone number on a piece of paper,' said Harish looking round for a scrap of paper. Ratnesh stopped him with a possessive hand on his shoulder.

'Don't bother now. Amit can contact me and I will of course be in touch with you.'

'So do you think this business Ratnesh talked to you about can be done?' asked Amit, wondering just how much Ratnesh had told Harish.

'You mean the importing of saffron through us. Yes, I think it is very possible although we have never imported anything on such a scale and we may have practical problems in arranging adequate storage space,' said Harish, thinking that if they went ahead with the deal, Zulfikar would probably have to give up his prayer room – a cozy room at the back of the store. Zulfikar had given up smoking just two months ago. Earlier that room had been his smoking room.

'Harish is excited about this new opportunity. He has always wanted to diversify into spices,' interjected Ratnesh, rushing to foreclose all hesitation.

Amit, gradually gauging more accurately Harish's station in life, was now inclined to be less deferential. He said, 'I will expect promptness and clean paperwork – squeaky clean – in accepting consignments, the clearing of goods through customs, invoicing and making payments. And, as in the case of any commercial transaction, complete secrecy. Particularly in our trade there are many competitors who will want to elbow in on the business.'

'Of course. But first, as I told Ratnesh, I have to discuss this opportunity with my partner Zulfikar. We need to see if we are capable of handing such a large deal or even if we want to. You see, Zulfikar and I have been growing our business slowly but surely – and are quite content with our progress. We know our many limitations and try to live within them. You have been generous in giving us this opportunity but we have to make sure that it does not affect the even tenor of our life and business.'

'Well, do decide and tell us by tomorrow. There are other importers who have approached Ratnesh. They are keen to do this deal,' said Amit, irritated that petty shopkeepers should have volition beyond the profit motive. Business schools did not expect them to.

'Well, I guess I should be leaving now. I will talk to Zulfikar about this tonight. I will be here by ten tomorrow morning and then after my interview we can perhaps go over to a café and discuss this opportunity again. Does that suit both of you?'

Amit did not like to be in the position of having to wait for a grocer's decision but seeing no alternative just stood and sulked. Ratnesh accepted on behalf of both of them, 'That should be fine. If you accept the offer, Amit will pay for the coffee. If you don't, you will. So please do convince your circumcised friend tonight.'

'Zulfikar and I will definitely go over this tonight. Namaste,' said Harish, bowing his head slightly to both Ratnesh and Amit. Not forgetting Seetha, he turned towards her with another namaste. He then walked slowly towards the lift, his brow a little more furrowed than usual.

'Harish is a simple person. I hope he is able to convince that Zulfikar. I don't know why he is partnering a Pakistani. Anyway, if Zulfikar does not want to go along with our plan – and he may not simply because it involves more Indians – I have other ways of convincing Harish,' said Ratnesh looking meaningfully at Amit.

Amit pursed his lips in a very American way – perhaps they now taught this at all B-schools worldwide – signifying that he understood but did not necessarily agree, that nothing more could be done or said for now and that he was keeping all his options open.

Ratnesh, an adept learner, imitated Amit in pursing his lips – he almost got it right except that he widened his lips too much and came too close to an old toothless crone's smile.

Chapter 14

Seetha had continued sitting while the three men stood near her and talked. While her eyes had wandered over the hall with its assortment of humanity she had listened with curious attention to the men's conversation. By the end of the conversation she had done some more slotting. Harish was a hard-working, old-fashioned immigrant. A little stodgy and a little slow but a good man all the same. She regretted having been so abrupt with him in the morning. Her liberal, Nehruvian heart warmed to his willingness to partner with a Pakistani. Ratnesh was a hard man, a con man, a rude man – out to swindle both Amit and Harish in some dubious business. Amit was a weak, pampered fop with intellectual pretensions.

Both Ratnesh and Amit seemed to rediscover Seetha at almost the same instant.

Amit turned to Seetha and smiled, his eyes asking her if she had understood and appreciated the tough business negotiations she had been privileged to witness. Ratnesh's eyes turned to her for an instant and then turned back to Amit – he had decided that she was of no importance.

'I'm sorry, I have not introduced the two of you. Ratnesh, this is Seetha – one of India's new crop of writers in English – darting thought and leaping language! Seetha, this is Ratnesh, an Indian businessman who is helping me put together a complicated deal.'

Seetha smiled a wintery smile. Ratnesh did not smile at all. 'We met this morning,' was all he said, choosing deliberately to stay with Hindi.

At that moment, the intercom boomed again, 'Mr Ratnesh Kumar, please come to the first counter.' All three turned to look at the Belgian officer holding the mike and looking over the other applicants directly at them. Ratnesh had clearly made an unforgettable impression on the Belgian.

'That must be the call for my interview. I hope the questions are not more constipated than usual. I'll see you in a few minutes,' said Ratnesh to Amit before walking towards the counter.

Amit sat down and stretched his legs. His face and body relaxed. He wasn't sweating but wiping his brow seemed an appropriate gesture and he did that, taking an initialled handkerchief from his pocket. He wondered what he had got himself into. He did not want to think deeply about it now. The time for that would be the next morning, in the silent luxury of his hotel room, over his second cup of morning coffee, after the *International Herald Tribune*. Now he wanted to relax. It was time for other sides of his multifaceted personality.

'Sorry to have inflicted the cut and thrust of business on you. As you saw, in that world one has to deal with a variety of people. The trick is to understand each person and his objectives and then shape the deal to meet all objectives.'

'Don't apologize. I quite enjoyed watching the sparring but I did not like Ratnesh. He is crude.'

'I don't like Ratnesh either. Unlike us, he will not be able to discuss the evolution of Indian thought after Sankara. But he is an Indian businessman in Europe. That's a tough role. And don't forget that today, behind every successful artistic or intellectual endeavour or institution there needs to be a rich sponsor or donor. They are mostly oily tycoons who have clawed their way to wealth a la Ratnesh. In twenty years time when you want to found an Indian Institute for Philosophical Studies, Ratnesh may well be the munificent patron.'

'I'd die first.'

'And in your next life, the gods may have you as Ratnesh's wife, who knows! Anyway, let's not spend more time on Ratnesh. This morning I was reading one of the Indian newsmagazine websites and a columnist had described our Laloo Yadav as being a Rig Vedic politician. I've always been curious about the Rig Vedic period. I once asked my grandmother why she never read me any hymns from the Rig Veda and she said that they would confuse me. Tell me something about it.'

Seetha had been thinking for some time that it was time to leave. She could put in a half day at the office before meeting Amit again. She had even wiggled her feet back into her shoes. Shoes were one of the things she disliked about the West. In sultry Chennai you were barefoot at home and wore slippers or sandals outside.

But now Amit looked at her so earnestly and the Rig Veda was one of Seetha's favourite texts. And he had invited her for a diplomatic dinner party. She stayed.

'Where should I begin? Maybe around two thousand years before the birth of Christ. That age saw the beginnings of what we today call Indian thought. The hymns of that age have come down to us in the Rig Veda. The hymns are wild and free: the work of poets really, not priests or scholars. The Rig Vedic people were primarily a pastoral people, successful in war, apparently confident and assertive and subject only to their gods. They reared cattle, rode chariots, fought their enemies, worshipped their gods and drank a lot of the intoxicating Soma juice.'

'Did they philosophize?' asked Amit in studied, trance-like attention.

'They did – in a very natural way as you might expect. They saw all around them in Nature, forces they could not control and did not understand. They also saw in Nature itself much diversity, variety. They assumed that there must be superior beings who controlled the elements and took care of such tasks as arranging for the sun to be charioted around the Earth every day. Since there was so much to do, there had to be many gods – and goddesses too.

Seetha noticed with some irritation that the inane expression on Amit's face was strikingly similar to that of Western tourists in India watching Indians at any traditional activity – women drawing water from a well, a Tamil housewife drawing a traditional kolam on the ground outside her home, urchins playing cricket on a street, Rajasthani women dancing a slow folk dance. The tourists' faces generally expressed, as Amit's did, a vacuous, craven wanting to appreciate.

Nevertheless she continued.

'The Rig Vedic men saw that nature was quirky and unpredictable and they gave their gods the same fickleness, particularly Indra and Rudra. But behind the seeming vagaries of Nature, Rig Vedic men thought they saw an underlying cosmic order and regularity. They called the cosmic order Rta and put a god, Varuna, in charge of it. Rta, you can say, was the thread which was to sew the crazy patchwork quilt of the universe together.'

There was mild confusion at the other end outside the hall, where a Far Eastern person of uncertain sex and age, either unwilling or unable to read the notice was trying to force open the bathroom door. Two other Far Eastern women seated inside the hall, shouted advice across at least twenty metres. The Belgian officer glared menacingly at the women. He had learnt the very British way of conveying strong displeasure without the assistance of words. Amit had schooled himself to be completely incognizant of such trifles. He sat transfixed, eyes glued to Seetha. She looked over at the women, hesitated and then went on.

'The Rig Vedic people intuitively saw a certain kind of oneness in the world. This was what over time crystallized into the Brahmin of the Upanishads and the monism of much of later Indian thought. But they could not ignore the obvious diversity all around them. They revelled in it and celebrated it. To many in the West, brought up in a world dominated by Judeo-Christian thought, polytheism seems to be a little crude and difficult to understand but a little closer thought will show us that monotheism, polytheism and pantheism are all stations on the same loop line which runs from unity to unity via diversity.'

Amit drew in a sharp breath. 'How?' he whispered.

'Through time, in almost every culture, the more thoughtful have been confronted with this paradox of unity and diversity. Some resolve it polytheistically, as the Rig Vedic people did, by positing a multiplicity of gods and an underlying, unifying cosmic order. Others opt for pantheism where one God is seen in everything, every diverse object. Other cultures opt for a stern monotheism and then offer a platter of reasons to explain why the one, eternal God should create so mysteriously diverse a world.'

They both looked up as they heard a door bang. It was Ratnesh leaving the interview room. He had a broad smile on his face as he came towards them.

Seetha thought he looked rather Rig Vedic. Would be able to keep Laloo Yadav company.

Chapter 15

The Belgian officer pointed Ratnesh to the second interview room. Ratnesh walked towards it. Ratnesh was practised in facing authority in its many manifestations. Never having been helped by authority, he loathed it and all whom it protected and nurtured. But he was practical. If you grow up poor and friendless in Bihar you cannot be otherwise. He had learnt to live with and under authority of all kinds. He had learnt to respect its power. Today he wanted his visa. That was all.

He made to smooth his hair but dropped his hand, deciding that it was not important. He opened the door of the second interview room and entered. Doug, already seated on the other side of the glass partition, reading Ratnesh's papers, looked up sharply and waved him into the chair. Neither man smiled or even greeted the other. They just had a job to do and neither was going to help the other.

Doug did not dislike all coloured people. He liked Seetha. He liked the idea of a multi-cultural Britain. He had voted for Blair and New Labour. He once had had a black girlfriend. He liked a Britain with Asian newsreaders, black footballers, Canadian tennis players, German royalty and Russian ballerinas. When he entered a restaurant or a pub, he liked to see a riot of skin colour, not just pasty white.

But Doug instinctively disliked one category of coloured people – poorly educated, young, single men recently arrived from the subcontinent. They stared, ate noisily, dressed in strange combinations, spat at street corners and scratched themselves. They loomed menacingly at night on lonely London streets. Recently, in the last few years, they had taken to flaunting their ethnicity in dress, demeanour and language. They spoke little English and seemed unashamed. If they had within them a whole world of thoughts, ideas, dreams and values, it was well hidden from Doug. To him, they did not seem to have a single redeeming feature. If his newspaper carried another story of Afghan or Sri Lankan men arriving in Britain hidden deep in six tonnes of mackerel in the back of a 24-wheel lorry, Doug would reread the article carefully, his thoughts dark and despairing.

Not surprisingly, Doug viewed with deep suspicion all applicants for tourist visas from that category of persons. His experience told him that it was unlikely that such a person would make the expensive journey to Britain just to visit the Lake District. In appraising applications he played it by the rules of course, but if discretion had to be exercised it was always on the side of caution.

He went through Ratnesh's papers. He looked at Ratnesh's photograph. Then he looked at Ratnesh. Ratnesh looked back at him coolly, appraisingly. 'He does not like people like me but he is a British bureaucrat and knows no other way than to play it by the book. I need not be nice to him but I must not slip up on any facts. I'm only applying for a short-stay tourist visa and I am eligible for that. If I am consistent, I will get my visa,' thought Ratnesh.

He knew he would have to speak in English and he knew his limitations in that language. Perhaps it was just as well. In Hindi he tended to be more fluently rude. He should stick to the facts, use the right nouns and never mind the rest.

'Why did you not apply for your British visa before you left India?'

'I had plan business trip to Germany, France and Belgium but my friend Sham who live in London phoned me few days ago and invited me strongly to spend two-three days with him in London. I would like to accept invitation, having come ninety percent of way already.'

'What is your profession?'

'I am a businessman – I have written already in my application form.'

'Do you have any documents – bank statements from India, contracts signed or proposed, company registration details – anything that establishes your profession?'

Ratnesh took his time to think.

'No. I did not expect being asked to prove my profession. Never happened before. Of course I have visiting card,' said Ratnesh, producing a shabby card that introduced him as the Managing Director of M/S Om East-West Traders – Imports and Exports – located in NOIDA Phase II. He slipped it into the bowl-shaped window at the bottom of the glass partition.

Doug took the card, gave it a quick glance and then placed it on his table dismissively.

'Of course if required, please you give me one day. I will phone my office in Delhi to fax to me or to you some supporting documents,' said Ratnesh confident that this would not be a difficult exercise.

Long experience told Doug too that this would not be a difficult exercise. He needed to probe other areas.

'Are you married?'

'No,' said Ratnesh. But he sensed the import of the question and quickly framed an appropriate supplementary answer, 'But I am planning to get married next year – I have fiancée in Delhi. Her name is Neeta.'

Doug's face showed both his complete disbelief as well as his frustration as being unable to reject Ratnesh's application on the basis of the applicant's transparent disinclination to distinguish between the plausible and the true. He was sure that if he asked Ratnesh to substantiate his claim of being engaged, Ratnesh would be able within 24 hours to produce a photograph and a phone number in Delhi that he could call to speak to a putative Neeta.

The Home Office manuals required that the applicant be given every reasonable opportunity to establish his intention to return to his home country. That now required him to write down in the space reserved for official use: 'Claims to be engaged and expects to be married in India next year.'

'How large is your company, Mr Ratnesh?'

'We have sales turnover of greater than five crores annually.'

'What is a crore, Mr Ratnesh?'

'Hundred lakhs.' Ratnesh liked being unhelpful.

'What is a lakh, Mr Ratnesh?'

'One hundred thousand rupees. Around fifty Indian rupees make one euro.'

'How many Indian rupees make a British pound, Mr Ratnesh?'

Ratnesh did not know.

'I don't know. All our contracts denominated only in euros

or US dollars. British pound not so important in world trade.'

'But you are a businessman, Mr Ratnesh, surely you would have a rough idea.'

Ratnesh did have a vague idea. He knew that a pound was worth more than a Euro – probably around eighty rupees – but he was not sure and did not want to guess.

'My Finance Manager in Delhi normally keep track of currency values. I don't. Too many things to worry about. I can call him and let you know.'

Doug had a feeling that Ratnesh was enjoying this interview.

Doug did a quick calculation and wrote down, 'He claims to be the MD of an Indian company with an annual turnover of around 800K Pound Sterling.'

Doug read the application form. It had been filled in a neat, clear, round hand. The English was British, not Indian.

'Have you completed this application form yourself, Mr. Ratnesh?'

'No. I jammed right hand yesterday so good friend filled it out for me.'

'Can you please show me your right hand, Mr Ratnesh?' asked Doug.

'Hurt completely inside. No mark on outside,' said Ratnesh, lifting and showing Doug his right hand. Turning it slowly, so that it would be visible from all angles.

'Is your visit to London entirely social or will you also be exploring business opportunities there?'

'Hundred percent social. I just want to spend enjoyable time with friend.'

Doug thought of Ratnesh and his friend in some seedy loft in Southall. Two lumpy mattresses on the floor, the air thick with smoke from cheap Indian cigarettes. Their whinging music in the background. They would be cooking a pungent curry in a noisy pressure cooker, drinking heavily and crudely discussing the British Visa Officers they had encountered.

'Does it not make sense for a sharp businessman like you to explore business in the UK having come all the way?'

Ratnesh took a few seconds to reply. 'I have no any plans to trade with the UK. British system very bureaucratic. British businessmen not having vision.'

Doug wrote down, 'Claims it to be a social visit???'

'How long do you plan to spend in Britain, Mr Ratnesh?'

'One week only. Have to go back to business in India.'

Doug looked carefully at the faxed letter from Sham promising to be responsible for Ratnesh and all his expenses in Britain. The fax had been received on an old home fax machine whose ink cartridge needed changing. Sham had faxed his work permit as well as his visa. Doug decided to get his office to verify them and make sure they were still valid. If they were invalid, forged or lapsed, even by a day, he would throw out Ratnesh's application with immense satisfaction. He would also look more closely at Ratnesh's application later in his office. He wanted to reject the application but must find sufficient grounds to do so. So far Ratnesh had not given him much room for that. Cheekiness was not room enough.

'Do you have your return ticket to India?'

'Yes, here, please see,' said Ratnesh handing over a Ukrainian Airlines ticket. London Heathrow–Kiev–Moscow–Tashkent–New Delhi. The last sector by Uzbekistan Airlines. The cheapest ticket to Delhi that money could buy. Doug did not know that even this cheap ticket had now been cancelled. A month ago Ratnesh had informed his travel agent in Delhi that the ticket had been lost. He would claim his refund later. Ratnesh saw no reason to tell Doug all this. Doug only needed to see a London–Delhi ticket.

'Thank you. Mr. Ratnesh. We need to run some background checks and may need to contact our High Commission in New Delhi too. Come tomorrow morning and we will let you know,' said Doug, getting up and turning towards his door. Ratnesh did not reply. He waited for Doug to leave the room, stared for a few seconds at the closed door, then slowly turned around, opened the door on his side and left the room. He guessed that he would get his visa the next day unless Sham had forged his work permit or visa. He walked towards Amit and Seetha in fairly good humour. He was hungry and was confident that he could get Amit to stand him lunch.

Chapter 16

Amit decided to notice Ratnesh while he was still some distance away. It spared him the need to respond appropriately to Seetha's peroration. He smiled broadly at Ratnesh. This time he was determined to be in control. He would not allow a country huckster to overawe him.

'So how constipated were the questions? Did your answers act as a laxative?' asked Amit with a wink.

Amit had spoken in English but Ratnesh replied in Hindi.

'It was okay. The bastards tie their own hands with their rules and that helps us. This particular bastard wanted to keep me out of his fucked up country but his own rules wouldn't let him. I could see the hate in his eyes but he has been wrapped so well in bureaucratic red tape that he could not do what he dearly wanted to do. I had my sponsorship letter and it came accompanied by my sponsor's work permit and residence visa. The poor fool pored over the documents, hoping to triumphantly announce that he had found a contradiction or a forgery. Not finding any, all he could come up with in the end was a weak play for more time – come tomorrow, he says. Of course I will – to collect my visa.'

'These Brits have a peculiar reverence for the written word. They think that while a person – particularly an Asian – may tell lies, he will not know how to write or print lies. The Visa Officer would not readily believe me when I told him I was a businessman wanting to travel to Britain to explore business opportunities but he was perfectly willing to base his decision on a fax which I am going to produce tomorrow – it will be a designer fax, made to order to help a British Visa Officer cough up a visa,' said Amit, straining to match Ratnesh's bravado.

'Yaar, what about lunch?' asked Ratnesh as if the thought had just occurred to him.

Seetha decided that this would be an appropriate time for her to leave. She found Ratnesh's words, style and jauntiness deeply distasteful, quite apart from the fact that he spoke almost always in Hindi. She also found that in Ratnesh's presence, Amit developed quite another persona and seemed to alternate between imitating and patronizing Ratnesh, and in the process became equally unlikable. She put her feet back into her shoes and stood up.

'I think I should be going. I need to put in at least an afternoon's work at the office.'

Amit was determined to be in charge. He was also very reluctant to lunch alone with Ratnesh.

'Seetha, you need to have lunch anyway. And there is so much more about Indian philosophy I need to know. Do come with us for lunch. You name the restaurant.'

Seetha's mouth was just curving into an apologetic smile of refusal when Ratnesh interrupted.

'Yes, please come, madam. It will be surely interesting listening to you speaking about your noble profession,' said Ratnesh, this time in English, smiling an impish smile. He had sensed that without Seetha, Amit might well drop the idea of lunch altogether. An ample lunch, at Amit's expense, even if it was in the company of a stuck-up bitch, pontificating about writing and philosophy was better than a drooping sandwich at a Gare du Midi kiosk which was all he could afford.

Seetha was too surprised to react immediately. Her half-smile remained frozen.

Amit drove into the breach. 'Yes, please. Here you have two men who will be hanging on to your every word. You can't disappoint them. Besides, you have just finished telling me about the Rig Veda. You can't go away without talking about the other three Vedas as well. Only then will I understand why Laloo is Rig Vedic and not Yajur Vedic!'

'I'm not sure if either of you is serious at all,' said Seetha doubtfully.

'Yes, madam, we are certainly. At least I am certainly. My uncle was a magician. Not someone big like Sarcar who comes on television and performs in air-conditioned halls with one hundred assistants. My uncle performed to live – for a living – alone – on streetside. He always began performances, standing dead still for one second, folding his hands together like this, resting them on his forehead and chanting like in his deep voice one-two Sanskrit slokas – which he said were

from Yajur Veda. After that I have always been interested like
a cat about the Vedas,' said Ratnesh, continuing in English
his charm offensive for lunch.

Like many wilful people, Seetha was difficult to oppose but
easy to persuade.

'I have a strong feeling that one or both of you are pulling
my leg, but I will humour you. Where shall we go for lunch?'

'You decide. You are the Belgian among us,' said Amit.

'I don't like fast food,' said Ratnesh, setting a minimum
bar, convinced now that he would not have to pay.

Being in the company of two other Indians, of uncertain
table manners, she decided to be circumspect and opt for a
restaurant which catered to tourists. One of the restaurants
on Rue Jourdan on the other side of Avenue Louise should
do fine.

They moved out of the visa section, Seetha leading the way.
In the street, the two men drew level and flanked her on either
side. Ratnesh and Amit were discussing the relative merits
of Indian and Belgian beer. Ratnesh had switched back to
Hindi. A little tired of having words like Kingfisher and Stella
Artois drilling into both her ears and a little disgusted at the
way Ratnesh frequently loudly cleared his throat, Seetha
drew back a little. The two men continued their animated
discussion, drawing closer together. They barely seemed to
notice that Seetha had slowed down and was now walking a
couple of feet behind them. Like a good Indian wife; like her
original namesake, thought Seetha.

Why do I get myself into such situations? I'm twenty-eight
and I still have not learned to say no, even to a fop and a
scoundrel. Pathetic. Anyway, there's no point moaning now.
Just relax and enjoy the lunch. They will probably have some
pasta. The two men will hopefully be on their best behaviour
and they seem to actually want to know something about the
Vedas. And it's a good chance to check out a restaurant. If it's
good, I can invite Luc here for a meal some day.

They reached Avenue Louise and the men had to slow down
and turn around and ask her for directions. Amit, belatedly
polite, drew away from Ratnesh and allowed her to draw level
with them.

At Place Stephanie they saw standing in their way an Indian

couple. They were obviously tourists. They must have been in their sixties. The man was dressed in an old-fashioned brown suit, a faded yellow shirt and a fraying blue tie. He carried an old Kodak camera. The woman was wearing a gorgeous silk sari but it was tied badly and half-covered by a grey shawl draped gracelessly. Like a number of Indian women of her age it seemed to be at least twenty years since she had felt any need to look good.

The two of them had the frightened, uncertain look that unescorted older Indian tourists in the West did. They had problems with the accents, not to speak of the languages. They had difficulties with the elevators, the knobs, the switches, the faucets, the door handles, the turnstiles and vending machines of all kinds. They strained to communicate accurately to waiters in restaurants that they were looking for vegetarian food – and yes, vegetarian food did not include fish or chicken or even a sweet corn soup if it contained meat stock. They struggled with cutlery and longed to use their hands. They wrestled with maps and guidebooks, coming as they did from a culture where any street vendor was a willing, living guide book and where any of the dozens of young unemployed men lounging on the streets would be glad to give you elaborate directions to reach your destination. Never mind that the directions were confusing or wrong. You could always ask another young man down the street to reconfirm. They averted their eyes from the sex shops and the couples kissing and snuggling on the park benches. They stood in long queues to tour palaces. They were the occasional brown faces in crowds of Japanese and American tourists gazing upwards through camera lenses and Handycam viewfinders at snarling gargoyles flanking the roofs of soaring cathedrals.

Seetha took one look at them and muttered to herself, 'Retired State Bank of India officer and his wife. Live in Hyderabad. Proud parents of a son who works with IBM as a software engineer at Charlotte, North Carolina. Went to the US to visit him. He sent the tickets. Stopping at Europe on their way back. First trip overseas. Longing to get back home but also glad to be taking back hundreds of bragging points and twelve rolls of film.'

The three of them passed the Indian couple. Ratnesh

ignored them as he did anybody and anything that was of
no use to him. Amit ignored them as he did anybody and
anything that somehow seemed inferior. Seetha dared not
smile at them because – frequent experience told her this –
they, lost as they were in an alien land and finding a pleasant
brown Indian face, would start a conversation with her. They
would begin with enquiring about the nearest rest rooms and
end with enquiries about her parents, her caste and her salary
because they were looking for someone suitable for their NRI
son and it appeared to them that Seetha came from a 'decent'
background and appeared to have retained our Indian 'values'
while also understanding the modern world. To boot, she was
pretty and their son had insisted that the bride they find for
him be that too.

The couple stood rooted and stared at the three passing
Indians.

Seetha was now once again between the two men. All the
way to the restaurant, she endured a conversation between
the two of them, this time on the slowness of the European
mind (in contrast to its nimble and agile Indian counterpart).
Ratnesh's loud opinion – fortunately in Hindi – was that it
was the cold which was to blame. It froze European brains
as it did their hands. While they wore gloves to keep their
hands warm, they could do nothing about their brains except
allowing them to work very, very slowly.

Chapter 17

At the restaurant, they chose a comfortable window table. Seetha chose the seat facing the window. If the walk to the restaurant was any indication, the two men were likely to be conversing most of the time – and on uninteresting subjects. She could at least watch the street – something she loved to do – even if it was a wet, gloomy street seen through a misted window.

The waiter was not unfriendly. He was not friendly either but Seetha did not mind. He knew the English of the tourist trade. Had he been very effusive and obsequious Seetha might have been anxious all through lunch – anxious that her companions not offend him in any way. This way it was just right.

They were all hungry. Seetha ordered the Indian vegetarian's staples in Europe – salad and a pasta. Amit opted to make an event of the ordering – he enquired about traditional Belgian fare, asked the waiter for suggestions and finally opted for Salade aux lardons and Lapin à la kriek. Ratnesh asked Amit to order for him meat and fries. Amit did so with aplomb. Ratnesh and Amit chose Grimbergen beer while Seetha opted for orange juice-presse.

The drinks arrived and the waiter served them with a flourish and a 'Voila'. Ratnesh refused to acknowledge him. Amit thanked the waiter profusely as if he had been done a personal favour. Seetha smiled prettily at him.

'Cheers.'

'Ah, the good life!' said Amit and meant it. Ratnesh grunted as he drank his Grimbergen. His moustache now sported a patina of foam but he did not seem to notice or care. Seetha wanted to tell him to wipe it but she was wary of an unpredictable response and held her peace. For Amit it was all part of the jolly atmosphere.

'I'm sure you think this as an improbable setting to expound the Yajur Veda but I would say it is perfect. Our minds are at rest. Our bodily needs are being well attended to. We are not pressed for time. And we have heard about the Rig Veda. Please to begin.'

Ratnesh seconded the request with another grunt.

Seetha decided that there was no escape. It had to be done and got over with. To tell the truth, she was in a fairly mellow mood herself. She thought she had the measure of her companions. She had an embassy party to look forward to and she was fairly sure she would get her British visa.

'Well, okay. Just remember that you asked for it!' said Seetha. She took a deep breath, collected her thoughts, assumed a professorial air and began.

'After the Rig Vedic period comes the Later Vedic age; that's the age of the last three Vedic texts – the Saama, Yajur and the Atharva.'

'When a people, be it the Vedic people or anyone else, conclude that Nature is controlled by superior beings called Gods, it doesn't need much imagination to guess what the attitude of such a people to their Gods will be. It will be one of cringing fear tempered with moments of gushing gratitude. That's what the attitude of the later Vedic people was and in this they were no different from men of so many cultures. The later Vedic people behaved towards their Gods the way they did towards their kings and anyone else who had authority over them. They tried to please and appease their Gods, they paid them homage and they sang their praises.'

Amit leaned forward and adopted his Thinker posture again except that his left hand held his glass of Grimbergen. Ratnesh was examining the considerable dirt in his fingernails. He proceeded to use the fingernails on his right hand to clean those on his left.

'For the later Vedic people appeasement meant sacrifice. If I had to describe Later Vedic religion in one word, that word would be "sacrificial". My second word of choice would be "propitiatory". A man sacrificed what was valuable to him – in that period it was normally a fatted calf, a young lamb, milk, clarified butter or honey. He hoped the gods would be pleased. Most Vedic sacrifices were burnt offerings

Ratnesh fished out a packet of cigarettes and lighted one. He looked at Seetha, lifted the hand with the cigarette and said, 'My fiery sacrifice.' Seetha assumed charitably that it was his way of showing that he was following her narration. She wondered if smoking was allowed in the restaurant. The waiter hurried over with an ash tray and set her mind at rest.

The waiter came and arranged the appropriate cutlery for each of them. Ratnesh asked for another Grimbergen. The waiter bowed his head in acknowledgment. The table was now beautifully set and Seetha couldn't help thinking that it resembled an Indian mandala. The waiter would soon return bearing the burnt offerings. He was their priest. They were the gods.

She continued, not breaking stride.

'Can't say whether sacrifice created the professional priests, the Brahmins, or the other way around. The elaborate rites of sacrifice required professionals who understood them and the Brahmin priests in turn needed an elaborate, esoteric ritual to justify their existence and confirm them as the sole intercessors with God.'

'All Brahmins are bastards.'

Ratnesh had indeed been following and had been moved enough to make this comment.

Seetha was stunned into silence for a moment. Her next thought was that Ratnesh had been drinking too fast. She also noticed that Ratnesh had used the present tense and not the past. She wondered if Ratnesh had figured out that she was a Brahmin, or was it just that his grammar was poor or was this a pet rant?

Ratnesh continued to stare at her belligerently. Amit wore a pained expression. He had moved his hand from his chin to his forehead. From a troubled Thinker to a pained one.

Seetha decided to take refuge in pedagogy.

'In Ancient India, the word Brahmin or Brahman is used to refer to a priest as well as the chant which accompanied sacrifice.'

Amit was conscious that he had been silent for too long a time. He was also keen to distance himself from Ratnesh's remark.

'I would have loved to be a Brahmin in the Later Vedic Age. A master of sacrifice. An intercessor with the gods. A diviner. Known from the Himalayas to the Vindhyas as the priest whose sacrifices never fail.'

Seetha smiled thankfully and continued, eager to take the discussion to a higher flight path, above Ratnesh's limited radar of understanding.

'We can also say that in India, elaborate sacrificial ritual was the precursor of elaborate philosophical speculation. In both cases the complexity of reality was sought to be captured. The elaborate site plan for a sacrifice drawn up by a Later Vedic priest found its echo later on in the complex charts of the body drawn up by Hatha Yogis and in the intricate analyses of reality by the Nyaaya schoolmen.'

'All bakwas! All mumbo-jumbo! Invented by Brahmins to make others fear them and feed them,' spat out Ratnesh.

Seetha and Amit looked at each other questioningly for a moment.

'It certainly was an unfair system,' ventured Amit cautiously.

Seetha was not having any of this – vulgar ranting or soppy, mild, post facto egalitarianism. 'I'm not sure I understand. If a system or society is not perceived to be unfair by any, I repeat, any, of the groups in that society in that time and age – Brahmins, Kshatriyas, Vaishyas, Sudras, those outside the pale of caste not excepted – I don't see much grounds for anyone today to be morally uptight and critical of a section of the dead.'

'Let the dead criticize the dead,' murmured Amit, his fondness for a neat phrase easily overriding any need he may have felt to argue consistently.

'But they are not dead, the Brahmins. They live and they continue to deceive and to deprive poor people of the little money they earn,' said Ratnesh, spoiling for a fight.

Just then the waiter arrived with their salads. Both Amit and Seetha looked at him thankfully and expressed delight with their plates. Amit asked the waiter a number of questions about the constituents of his salad. The waiter answered in the Brussels tourist argot which was a combination of English nouns and French grammar with a hint of Dutch. Ratnesh brusquely ordered another beer.

The waiter left, having blessed the table with a generous wave of his right arm and a sonorous 'Bon appetit'.

Silence reigned in his wake. Amit and Seetha concentrated

on their food. Ratnesh's fourth Grimbergen arrived and was consumed.

'Madam Seetha,' continued Ratnesh, leaning forward and switching to English to make sure Seetha understood him, 'It is nice hobby to discuss and analyze society to which one does not belong. It could be society of olden days or it could be society of another country. I have that hobby also. For example I like to look at these white people – at their churches – and I see that only old people and immigrants go to them. I think to myself that once men become rich and comfortable and have no problems except what they create for themselves they don't need God in lives. I think like this a lot to myself and I wonder if things will be different if there was sudden calamity – World War 3 or 9/11 version two or global freezing or something like that – but for me this thinking is simply timepass. But about India, about Bihar, about the arrogant officers, corrupt politicians and deceitful Brahmins – all motherfuckers – I also think a lot, not as a hobby, and not so much now. But earlier in Patna I used to think a lot – not timepass but because I had to understand them and fight them to survive.'

Seetha had not anticipated his grasp of and interest in society and she was fleetingly impressed but then her mind was occupied with trying to think of a response. Seetha disliked politics and messy current social issues. She was loath to enter into a discussion about them, particularly with someone like Ratnesh for whom her dislike was steadily increasing. Also, like most thinking Brahmins, she carried in a corner of her mind a tiny, little jewel bag of ancestral guilt.

Amit, also squeamish about any jagged discussions, came to her rescue.

'Arrey yaar,' said Amit, slapping Ratnesh on the shoulder. 'There are bastards in every community. A community may not have a saint but it sure will have its share of bastards.'

'Amit, my brother, you don't understand,' said Ratnesh, putting his hand on Amit's shoulder and keeping it there. He switched to Hindi, the better to express himself. 'I am a Berhaiya. Do you know who Berhaiyas are? They are basically poor, subsistence farmers and wage labourers. Just a little higher in the hierarchy than the Harijans – Dalits as they call

themselves now. As long as I remained in the village helping
my father in the fields it was all right – our village was mostly
Berhaiya anyway. But I did not want to farm. I wanted to see
the world – to experience – to become rich – even perhaps
like Seetha madam to study philosophy. So I came to Patna.
And in Patna the Brahmins and Kayasths had a stranglehold
on business, education, sciences, the administration – on all
white collar jobs. It was a long hard struggle to get to where
I am now. Don't tell me that caste is dead. In Bihar it is alive
and in great shape.'

Seetha noticed that Ratnesh's speech was beginning to slur
and his tone was now more maudlin than angry. She relaxed
just a little and concentrated on gathering the stray ears of
corn on her plate with her fork. Let Amit calm his friend
down.

'My friend, I understand. What you are saying is important
and is about real life. On the other hand, Seetha is talking
about the past. About our religion, our people and their
thoughts through the ages. That is also important,' said
Amit.

Ratnesh shook his head, both to clear it and to show
Amit that he disagreed. 'You have to give it to them, the
Brahmins. They managed to hoodwink a whole fucking
country, a subcontinent, into rank submission for a couple
of thousand years – without much use of arms, torture or
any bloody crudity. They gave each little tribe, each clan,
each occupational group a crummy station in life, convinced
them that they deserved it and then kept them there. That
was the awesome power of Indian philosophy – Brahminical
ideology. It was a breathtakingly elegant conquest. The only
other example in history of a non-violent ideology keeping
a vast, barely surviving majority in thrall to a small stinking
rich minority is today's fucking capitalism. I have had the
great good fortune to have been at the receiving end of both
these vicious ideologies.'

Amit was uncomfortable. He was clearly a beneficiary
of both vicious ideologies as Ratnesh had described them.
Seetha continued to be surprised at Ratnesh's social and
historical acumen but made no attempt to relieve Amit or to
continue her narration. Amit was embarrassed at Ratnesh's

hijacking Seetha's elegant survey of Indian philosophy and lowering it into snarling, personal argumentation. Amit tried to think of a way to make the debate once again more arcane, more toothless.

Seetha just wanted the lunch to end. Once again the waiter bailed them out. He came to clear the salad plates and then brought in the main course. He looked at Ratnesh and asked if monsieur would like another beer. Ratnesh's reply was brief and immediate: 'Yes.'

Silence continued. Ratnesh's beer, his fifth, arrived. Ratnesh drank deep. He wiped the foam off the corner of his mouth with the flat of his hand. Foaming at the mouth, thought Amit, but kept a straight face.

Ratnesh continued, 'I am a hater of laws, codes of behaviour, ethics, ideologies, systems – all fucking thought up by effeminate men who wanted to justify or perpetuate some injustice which benefits them. Take this fucked up visa shit. What an extraordinary concept the visa is. We won't let you in because if we do, you famished, scrounging, slaving, saving, miserly sod from dirty India, you will work harder and longer than us, since you don't know better and have nothing better to do, and we will end up losing our jobs or having to work harder too and we don't want to do either. The only people from the Third World we will grudgingly accept are computer programmers and refugees. Computer programmers are technical slaves and we chain them to their computers. And refugees, in very small paediatric doses, are good for the vestigial remains of our Christian consciences,' shouted Ratnesh.

Heads were beginning to turn and Seetha's face was reddening with embarrassment. The only saving grace, she thought, was that he was orating in Hindi. Amit was back in Thinker mode with another variation this time: he was slowly nodding. It was all he could think of doing.

Fortunately for them, the restaurant was soon distracted. A man entered the door, wearing a ten gallon hat, a leather jacket and a dress shirt, both unbuttoned enough to show the hairy chest its owner seemed to be proud of. The man's arm was around the waist of a very fair blonde. She seemed to have spent a lot of money trying to dress the way some

American tourists thought fashionable European women dressed. They must have both been in their fifties. They stood at the doorway and looked around boldly, appraisingly. Amit noticed that the woman was not wearing a bra and that the man's trousers were very tight at the crotch. Seetha guessed that they were Americans, now single, both previously married and divorced, holidaying in Europe – six countries in twelve days, a last spurt of tired adrenaline and hormones. Through his haze of liquor, Ratnesh noticed that the woman wore a gold chain and the man a gold watch.

'Kinda neat place. I figure they'd understand English here,' said the man loudly enough for everyone in the restaurant to know that he was American. The couple held the attention of the restaurant.

'They'll understand enough English to know that I want a salad and a Coke,' said the woman. 'Let's eat here, hun.'

They moved to a table in the middle, followed by disapproving European eyes and curious Indian eyes. The table had a small sign on it that said 'Réservé'. The Americans disregarded it and sat down. A waiter came up to them, hesitated, pursed his lips and then removed the sign from the table.

Amit and Seetha continued to look at the Americans for as long as they politely could and then turned their heads slowly back to their table. Ratnesh was waiting for them. His mouth was twitching and he seemed to be making a great inner effort of some kind. Seetha was immediately alarmed, convinced that he was going to throw up on the white tablecloth in that restaurant in front of fifty white people and she would have to help him clean up and everybody would assume that she was his girlfriend or wife and look at both of them with contempt... And what if he passed out after throwing up? She and Amit would have to carry or drag him to a taxi and then where?

Ratnesh ended her quick nightmare by finally blurting out in a slur that was becoming more difficult to follow each minute, 'Let me tell you something. It's a secret and you are swearing to keep it so.' Ratnesh looked around belligerently challenging anyone to refuse. Seetha was glad that he had lowered his voice to a stage whisper. A very slurred stage whisper it was too.

'I'm going to beat the bastards at their own game. You know

they have with their fucked up visa rules made it impossible for an honest Indian businessman like me to live in London and carry out my business. But if I pretend to be a refugee and come up with a convincing story of oppression and misery, then they will let me live in Britain... give me asylum... and that too permanently... forever. So what I am going to do is to go to London as a tourist... on a tourist visa... and once there I'll apply for asylum. I have a convincing refugee story to tell.'

Embarrassed silence reigned. Seetha wondered if all this was just drunken bragging or was it really a drunken confession of intent to commit a crime.

The waiter came and cleared the plates. He wanted to know if madame or the messieurs would like some dessert. He suggested the Chocolat Mousse. Seetha, smiling, refused and asked for coffee. Amit followed suit. Ratnesh hurriedly nodded and then impatiently waved the waiter aside. The waiter wasn't sure what Ratnesh meant but decided to bring him some coffee too.

Ratnesh looked angrily at Amit and Seetha, willing them to ask him to narrate his refugee story. Amit obliged.

'Tell us your refugee story. And we will let you know if it is any good – if it will get past the likes of the British Visa Officer we all had the privilege of meeting today,' said Amit smiling desperately and trying to make the atmosphere more convivial – friends exchanging yarns over a few beers.

'I am a poor Dalit, an untouchable from the unimaginably backward, feudal and poor Gaya district in Bihar. In my village my family lived in the Dalit quarter on the outskirts of the village. My parents worked as day labourers on an upper caste landlord's farm. We owed him money and he kept the accounts. Although we had been repaying for years, there was always more to repay. We almost worked for free. We Dalits could not use the village well, drink tea in the village tea shop or worship at the village temple. There were a million other indignities we suffered but this will suffice to give you an idea. In the village school, we Dalits sat at the back of the class. I happened to like books and knowledge. I read whatever I could. I dreamed big dreams. I did not want to live as my father and other Dalits did. When I was twenty I ran away to the city – to Patna. The discrimination there was more subtle but just as real. I saw that most rickshaw-pullers were Dalits. They had no rights, no hope, no life. I organized them. We struck work when one of us was arrested by the police and thrashed for daring to refuse to carry a policeman's family gratis. The local police knew I was their leader – they framed me on a trumped up charge of murder. Apparently I had murdered a policeman's wife. She had been murdered a few days before the strike and everyone in Patna knew that she had been murdered by her husband who had come home unexpectedly one afternoon and found her in bed with the milkman. He had strangled her with his police belt. But the police had rented witnesses, concocted evidence. I had no chance. They came to arrest me. I ran away. There is a police warrant out for me. The maximum sentence for premeditated murder in India is death. The European Union is against the death penalty. Surely you are not going to send me back to India where I will be hung for a crime I never committed?' Ratnesh had been speaking urgently and fast.

'Well done. You have a case, my friend,' said Amit leaning forward to slap Ratnesh on his back. Ratnesh leaned back, relieved. He appeared flushed – partly from satisfaction and partly from drink. Seetha disgustedly looked out of the window. She saw a Belgian policeman pass. He looked smart in his blue uniform. She wondered what he would do if he found his wife in bed with the milkman. She was sure there were adulterous policemen's wives in Belgium – but were there any milkmen?

'But you said you were a Berhaiya. Berhaiyas are a backward community but not Dalits. Won't you get caught out?' asked Amit, falling into the role of a trusted confidante playing devil's advocate.

'These white bastards don't know the difference between a Dalit, a Berhaiya, a Brahmin and the backside of a water buffalo. But to be safe, I have a caste certificate issued by the tehsildar of the tehsil my village lies in, certifying that I am a true blue Dalit. You know how it works, don't you? All these clerks in the tehsildar's office are corrupt to a man. If you need a caste certificate, they will give you one. If you want to remain true to your identity, in my case Berhaiya, the certificate will cost you two hundred rupees. If you would like to assume another caste, you can choose what you like – Dalit to Brahmin – the certificate will cost you five hundred rupees.' Ratnesh laughed and Amit joined him. The laughter of men who understood the world and were sure they had its measure.

Seetha could not restrain herself any longer. She turned from the window and looked straight at Ratnesh, black eyes brilliant with fury, 'I find your story, your attitude, your feeble attempts at philosophical justification of blatant, self seeking dishonesty all deeply loathsome. I can't understand how men like you live with yourselves.'

Ratnesh's eyes bulged as he sat up from his slouch and replied, slowly, softly and coldly, 'Don't trouble yourself, memsahib. You can't and won't understand. How can you, you Brahmin bitch?'

Seetha gazed out of the window. Her look was fixed but her heart was hammering with a kind of fear. Had she crossed the line again?

Don't respond. Don't respond. Just shut up. Another five minutes and this wretched lunch will end.

Ratnesh continued, switching to English to make sure Seetha understood. 'I have zero need to justify myself to you, to you of all people.' Here Ratnesh snorted mirthlessly. 'But just to make you happy, let me give argument in your style. You agree of course that all laws must be observed in spirit particularly, more than in each letter. All great men including Brahmin great men have said that same thing. Right? Okay, then let me tell you that my life in Bihar worse than Dalit. I have suffered every indignity. If you put all castes and subcastes in rank from one to hundred, then Brahmin will be number one and all Dalit castes will be from 95 to 100. Berhaiya will be 94. But there is big difference. Indian Government gives all kinds of benefits, loans, reservations in jobs, in colleges to Dalits. Nothing for Berhaiyas. There is also law. If anyone abuse Dalit using caste name then he will go to jail. But anyone can abuse any Berhaiya. And all people abuse Berhaiyas daily. And what I said about police is also true. If I without Godfather try to come up in Patna, police will chargesheet me for something or another thing. British government when they thought of refugee law, they thought about people like me. I have right to use it.'

Seetha didn't really try to follow Ratnesh's argument which apparently had been in her 'style'. Her intense dislike for him meant that her mind concentrated on vindicating her dislike. And there was much in Ratnesh's diatribe to help her: his intimidating manner, his article-free English, the way his lip curled every time he mentioned the word Brahmin, his undisguised self-interest, his absurd attempt to interpret the British Government's thinking.

She did not consider responding. She recoiled from a debate with him. She continued to look out of the window into the dull, stolid street. A light snow was now falling.

As Ratnesh had been speaking, Amit, for one brief moment wondered how he had let this common, low, bazaar con man into his life and whether he should push him out quickly without any further ado. But thoughts of such messy action were always quickly pushed out of Amit's mind. He couldn't look Ratnesh in the eye, never mind throw him out.

The coffee arrived. Seetha noticed absently that she and Ratnesh had something in common. They both needed lots of milk and sugar in their coffee – the Indian way. Amit had his coffee black.

The American man with the unbuttoned shirt and ten-gallon hat sent back his steak. In a voice that complained and carried, he said that it was too well done.

The coffee seemed to clear Ratnesh's head. He remained silent but his movements appeared more directed. He looked at his watch, then poured himself another cup. He inspected his now slightly cleaner nails. He seemed to be brooding over his recent drunken outpouring, perhaps trying to recollect just how much he had told his listeners and whether any of it would compromise him or his plans in any way. He wasn't worried about Seetha. He didn't think much of her capacity to either help or hinder. But he was concerned about Amit. He wasn't sure how Amit had taken his refugee project. He did not want Amit to chicken out of the saffron money laundering. Best to embarrass Amit into continuing their relationship.

Ratnesh stretched, deliberately yawned and turning to Amit, said in a friendly, even tone, switching back to Hindi,

'Well, that was certainly a winding discussion. I think I must apologize for barging into Seetha madam's interesting discourse like a buffalo barging into a room full of women singing bhajans. I don't know how we ended up discussing how one could possibly hoodwink the British and attain the exalted status of refugee. The world is a maze of laws and rules and codes and we need to wend our way through them. Which reminds me of our project to get your father's money back to India through another set of absurd rules – India's taxation and foreign exchange control rules. With Harish's help, you and I are going to find a way to do that with saffron. I will convince Harish tomorrow and then we need to spend some time discussing the exact modalities of payment.'

'Yes, certainly,' replied Amit, starting guiltily.

Seetha pretended to be absorbed in the street, where a white van, hazard lights flashing, back door open, was unloading some goods for the shop opposite. It was blocking a lane and other Belgian motorists were expressing their displeasure with a flurry of horns. She wondered what dubious transaction Ratnesh and Amit were involved in. She was sure it would be dubious. She idly hoped that Harish would not be convinced of whatever Ratnesh wanted him to be convinced of. Harish seemed to be a good sort.

'Well, I must be going. I have to meet a business associate at the Bristol Stephanie. I'll leave you to Seetha madam's enchanting company and I am sure you will have a more intellectual discussion without my crude interruptions. Goodbye, Madam Seetha. Doubtless we will meet tomorrow at that Temple of Justice, the visa section of the British embassy.'

Ratnesh pushed back his chair to stand up and leave. He pushed too hard and the chair fell over. Ratnesh bent down to pick up the chair and fell down himself. He got up unsteadily before either Amit or the waiter could help him up. Seetha stared beyond Ratnesh fixedly with frozen disgust. Ratnesh left the restaurant without another word or look or mishap.

'I'm sorry, Seetha. If I had known that he would make such a spectacle of himself, I would not have suggested this lunch. He's an interesting character though and I guess he has seen some hard times.'

Seetha turned sharply to look at Amit. 'I can't understand why you are holding a brief for him. He's just a common garden-variety rascal.'

'He's a brightly lit pirate ship that has happened to pass me in the night. He can help me in my business. I do not know his whence or whither and I don't really care.'

There were a few minutes of silence. Seetha became calmer. Maybe that was how one should look at Ratnesh – as a brightly lit pirate ship passing in the night. And then, her pasta had been just right. Not too cheesy or creamy. The sauce had been delicious. And she had told Ratnesh just what she thought of him.

Seetha felt a little surge of excitement as she suddenly remembered that she had an embassy party coming up in the evening.

Have to change. Can't wear this sari although it would have been just right. I don't have any formal Western evening dress. I'll probably have to make do with a business suit.

They asked for another pot of coffee. The waiter brought it and asked if they would like a liqueur to round off the lunch. Amit chose a cognac. Seetha demurred.

'You should not let a – to use your words – common garden-variety rascal derail you. You should continue with your narration. You were at an interesting point. You were talking about sacrificial ritual being an attempt to capture the complexity of reality.' Amit adjusted his spectacles and became the Thinker again, and looked at her expectantly.

'I'm sorry, Amit. I just can't go on. I'm too tired mentally. Too many new experiences today I guess.'

'Not to worry, Seetha,' said Amit gallantly. 'Just relax and enjoy your coffee when it comes. I'm worn out too from Ratnesh's unexpected viciousness.'

Seetha paused as the waiter arrived, bringing Amit his cognac. Amit took a sip, closed his eyes and sighed with satisfaction. Seetha looked around and noticed that the restaurant was almost empty. Most of the tourists who had come for lunch had left. By now they would be tramping around the Grande Place, building an appetite for dinner. Seetha pictured the American couple back in their hotel room. She looked at her watch. It was almost three.

The restaurant was quieter now. In the far corner she saw a pretty alcove with a small table set for two.

If I come here with Luc that's where we should sit.

The waiter hovered beside their table. He was impatient for them to leave and showed it. Amit looked up at him and he immediately stepped forward and asked if madame or the monsieur would like anything else.

'Not for me,' said Seetha looking at Amit. 'We really should be leaving.'

Amit asked for the cheque.

Seetha insisted on paying her share. That left Amit having to pay for his own lunch as well as having to foot Ratnesh's considerable bar bill. Seetha tried not to look but couldn't help noticing the tip that Amit left for the waiter. It was all of ten euros, a princely sum for a tip in tight-fisted Belgium.

A fool and his money.

For all Amit's generosity, the waiter did not see them out.

Chapter 18

Leaving Amit outside the restaurant and firmly turning down his suggestion that they proceed next to the Musee des Arts Ancien, Seetha had taken a taxi home, impatiently pulled off her sari, left it as a bright puddle on the floor, changed into a dull, grey business suit and caught a tram to Expobel. Her morning had been more eventful, multihued and uncharacteristic than any morning so far in Brussels and her head had a very limited tolerance for the colourful and unusual. And there was still the embassy dinner ahead.

Seetha entered the chrome and glass Expobel office tower, letting herself in with her Contractor badge. She took the lift to the third floor and in the Finance Section walked briskly down the long aisle between rows of workstations. She reached her workstation, sat down and straightened the tiny India flag which the cleaning lady inevitably left awry. She powered on her desktop and then leant back, letting the peace and predictability of the office soothe her nerves. She discreetly stretched her arms and legs and breathed deeply in an abbreviated, sitting-on-a-chair version of a pranayama exercise she had been taught in the yoga class she had attended at the Paramananda Ashram in Mylapore.

She had come to the office not so much to work as to reconnect with her everyday business world, the morning having been so disorienting. She reached out and held the mouse – in touch and regaining control.

She started up Microsoft Word and brought up a draft design document for Sales Invoice Cancellations that she had been working on. It was comforting to look at the familiar formats. She then switched to her project control file and flipped idly through time charts, process flow charts, Gnatt charts and data element tables. The world of Bihar policemen who murdered their wives seemed to be light years away – an imaginary, mythical world. Almost as far away was the world of men like Ratnesh who used the life stories of such Bihar policemen to claim asylum in Britain.

Idly scrolling through the document, Seetha went over the morning. She revisited her interview. She was reasonably pleased with her performance. She had read somewhere that doctors schooled themselves not to think of any of their patients except when they were actually treating them. She wondered how it was with Visa Officers. Would Doug have thought of her anytime after her interview? Would he perhaps be thinking of her now? Seetha, in an offhand way, knew and relished the power she had to make an impression. She would have been disappointed if she had never figured in Doug's thoughts after her interview.

She thought fleetingly about the basic dishonesty of her visa application. But she and her conscience had already hammered out a defendable document of understanding. She let that rest undisturbed.

She looked at her watch. An Indian Titan calendar watch. 4:30pm. It would be nine in the evening in New Delhi. Time to call Raghunath Singh. She extracted her little brown diary from the clutter in her handbag and found Raghunath's home phone number. She hoped he was at home. Often he wasn't. She could hear the phone ring at the other end. The tring-tring of an Indian phone, not the long, single trill of the West.

'Yes,' said Raghunath picking up the receiver.

'Good evening, sir. This is a fan calling from miles away. Do you recognize my voice?'

Raghunath perked up. When he had heard the phone ring, he had thought the call was from his mother.

'No, I don't but it does sound enchanting.'

'I'm Seetha Subramanium, sir. If you remember, I wrote a short story which figured in *Stories Which Bend Belief*. I last saw you at the Book Fair in Delhi two years ago and I remember you berating me for preferring – as you put it then – the rustle of high denomination currency notes to the rustle of pages in a slim volume of poetry.'

'Of course, I remember you. I even remember that you were looking lovely in a blue kameez that day. Talk about images etched in memory. And where in the world are you now?'

'I'm in Belgium, sir – in Brussels. I'm on a contract here, on an assignment to design application software for a Belgian company. Before you start to scowl, sir, let me tell you some news that I'm sure will be well received. I've begun work on a novel – a philosophical novel.'

'That's wonderful news. There is hope yet for you and for us. Whenever I thought of you, I used to shed copious tears thinking of the rare talent the Humanities had lost and crass computing had gained. But I always had a feeling that you would come back. I knew that we were not going to lose you for just a handful of silver. What is the novel about?'

Half an hour later, Seetha replaced the receiver, smiling to herself. It was nice to speak to people like Raghunath, never mind the pomposity and mild flirting you had to put up with. When the British embassy official called Raghunath the next morning, Seetha was sure that Raghunath would pronounce her a writer of unusual promise – one whose coming novel would be a bestseller – a novel which would span the thought and mores of two cultures and which would necessarily require her to stay and write in London. She only hoped that he would not be too extravagant in his praise, suspiciously extravagant.

Mission accomplished. Now for some coffee and then for some Luc.

Luc, oh Luc. Prescribed by doctors worldwide as an antidote to the malignant Ratnesh virus.

Does Luc know anything about Brahmins or Berhaiyas or Dalits? Has he heard those words? Does he know what I am? Does he care? How would he react if he heard Ratnesh's story? Either the real Berhaiya story or the Visa Officer special – the Dalit story. Being the credulous, big-hearted fool he is, he will actually believe Ratnesh, whichever story Ratnesh chooses to tell. There is a lot I need to warn Luc about before I take him to India.

You've completely lost it, girl. He's just a colleague. A colleague you know next to nothing about. And you're fantasizing about taking him to India. Take him along as what? You're finding it difficult to bring yourself to even enunciate that word. You know it's so absurd. What's absurd about it?

Well, dream about him if you want to. As long as you know that you're fantasizing. Recreational activity. Harmless castle building. As long as you know and don't forget. But I'm not sure I can trust you to always remember.

Luc does not talk to me the way he talks to his other colleagues. Maybe it's because I'm the only one he talks to in English. No, that's not the only difference. With me he is gentler. Less business-like.

She walked over to the coffee machine and made herself a cup. She needed to press the milk button thrice and the sugar button twice. She walked over to Luc's desk, coffee in hand.

Luc Dubois was a manager and had a large cubicle, sixty square feet of office space, all to himself. His desk was not hemmed in by other desks the way Seetha's was. She sat on the edge of Luc's table.

'Hi, Luc. Am I disturbing you? Don't say I am.'

Luc looked up and took his hands away from his laptop keyboard and folded them. His hands were indeed big. He smiled. He pushed back his chair and swivelled to face her.

'Luc, I've got to tell you this. This morning I met two colourful Indians. One was the nephew of the Indian Foreign Minister. A business school product. Pleased with himself. Pleased with the world. No angles, no aims. The other was a scruffy, scheming, mean, amoral man who pretends to be a businessman but is actually a trickster.'

'You have learnt a lot about these two men in one morning.'

'We spent most of the morning together – in the British embassy visa section and then at lunch. I had gone there to apply for a tourist visa to go to Britain – I did tell you that I planned to visit London before returning to India, didn't I?'

'Yes, you did. But I am surprised that you can learn so much about two men in the waiting hall of the visa section of an embassy. You have used so many specific adjectives to describe these men. You see that man walking towards the door – that's Robert van Straelen. He is a Finance Analyst. I have worked with him for the last two years. We see each other almost every day. Yet, I do not think I know anything about him. I would hesitate to describe him in any way.'

'I can tell you all about him,' said Seetha, giving Robert's broad back a good look. 'He's Flemish. He studied Finance at the Vrij University in Brussels. He lives near Ghent in the old farmhouse they bought and renovated last year. His first

marriage – to a completely unsuitable woman he met at college
– did not last long. Now he has remarried and is devoted to
his second wife who was his childhood sweetheart. They have
twins – five years old. Robert and his wife like French wine
but not the French. On Saturdays you can see him helping out
at the local junior football club. He reads *De Standaard* and
on Sundays he takes *The International Herald Tribune* too.
He goes to the local pub just once a week, usually on Sundays,
and then it's only after a couple of hours of strenuous cycling
by the Skelde, and it's always just a couple of Duvels. They
spend most of their year planning their summer holiday –
always in Europe, preferably Northern Europe – 'the South
can be a little too hot and a little too foreign, you know'. I
solemnly swear that all of the above about Herrn van Straelen
is likely to be true to the best of my knowledge, give or take a
fact or two.'

'You are an Indian guru – or do they call a female guru a
guri or gurini – and can look into people. I am a poor, prosaic
European,' said Luc smiling his adorable smile.

Seetha extended her hands slowly towards Luc, palms
facing up and fingers extended in the manner of an Indian
tantric. Eyes fixed, she whispered, 'Luc, I can now look into
you, I'm now travelling through your mind, stopping to read
some of your thoughts.'

Luc's smile was now a little unsure and his eyes showed
some alarm. He was relieved when she burst into laughter.

'It's so easy to play an Indian godman or godwoman. You
Europeans are so easily taken in. If for any reason you cancel
our software development contract, I think I am going to don
saffron, shave my head, get a staff, a coconut shell as a begging
bowl and sit cross-legged and motionless under a tree in the
Parc Royale. I'm sure I will have a dozen disciples in a month,
a hundred in two months and in a year my disciples would
have built me an ashram on the coast near Ostend.'

'I'm afraid that long before that happens the Park
Authorities and the Belgian police would have removed you
from the park without much ceremony. I may have to come
and bail you out.'

'I'm not so sure. Maybe I can convince the Belgian
authorities that I can quickly become a new tourist attraction

– there aren't too many in Brussels anyway. I can probably do some magic – pull things out of the air. They can then charge for admission to the Park,' replied Seetha, grinning.

Luc's phone rang. He excused himself to take the call.

Seetha looked at her watch. 5:30pm. She ought to be leaving. There was an evening to look forward to. She wondered what it would bring. The morning had brought her the nephew of a foreign minister, a Bihari buccaneer and a story of a lecherous policeman's wife and a horny milkman.

Luc finished his call and put down the receiver. He smiled in apology.

'Are there milkmen in Belgium, Luc? I mean, men who deliver milk in bottles to homes every morning?'

'Yes, there are still milkmen in some rural areas around Ghent and St. Nikolas who deliver milk in small delivery vans to homes. But in Brussels, I'm yet to see a milk van. But why, do you want to have fresh milk delivered to your home?'

'Oh no, no, I was just curious. Luc, would you like to join me for lunch tomorrow? I have to be at the British embassy again up to around 1pm I guess. After that, we could have lunch somewhere in that area. Tomorrow's Friday.'

The words had just come tumbling out and Seetha was a little surprised by her daring. She was also petrified that he would decline.

Being Luc he took those few extra seconds to reply.

'I'd be very happy to. There is something I had wanted to talk to you about and maybe we can do that over lunch. Maybe it would be best if I picked you up at the British embassy. I know where it is. One o'clock did you say?'

'Yes. But if there is any change in our plan forced by the red tape which tightly ties Her Majesty's government I will call and let you know. Otherwise I will see you at one at the embassy.'

A few minutes later, Seetha left her office, humming to herself. She had regained her composure and her compass. And she was going to have lunch with Luc. A little early but unmistakably, spring was in the air.

Her heart was singing a little. It always did after she met Luc. She wondered what he wanted to talk to her about – at lunch, away from work.

Chapter 19

Amit hailed a taxi to take him back to the Hilton. He had no idea how far or near the Hilton was and he did not care. The experiences of the morning and the beer and cognac had left him in a state of mild euphoria. His trip to Europe seemed to be on the verge of becoming what it had always held the promise of being – an exciting coming of international age.

At the Hilton, he savoured the commissaire's greeting, the courteous smiles at the reception and his being handed his room key without being asked his room number. He took the lift and was happy to absorb that all signs at the Hilton were in English. He smiled indulgently at his reflex action of stopping scratching his armpit on seeing a sign that informed users of the lift that they were under 24 hours surveillance. He looked up to see if he could locate a hidden camera. He could not.

In his room he was pleased to see the little red flashing message light in his telephone. He listened to the messages. There was one from Promod Khera confirming that he would be picked up from the hotel at 8pm. There was another message from the Ambassador's secretary leaving a phone number and asking him to call if he needed any assistance from the Ambassador's office. The messages furthered Amit's sense of contentment. He went over to the minibar, took out a can of Heineken, opened it and flopped into the large armchair. He switched on the television, surfing channels till he found one which featured scantily clad girls participating in some kind of game show which involved a shallow pool of water, many rubber ducks and an avuncular gent in a three-piece suit. There was much merriment, excitement and flesh. The language appeared to be Italian but he wasn't sure. He pressed the mute button and continued to watch idly. His fingers drummed on the armrest.

He knew he should be thinking about the whole arrangement with Ratnesh. It was a little black cloud on his horizon. But this was not the time for serious thought. It was the time for mindless reflection. His thoughts wandered over the morning gone by, a vacant smile on his face.

Amit thought about Seetha. He found her pretty, pert and poised but not sexy. He thought he would love to have her on his arm at a party but not in his bed. He wondered why. He was rather catholic in his tastes as far as women were concerned. But there was something forbidding about her. Maybe it was her guarded manner, her formidable intellect, the hint of frigidity. Would she laugh – full-throated laughter – if he told her the joke about the three sardars in a Paris brothel? He thought of her mouth. When she spoke, she enunciated each word exactly, her lips – no lipstick – moving in precise textbook style. He tried to imagine those lips doing other things. He could not. The thought began by being too salacious. Quickly it changed to being almost sacrilegious.

He thought of the email he would send his father later tonight. At last after two previous bland emails with general waffle about how he was making progress in a hostile and unfamiliar business environment, he now had something concrete to report. For a moment he considered phoning his father but Trehan Senior had the ability to make any caller including his son feel diminished at the end of a call, irrespective of what the caller had to report. No. An email was what was in order.

He could not restrain himself. He decided to send the email straight away. He slowly fetched himself from the depths of the armchair and moved a little unsteadily towards the little guest safe under the writing table. On the TV, the game show involving rubber ducks had given way to another, this one featuring enormous beds on castors. The girls and the avuncular gent remained the same. Amit saw that the game scoreboard had the two teams labelled Uno and Duo. It was indeed an Italian channel.

He opened the outer door of the guest safe, keyed in the secret code he had set (always 2309 – the day in 1987 when the DOW registered its largest ever single-day points gain) and took out his IBM ThinkPad. He set it up on the writing table and plugged in the telephone jack. He composed his mail slowly, choosing his words carefully, backspacing often, deleting, reordering, cutting, pasting. Done, he read it one last time with some satisfaction before clicking on the 'Send' button. The tone was right. The note was short on specifics for two reasons – Amit had very few at this moment and secondly, the note had to be non-incriminating. It was after all a money laundering project that Amit was organizing. The note read:

Hello Papaji,
Working with business associates here I have chalked out a plan to effect the funds inflow needed for our Indian projects. We will be working out implementation details over the next few days. I am working on this project with an Indian exporter-importer and a local Belgian-Indian retailer. As you can imagine, the negotiations were tough and prolonged but I think I have been able to cover all risks and arrange for the funds at a very low cost.
The Ambassador and his officers have been very helpful and I am working on some large export opportunities. I plan to travel to London this weekend and work on some opportunities there too. Though I did not get a British visa in Delhi as I am supposed to do, I have been speaking to the British visa officer here and, while they were initially very reluctant, I did make out a strong case and they are willing to make an exception in my case and stamp a visa on my passport here. They want some paperwork done and the embassy is helping me with that.
The days here are very short – it is still winter – and they appear even shorter because of all the work that needs doing.
I have not forgotten the Johnny Walker Blue. Will buy that at Heathrow.
Respect and love to you and Ma.
Amit

The email sent, Amit returned to his armchair and the Italian channel. The liquor he had consumed and the antics of the avuncular gent soon had him dozing.

He awoke some time later with a start and a mild headache. It was dark. He looked at his watch. It was seven-thirty. Seetha and Promod would be coming at eight. He groaned.

He would have given a lot to go back to sleep. He thought wistfully of the reinvigorating massages their old family retainer, Mangat Ram, would give him from time to time. He could do with one just now. But he was in Brussels and the closest thing to a good old Indian massage was a hot shower. Stumbling to the bathroom, he undressed, drew the shower curtain, fiddled with the elaborate shower water control, naked and shivering, till he managed to get the water the way he wanted it – really hot, just short of scalding – and then stepped in. The water pierced his skin like hot needles. Water acupuncture – treatment for high-life fatigue.

He dressed quickly, deciding against a suit and opting for grey trousers, a pale blue tailored silk shirt and a dark blue jacket. No tie. He sprayed a little cologne on himself and used a mouth freshener. He wanted the Indian Foreign Service community he was going to meet that evening to know – if only in passing – that he was one of the new breed of Indian businessmen who did not wear ill-fitting white safari suits, slick back their oily hair or smell of the fried pakoras they had had for tea.

Buoyed by the shower and mellowed by the warm, lingering afterglow of the morning, Amit was ready for the evening.

Chapter 20

Ratnesh had spent the last two hours wandering up and down Avenue Louise.

Leaving the restaurant on the Rue de Jourdan he had initially walked briskly towards the Bristol Stephanie, for no other reason than that he had mentioned it to Amit and Seetha as the place where he was to have met a business associate. The business associate did not exist and neither had Ratnesh the money to dine or snack or drink at that hotel but it had seemed a suitable exit line at that time.

It was becoming darker and colder. And a biting cold that Ratnesh was not used to. His teeth chattered and his limbs shivered. He pulled the overcoat that Mabel had given him close around him and tightened its belt. He drew up its collar. It did not seem to make much difference.

He wanted very much to get out of this city and this country. Here he had no money, no room and no language in common. He had not bathed for a few days, his clothes were dirty, his face was unshaven... and he was tired. Very tired.

First there was the physical exhaustion. He had moved around Europe for the last three months, visiting every country in the Schengen zone –.for he had a Schengen visa – relentlessly probing for opportunities, any kind, any type, all comers welcome.

In each city he visited, he first sought out the local Indians. Arriving by train, as he usually did, he would check his luggage into the train station cloak room and then wander out, looking for Indian faces. Normally it was not long before he found an Indian newsagent or an Indian restaurant. His cocky armour in place, he would chat with the local Indian, weaving stories about himself as the spirit moved him, then ask for suggestions, names, business contacts, perhaps a place to stay, at the least a free meal, at the very least a free cigarette. Often he was rebuffed, ignored, politely told to go away, misled; but, surprisingly often, he was taken aback by the generosity and warmth that some fellow Indians showed to a complete stranger. He would be taken home, plied with pakoras and sweet tea, asked to explain the latest turn in Indian politics (and there were many), given a warm meal and welcomed to stay for the night; even though there were already five persons at home, just two rooms and just one bed.

He found that it was generally the less well off, often first-generation immigrants – the corner newsagents, the small restaurateurs, the taxi drivers, the airport cleaning staff – who were the most welcoming even though they were often struggling to make a living themselves. The more comfortably placed Indians like the new wave of IT professionals, businessmen and financial experts had no time for Ratnesh and if he forced his attention on them, they immediately searched for a quick getaway line. They found his presence disturbing, an embarrassment, at odds with the image they had of themselves as accomplished world citizens – an image that many of them expended a great deal of effort and care in establishing to their European colleagues, neighbours and the local authority.

Ratnesh noted the differences. He accepted the hospitality where given, quickly turned away from those who turned their eyes away from him. He had survived but it had been grim, joyless. The winter weather made everything bleaker. The only pleasure his quick mind had found had been in noting and trying to understand European ways of thinking, habits, customs, manners and mores. It never occurred to him to adopt those manners and mores.

Ratnesh had come to Europe with just fifty euros. To stay alive and travel for three months he had had to wheedle, cadge and twice even steal from homes where he had been generously invited to spend the night. Once they were sleeping on mattresses on the floor, five in the room. He had noticed one of the others keep his wallet on the table on the far side before retiring. Just past midnight, Ratnesh had cautiously stood up, gingerly tiptoed across four forms shrouded in blankets, extracted all the notes he found in the wallet and tiptoed back into his own blanket. The next morning he woke at crack of dawn, shook awake his host, whispered that he had to leave to catch an early train and vanished before the others awoke. His need was greater than theirs. They would be able to bear the loss.

He had not been able to make a single business deal. He had brought with him to Europe a suitcase full of samples of Moradabad brass handicrafts. Exporting handicrafts had been one of the options he had pursued. He could meet very few importers and those few had been singularly unimpressed by his unsubstantiated stories of factories in three states employing row upon row of skilled artisans, sitting crosslegged, chiselling away at brass and ivory and sandalwood. Most of these importers were hard-headed men and women who had travelled to India, had their own suppliers and had developed a fine ear for exaggeration and untruth.

One blustery morning, after yet another futile meeting in Paris, (this one had been particularly humiliating – the importer did not even invite Ratnesh to his room but had met him at the reception, taken one look at Ratnesh's samples, told him that he was not interested, thanked Ratnesh for coming and turned back to his room) Ratnesh had dropped his suitcase of samples into the Seine while walking across a bridge near the Musee d'Orsay. The bag sunk quickly; Moradabad brass was heavy. Ratnesh then tried to work on other export possibilities – seafood, manpower, spices, gems – but few importers seemed inclined to do business with an individual short on proven experience, genuine references and demonstrable industry knowledge. Only Ratnesh's long acquaintance with frustration led him to persevere and kept him from catching the next flight back to India.

Then in Brussels he had met Mabel and what had begun as just another interesting account of his life, thought up on the spur of the moment, had sowed in his mind the seeds of a plan to become a refugee in Britain. From being an unsuccessful Indian businessman to becoming a successful refugee in order to eventually become a successful British businessman. This was the new plan.

If all went well and he got his visa the next morning, he could be on the Eurostar to London that evening.

He saw the entrance to INNO and decided to walk in. Ratnesh liked the anonymous legitimacy of a shopper. It was warm inside and that was nice too. He stopped shivering and wandered around the shelves looking a little at the goods on display and more at the shoppers looking at those goods.

Ratnesh strolled through the women's wear section, ignoring any stares thrown his way. A woman who must have been in her sixties had come to buy herself a new jacket and she was making an event of it. She had commanded the help and attention of two salesgirls and had entered the trial room for the third time since Ratnesh began watching. She was going to be there all evening.

In the liquor section a table had been set up and they were serving shoppers a newly introduced South African wine in small sample glasses. Ratnesh joined the small group gathered around that table. He took a glass, smelt its bouquet, then took a small sip, rolled the wine around his tongue, seemed to be lost in concentration for a few seconds, then swallowed, looked up at the aproned salesgirl across the table and nodded very briefly a few times. The wine had met with his approval. Ratnesh knew nothing about wines but had been carefully watching an old gentleman who was at the table before him and had copied him perfectly – to the last nod.

Ratnesh noticed that the store seemed to have adopted elaborate security measures. There were a number of overhead cameras and uniformed guards were making frequent rounds of the floors. Ratnesh guessed that there would also be a few plainclothes detectives on duty. Ratnesh wondered why anybody in the West would want to steal. The reason could not be want. It seemed to Ratnesh that anybody who wanted to acquire material wealth in the West badly enough could do so in a hundred legitimate ways. It was all right to steal in India where for millions of people there was simply no opportunity to earn a decent living but here – Ratnesh pursed his lips puritanically – here it was only those who were too lazy to work who stole.

A single, coloured man like Ratnesh who did not seem to be buying anything soon attracted the attention of store security. A guard watched him fixedly keeping a discreet distance. When Ratnesh moved, the guard did, always keeping Ratnesh, particularly his hands, in view. Ratnesh, with his long experience of playing cat and mouse with a variety of law enforcement agencies, had noticed the guard almost as soon as the guard had noticed him. Ratnesh smiled to himself and moved rapidly down the aisle to the kitchen goods section and pretended to examine a shelf full of Tefal pans. He acted as suspiciously as possible, taking his hands in and out of various overcoat pockets, turning around and peering furtively now and again. The guard had moved close to the Tefal shelf too, keeping his distance, but watching Ratnesh closely with growing suspicion. Ratnesh moved again, this time to a shelf with a range of cutlery. The guard followed. Ratnesh took up spoons, one by one and examined them carefully hiding his hands from the guard by turning his back. The guard moved quickly to try and peer around Ratnesh, trying to make out if Ratnesh was replacing the spoons he was picking up or stuffing them into his overcoat pocket. Ratnesh continued this game for a few minutes, moving from the cutlery shelf to the crystalware shelf. The guard moved with him. Then, having had enough of the game, Ratnesh turned around, looked directly at the guard, smiled a big smile and moved out of the kitchen section. The guard stared at Ratnesh, too wary to smile back, too startled to react in any other way. As Ratnesh passed the guard, he saw him take out his walkie talkie and urgently speak to someone. Ratnesh guessed that he might be frisked when he left the store.

Another half hour of aimless wandering past shelves on three floors left Ratnesh a little tired and wanting a change. The large amount of beer he had had was also telling. He took the escalator to the third floor, used the toilet and then bought himself a cup of coffee in the Lunch Garden cafeteria. He sat down in a warm corner, his back to the wall. He liked to look at the motley crowd streaming in and out of the cafeteria. He looked at his watch. 6:30pm. The store would close in an hour. Nursing the warm cup in both his hands, he wondered what he could do with the rest of the evening. He took out this wallet and counted out his money. He had eighty-two euros, most of which Mabel had given him. Fifty was the visa fee. Mabel had promised to buy him the Eurostar ticket. He should keep at least twenty euros for any eventuality in London. That left him with just twelve euros to spend in Brussels. Too little for a whore and dinner. Too little for just a whore even. Enough for a reasonable dinner. As for a bed, he could try Hamid again, but the odds were that he would end up sleeping once again on a bench in the Gare du Midi. Hopefully this would be the last night. Tomorrow night he should be in Sham's flat in London. Hope Sham's flat had heating which worked.

Reluctantly he got up to leave the restaurant. It was a self-service restaurant and he saw signs – thankfully pictorial – requesting him to clear his own tray but the tray bin was at the far end of the hall. Noticing an abandoned tray on another table, he left his own too and walked out of the cafeteria. He took the escalator down to the ground floor, buttoned his overcoat and approached the exit doors. They opened and he was in Rue Neuve again. He was surprised that he had not been searched when he left the store.

The cold hit him. He felt as if he had been suddenly seized by a giant trembling hand of ice. It took him a couple of minutes to stop his teeth chattering audibly. He walked briskly towards the Metro station hoping to warm himself that way. If his asylum plans succeeded he would have to learn to live with European weather. He would get used to it after a couple of winters – he would by then also have the money to buy warmer clothes. Right now he could do with woollen socks, thermals and a pair of gloves.

Ratnesh watched curiously as what appeared to be an unattended pram seemed to be moving slowly towards him. It was often hidden by hurrying pedestrians. As it came closer, Ratnesh saw that it was not a pram but an old lady, shrunk with age, bundled in layers of clothes, slowly shuffling forward, stooping, clutching a small bag or purse in her left hand and with her right pushing a little trolley with what appeared to be bags of groceries. Ratnesh watched her curiously. Must be poor and probably all alone in the world save for her cat. He wondered if she lived in a home for senior citizens. Lonely old people who took care of themselves were a rarity in India. He wondered how he would find growing old alone in the West. But he would not grow old alone. He would marry late – a much younger girl.

Suddenly a big man – Ratnesh noticed that he wore a leather jacket – grabbed the old lady's purse. She screamed and held on to it. He pushed her – a little reluctantly, it seemed – and as she fell, he took the purse and ran. Some passers-by did not notice. Some did but hurried on. Some froze. One young woman ran to help the old lady who had fallen.

Ratnesh reacted instinctively. As the big man ran past Ratnesh towards the Palais du Justice, Ratnesh stuck out a leg and as the man fell heavily, Ratnesh kicked him hard in the ribs. Two young men joined Ratnesh and they pinned the big man to the ground. They checked his pockets for a gun or a knife. The old lady's purse had fallen from the man's hand. Another man picked it up and took it to the old lady who was now standing helped by the young lady. Someone had called the police and within a minute a patrol car was at the kerb, siren wailing, lights flashing. Two policemen jumped out. One of the policemen had a gun in his hand. They looked at the big man and then at Ratnesh, not sure who they needed to apprehend. The two young men with Ratnesh spoke to the police in rapid Flemish. The policemen handcuffed the big man. One of them then walked over to the old lady and talked to her. A small knot of people had formed. One man patted Ratnesh on the shoulder. The two young men who had helped him pin down the big man shook hands with him. Having taken the old lady's statement, the police left with the big man in the back of the patrol car.

The small knot quickly dispersed. Ratnesh walked on. The scuffle had warmed him. He was also happy to observe that a deftly outstretched leg has the same effect anywhere in the world. And he was glad that he had helped in seeing justice done. A big, healthy man with enough money to buy a leather jacket had no business robbing a poor old lady.

Chapter 21

The phone rang again in Amit's room. He picked it up. It was Promod Khera calling from the lobby.

'Good evening, sir, I am calling from your hotel lobby. Shall I come up to your room or shall I wait for you here, sir?'

'Do come up, Promod. We have to wait for a friend of mine, Seetha, to arrive. I have invited her to the dinner as well. I hope that's okay.'

'That is perfectly fine, sir. I'm sure that DCM will be delighted to have your friend joining us at today's dinner. I will be up in a moment.'

In the lift, Promod looked in the mirror, brushed back his hair and smoothed the knot in his tie. He somehow never seemed to get it right. He had even looked up 'Tie knots' on the internet. Google reported 11,078 matches. A few webpages had diagrams. One even had an animated clip titled 'The Perfect Knot'. His mind could follow the instructions but apparently not his hands. It was one of those things he had to live with.

He wondered who this Seetha was. Girlfriend? Just a friend? Travelling together? Does the Ambassador know? Does Amit's father, the minister's brother, know? Was it right for him to have accepted on the DCM's behalf her coming to dinner? Are there any security or Foreign Office rule book issues involved? Forget it. Amit was the foreign minister's nephew and the Ambassador was doing all he could to roll out the red carpet. Promod was only a bit player doing his bit.

Promod knocked on Amit's door. A deferential knock. A hundred years ago he would have been the perfect courtier. Promod thought he heard a faint 'Come in' but he could not be sure and decided that it would be safer to wait. The 'Come in' was repeated, this time louder and more irritably. Promod turned the door knob and entered.

Amit was sitting in the room's only armchair. When he had heard the knock he had hesitated briefly, wondering whether he should go and open the door. But laziness and his own sense of propriety had made him shout out a 'Come in'.

'Good evening, sir,' said Promod, lingering near the door.

'Come in, Promod, do come in and take a seat. You have a choice between the straight backed chair near the desk or the bed – which has no back at all,' said Amit in good cheer, pointing with a drooping hand, not bothering to get up.

'Not a problem, sir,' said Promod, choosing to sit on the edge of the bed

'Just call me Amit. Have you been in Brussels long?'

This was the perfect opening that Promod had been waiting for. And he had to be quick, before that unknown quantity, Seetha, arrived.

'I have been here for three years, sir – Amit. I have just applied for an extension here. You see, Amit sir, the Brussels diplomatic world is a maze. The Belgian federal government, the Belgian regional governments, the EU, NATO – they're all headquartered here. It takes a diplomat at least three years to know his way around and develop the right contacts. From an Indian government's perspective, Amit, it would be a waste if I were to be transferred now simply because of the Foreign Office three-year rule.'

'Where is your next posting likely to be?'

'Africa, sir, probably Lagos. It's not that I have a problem with Africa, Amit. It's just that I can see that my replacement here will take another three years to reach my level of comfort with the diplomatic world here and that would not be good especially given that the EU-India strategic partnership has just been finalized and needs to be exploited fully, sir.'

'Yes, of course,' said Amit, appreciative of his own searching questioning.

There was a moment's silence. Promod had deftly succeeded in slipping in a word about his application for extension of his tenure in Brussels into the ear of the foreign minister's nephew. You never knew who could influence whom and what chance conversations might take place in the upper reaches of Delhi's South Block. Having accomplished his task, Promod did not want to too obviously appear a favour seeker. He decided to change the subject.

'Amit, have you found time to see some of Brussels's

sights?'

The phone rang and Amit was spared the need to think of a sufficiently witty reply.

It was Seetha. She had arrived at exactly 8:05pm. Not late enough to be impolite but late enough to allow her to remain in the lobby and decline any invitation to come up to Amit's room and have a drink before leaving.

Amit and Promod came down and met Seetha in the lobby. Seetha had changed into a dark trouser suit and high heels. On her arm was a smart black overcoat. Amit thought she looked like an anchor on a business channel (weren't Asian anchors the current rage on television?) just arriving for another work day in front of the studio lights, replete with weakening dollars, strengthening euros, the wavering FTSE, the restless DOW, jobless growth and oil prices rising on threats of disruption in supplies.

To Promod, Amit introduced Seetha as a computer whiz, a philosopher, a writer and a friend with whom he shared many interests. He omitted to mention that he had met Seetha for the first time just ten hours ago. To Seetha, he introduced Promod as the Commercial Attaché at the Indian embassy. The unvarnished title sounded good enough.

They moved towards the large glass front door. Promod moved quickly to open the door for Amit. Amit moved aside gallantly to let Seetha through first. Seetha went through, her face a little flushed from the unusual attention and the exalted company.

In the car, Amit and Seetha rode in the back. It was the embassy Mercedes and they had a chauffeur. Promod sat in the front passenger seat. Promod was pointing out various Brussels landmarks as they drove on. Seetha gritted her teeth when she heard Promod pronounce Bois de la Cambre as Boys deela Cambray.

It was dark and cold outside. It was not snowing though. Seetha wondered if the temperature was below freezing. She looked to the front panel to see if there was a temperature indicator. There was one. With German precision it told her that the temperature outside was 2.6 below freezing and that inside it was 20.5 Celsius. This was the first time Seetha had ever ridden in a Mercedes. The car appeared to be a smooth, sleek bubble of luxurious warmth and good cheer.

Promod was telling Amit that Belgians spoke little English and if at all they did, it was a peculiar brand of English, literally translated from French or Flemish. For example, said Promod, they never say 'You can do this,' instead they say, 'You have the possibility to do this.'

The Belgian chauffeur held his peace and looked straight ahead.

That's true, thought Seetha. Even Luc often uses that phrase. So what's wrong. We all have our national turns of phrase. Indian English has its fair share.

'The other day,' continued Promod, I saw a copy of an internal European Commission note which was addressed by a Spanish officer to his colleagues. It began with the salutation, 'Estimated Colleagues'! They laughed. The easy laugh of Indians who knew better.

'In India literal translation is what makes so much of Indian English delightfully different. Many trucks carry a little sign to ward off the evil eye – Buri nazar wale, tera mooh kala. Last month, near Gurgaon I saw a truck with the English equivalent. It read: Evil look person – your face black,' said Amit. They laughed again.

Seetha said that she thought that misspelling and mispronunciation – or rather different pronunciation – was what led to bizarre transformations of English words. She added her own account of a photograph she had seen of a restaurant and bar in Bihar which announced through a large signboard that 'Child Bear' was available in plenty in the shop. The laughter in the car was uproarious.

Promod chipped in with an account of buses in Meerut which had signs painted above a few seats indicating that they were reserved for 'handicrafts.' Promod had assumed that since Meerut was known for its hand-worked brass articles the local bus company must had decided to allot two seats to workers carrying handicrafts. He had to quickly revise his assumption when he saw a man, disabled in his legs, slowly sit down in one of those two reserved seats. Promod and Amit laughed or rather Amit laughed and Promod sniggered obsequiously, looking at Amit. Seetha managed a small smile – she was not quite sure if it was appropriate to laugh at jokes involving the differently abled.

They arrived at the house of Rakesh Bimal, the Deputy Chief of Mission, in good cheer. It was in the affluent commune of Sint Genesius Rode. The chauffeur turned into the driveway of what appeared to be a large house set in a much larger garden. A long line of cars were already parked along the driveway. Seetha took it all in, excited, just a little apprehensive.

The car stopped at the front porch. The chauffeur opened Seetha's door and she alighted. She wondered if she needed to thank the chauffeur or just look straight ahead and walk on as all important people seemed to do on television. She decided to err on the side of politeness. The chauffeur smiled and winked leaving Seetha a little disconcerted. What on earth did he mean? The sudden cold outside slammed her and she concentrated on trying to suppress the boorish chattering of her teeth.

The three of them walked up to the front door which opened before they had time to find the door bell. A tall Indian gentleman in a dark suit welcomed them into a small, rectangular hallway, shut the front door behind them and offered to take their coats. For a moment Seetha thought he was the DCM but he appeared more servile than what was par for an Indian bureaucrat. Seetha also saw that Amit and Promod barely noticed the gentleman as they gave him their coats. Amit helped Seetha out of her black overcoat and handed it over to the gentleman. Butler? Embassy flunkey? Hired help all the way from India?

They waited while the gentleman went into an ante room to deposit their coats. The lobby where they were standing was warm and stopped Seetha's shivering. She noticed a framed Ravi Varma reproduction on one wall facing a Rubens on the opposite wall. Both prints were the same size, had the same style of frame and both depicted women. She found the woman in Ravi Varma's print to be the more sensuous while Rubens's woman was the more nuanced. She made a mental note to find out if any Western critic had reviewed any of Ravi Varma's work. Amit and Promod were looking at their watches.

The gentleman returned from the ante room and hurried to

open the double door leading into the salon and show them in. Seetha tried to slink to the back but Amit waited till she was at his side and that was how they entered, with Promod Khera bringing up the rear.

The first impression which Seetha had was of entering a reception hosted by the President at Rashtrapati Bhavan in Delhi. She had seen news clips of such receptions on Doordarshan in Madras and this salon seemed to be equally grand, rich and sophisticated. It was very large. The walls were panelled with oak. The carpets were Kashmiri. The furniture was rich, antique Belgian. There were a large number of people in the saloon. The men were mostly in dark suits, the women in rich, silk saris and pashmina shawls. Two Filipina maids were serving drinks and cocktail snacks. Seetha saw only one white face. Everyone else was Indian. The men were standing in a number of little groups, drinks in their hands. The women seemed to have mostly congregated into a single large group, seated on sofas and chairs arranged in a wide irregular square near the middle of the room. With relief, Seetha noticed that only a couple of the women had drinks in their hands. There were a number of plates of snacks on small tables near the sofas. Seetha could make out her favourite cocktail vadas but this was not the time to dwell on them.

The level of noise was high – soft Amjad Ali Khan in the background and fashionable chatter in a Hindi-English polyglot in the foreground – and hit them as they entered the room. Their entrance had an immediate effect. The noise decreased suddenly and most faces turned towards the door. After all, the party was for Amit. Only a couple of the embassy officers had met the foreign minister's nephew so far and everyone else was curious. Being Indians no one hesitated to show their curiosity. Seetha's face coloured on finding that as many people were staring at her as at Amit.

A tall man with a neat, pencil moustache, dressed in a pinstriped suit, quickly put down his drink on a nearby table and hurried towards them, his hand outstretched. Seetha guessed that that would be the DCM.

'Good evening, Mr Trehan. Welcome to Brussels. It is a pleasure to have you with us today,' and turning to Seetha, 'and... er... Madam, good...'

'This is Seetha, a friend of mine who lives here in Brussels. She is one of those rare people who combine prodigious skills in application design with literary flair,' interrupted Amit.

Seetha, floating on a cloud of new experiences and excitement, was not as revolted by the introduction as she might otherwise have been. In a corner of her mind though, muted alarm bells were beginning to ring. She had a growing feeling that she was being perceived by everyone to be the minister's nephew's moll.

'Good evening, madam. It's a pleasure to have you with us today. You know, it's our responsibility at the embassy to get to know prominent Indians in this country but sometimes we are amiss.'

Seetha smiled a forgiving smile. It was nice to float on a make-believe cloud in a make-believe world. He used the word 'prominent Indian' to describe me! Pinch yourself, Seetha girl.

'Come, let me introduce you both to our embassy community here. They are very keen to meet you both,' said the DCM, shepherding them towards the closest little knot of officers.

On seeing them approaching, the officers abandoned their conversation and turned to face them, their expressions those of eager schoolboys seeing the headmaster approach escorting the school's annual day chief guests.

The DCM introduced them and they all shook hands. The officers shook hands with them in what over the last fifty years had become the standard Indian government regulation style of shaking hands with ones' betters. The hand was outstretched but otherwise the body was crouched deferentially in a manner most appropriate for tugging at a forelock.

Amit made a few fatuous remarks about being happy to meet the cream of the Indian foreign service. The officers smiled politely. The DCM soon led Amit away to meet someone who he said was a very successful diamond merchant in Antwerp's diamond bourse. Seetha hesitated, unsure whether to follow Amit or stay. She finally stayed, deciding that it would be a good idea to put some distance between her and Amit.

With their boss having left, the officers returned to their normal selves – bright, well informed, savvy diplomats. They

had the real delight in diverse knowledge and information
so common in more than a few Indian civil servants. Once
they discovered that Seetha was not just a dumb piece of
decoration, they were genuinely delighted to talk with her
about her work and her interests. In talking about herself
and answering questions, Seetha found herself in unexpected
confusion, stuttering sometimes as she found herself hopping
dangerously between her two personas – one mundane and
the other exotic. One real and the other largely imagined with
a few slivers of reality. One that of a junior Indian business
analyst and IT specialist on a short-term contract assignment
in Europe and the other that of a recognized writer of
philosophical fiction. But this was an intellectual challenge in
real time and Seetha relished it.

One of the maids came with a tray of drinks. The officers
pressed Seetha to have a glass of wine. She declined. She was
a teetotaller – could a Mylapore Tamil Iyer girl be anything
else? – and anyway today she was heady without a drop. The
officers took stout glasses of Belgian beer.

One of the officers, Pradeep Upadhyay, was boyish and
nerdish, with kindly eyes, Trotsky spectacles, a Stalin
moustache and a nervous tic. He was the kind of person who
would look a graduate student until his late forties: one who
you would not be surprised to meet in an IIT library, hunched
over back volumes of journals on fluid mechanics, engrossed,
oblivious of pretty co-eds and leaving only after the second
closing bell. In reality he was the second secretary at the
embassy with responsibility for Political Affairs. He was
a school teacher's son from the Ujjain in Madhya Pradesh.
His quick mind, his long hours of study and his perseverance
– he had succeeded only on his second attempt – saw him
qualifying for the foreign service eight years ago. He was
one of the very few Indian diplomats who had attained
a reasonable knowledge of French and he had rapidly
acquired a reputation within the Foreign Office of being an
astute analyst of European politics. The Foreign Secretary
was said to know him by name and had recently asked for
his analysis of the European reaction to the proposed Indo-
Iran gas pipeline. The placement of words in his English was
unashamedly Indian.

In talking to Seetha, the first time he used a Hindi phrase in a sentence he took the trouble of turning to her and asking if she understood Hindi. That won Seetha over completely and she replied that she did follow some Hindi and he was very welcome to speak in it.

Pradeep had studied philosophy in college and had chosen it as one of his optional subjects in the Civil Service qualifying exams. He and Seetha were soon duelling about the Hinduness of India's modern godmen, especially those who had won large international followings. Another officer with a beer belly and a cheerful face butted in. His silk tie showed tiny purple elephants rampaging on a yellow background. He held that today's godmen were indeed Hindu but in an Upanishadic way which really was quite different from a Puranic theistic way.

Around them the diplomatic evening swirled. Seetha saw Amit in the distance. He was holding forth at the centre of a large group. The group laughed uproariously at something Amit said. A few of the women had left their group and joined the men. One of the women was very pretty. She was wearing a fiery red Dhaka sari. She seemed to be laughing the loudest.

The Filipina was back again. This time her tray bore a plate of pakoras and another of cheese balls. Seetha was tempted by the pakoras. On the tray were small picks, forks and napkins. The officers and the philosophy having made her feel at home, Seetha opted to pick up a pakora with her fingers. She dipped it in the little bowl of green coriander chutney and then ate it. It was delicious. She had not had a pakora for three months.

Seetha saw the pretty girl in the red sari coming towards them.

'Intuition is so subjective...' began Pradeep when the girl in the red sari tapped him on the shoulder.

'Excuse me, I'm sorry,' she said to them in general, flashing a quick smile. Then turning to Pradeep, she said, 'Do you have Kamdar Uncle's phone number at home? Mr Amit Trehan is going to London and he wanted to meet an Indian in the food processing industry there. Kamdar Uncle will be the right person.'

'We have not met Kamdar Uncle for years but *haan*, Rita, he is the right person. He is also something important in the

Indian Businessmen's Association in London. I don't have the number here. I have it in my Filofax at home. We can call Kamdarji tonight and ask him to call Mr Trehan in London. I think he will be glad to do that. And Rita, I want you to meet Seetha here. She is a computer professional as well as a professional philosopher. Seetha, this is my wife, Rita.'

'Hello, pleased to meet you,' said Seetha putting out her hand.

'Good evening. Glad to meet you too,' replied Rita, flashing another smile – she seemed able to produce them on demand – but she declined to take Seetha's professed hand and instead chose to fold her hands in a namaskar. Seetha coloured and the diplomatic world seemed unfamiliar and closed once again.

Rita turned brightly to the officer with the elephant tie and said, 'Samir, you should bring Prakriti home sometime next week. She and I have a lot to talk about. Pradeep, why don't you and Samir fix a day next week. That's a lovely tie you're wearing, Samir. Well, I'll catch up with you later. I told Amit I'll be back in a minute.' Another smile which took in everybody (Seetha thought it had not included her but she was not sure) and she was gone, silk sari shimmering in the party haze.

There was silence in her wake. Neither Samir nor Pradeep seemed inclined to confirm a day as Rita had suggested they do – at least not immediately. Seetha was unsettled. She felt she had been shown her place. Pradeep sensed her discomfiture and tried to ease it by noting that the pakoras were very good indeed and that they had probably been made by the new cook the DCM had recently hired and brought to Brussels from a small town in Rajasthan.

'And arrey, I must tell you what happened last week,' continued Pradeep. 'This cook, Moti Ram, is an excellent cook and he comes cheap but he has spent all his life in a traditional haveli in Barmer, living a traditional Rajasthani life and wearing traditional Rajasthani clothes – dhotis and kurtas. Here in Brussels, the DCM instructed him to wear Western clothes – trousers, shirts and coats – and Moti Ram reluctantly complied. Last Sunday, being his weekly day off, Moti Ram decided to wear his old, comfortable dhoti, kurta and shawl and take a walk in the park. It was a windy day and you know our dhotis. Moti Ram's fluttered and flew in the Belgian breeze and two policewomen on their rounds arrested him – for flashing! Moti Ram had no knowledge of any of Belgium's three official languages or indeed of English and he wasn't carrying any ID – he just kept repeating the words – Indian embassy, Indian embassy. Fortunately he remembered the DCM's phone number and a very irritated DCM spent his Sunday afternoon at the Sint Genesius Rode police station explaining to two sceptical policewomen that men in Indian villages wore dhotis which could, to Western eyes, appear be very daring garments. The DCM went on to explain that these rustic, ignorant Indians wearing dhotis were wont to reveal some very private parts of themselves quite nonchalantly and absolutely without any malafide intent. The DCM's diplomatic status and the terrified look on Moti Ram's face convinced the policewomen that sexually inappropriate behaviour was the last thing on his mind. They let Moti Ram off with a warning and a pair of lock-up pyjamas. Apparently the next day the DCM confiscated all Moti Ram's dhotis and sent him in the embassy car to the giant Macro store to buy several pairs of trousers.'

They were still laughing when the DCM came over to their group. His arrival doused their laughter.

'Excuse me, gentlemen, for interrupting, but can I take Ms Seetha away from you? Gopal and I would like to pick her brains about our problems accessing the Foreign Office network. It is not often that we have an IT whiz with us.'

'I'd be glad to help if I can, Mr Bimal. But I must warn you that I am a systems analyst and not a communications specialist,' cautioned Seetha as she was led away to meet Gopal.

Gopalakrishnan was standing alone, his snazzy new full-feature mobile phone in hand. Gopal was reading an email message from the Western Europe section at the Foreign Office in Delhi. Gopal was a career diplomat specializing in multilateral organizations, particularly the UN and its organs, but he was also one of the countless people across the world who had been seduced by the wonderful world of computers and communication. He lived and breathed ICT. He changed his laptop every year. He added gizmos, hardware and software every month. He downloaded and uploaded millions of bytes each day. His cell phone was a marvel. He had got a reluctant embassy to subscribe to *BYTE, PC World* and *Home Computing*. His email password was jobs4steve.

Gopal had volunteered to help the embassy with their computing and communications infrastructure and had been frustrated by their inability to be online and smoothly integrated with the Indian Foreign Office Network. The technical help available to the embassy from New Delhi was limited. The embassy had also tried contracting with a local IT support firm but language difficulties, security considerations and unfamiliar technologies had frustrated the efforts of the contractor.

Soon Gopal and Seetha were deeply immersed in conversation peppered with bandwidth, gateways, protocols, optimum routing, switching technologies and all seven layers of the ISO. Both had intuited that the other was a Tamil Brahmin – you can always sense your own – and they were soon speaking in a Tamil-English argot. They were however both too far removed from the agraharams of Tamil Nadu to begin tracing family trees. Their parents would have done that.

The Filipina maid was back again. This time she caught Seetha's eye and smiled. Her tray now bore a plate of pickled olives and another of tiny sandwiches. Seetha passed. Gopal asked the girl what sandwiches they were. On being told that they were chicken sandwiches, Gopal declined, his right hand raised in front of him, face open in refusal. Seetha thought he looked like a traffic policeman making a stop sign.

The background music had changed from Amjad Ali Khan to Geeta Dutt singing 'Mera Naam Chin Chin Chu'. The song had many bald heads nodding, hands strumming on beer glasses and polished toes tapping on the polished wooden floor. The music seemed to move the men more than the women. Or perhaps it was just that their appreciation showed. Around Gopal and Seetha the little knots formed and reformed. The Filipinas glided around, tying the knots together. The two of them were busy, little tug boats provisioning noisy steamers which were not anchored.

Gopal and Seetha talked at length. Neither seemed to want to move away. From the foreign office network, their conversation moved outwards in ripples to encompass the whole dizzy world of IT and Communications. Gopal was in his element. Seetha was not equally enamoured of technology but she was knowledgeable and both Gopal and technology seemed to give her a safe haven in this rather intimidating evening. She was almost afraid that Gopal would suddenly move away and leave her alone. She wished that Amit would come over and talk to her, validate her presence in the party and introduce her to a few more people. But Amit was holding court in a far corner and he seemed to have quite forgotten Seetha.

Rita swished from knot to knot. To Seetha, her red sari appeared to be a warning flag – of what, she had no idea.

Chapter 22

Amit was enjoying the evening. He was in the home of the Deputy Chief of Mission of the Indian embassy in a Western European country at a party thrown at least partly in his honour. He was surrounded by the cream of the Indian diaspora in Belgium – intelligent, polished foreign service officers, suave diamond merchants who had driven over from Antwerp, a British MEP of Indian origin, two officers working at the NATO headquarters (American citizens but Indians in origin and inclination) and a sprinkling of academics from Leuven and the University Libre de Bruxelles. There was even a judge from the World Court of Justice at the Hague. And Amit was quite the centre of attention. He had met so many new faces today, he found it difficult to remember the names. But it did not seem to matter – they were all equally personable and deferential. And there were some very pretty women. One in particular, in a striking red sari, had been most helpful too. She had given him the name of a successful British businessman of Indian origin in the food processing industry – her husband's uncle apparently – and had promised to arrange that the businessman met Amit in London.

Amit had told the DCM of his need for faxes of invitation from a couple of British businessman. The DCM had immediately called the embassy third secretary aside and asked him to call the Indian embassy in London and ask them to find suitable businessmen and ensure that the faxed invitations to discuss potential business relationships reached Amit by the next morning. 'Involve Promod Khera too, if you need to,' added the DCM. The DCM reminded the third secretary to make sure that the Indian embassy in London understood that it was the foreign minister's nephew who needed the faxes.

Amit had been shepherded from knot to knot. First by the DCM and later by the lady in the red sari. It wasn't quite clear if the DCM had assigned her the responsibility of escorting Amit but nevertheless she performed the role with panache.

Amit now noticed her coming towards him – he tried to remember her name but could not. He noticed that she had tied her sari well below her navel.

'Dinner is waiting, gentlemen. The ladies have helped themselves so please do come. The paranthas are worth dying for,' and turning to Amit she repeated in a softer voice: 'Please do come, Amit, I'll show you the way.'

The group broke up, most meandering towards the buffet tables. Amit meekly followed her. It was pleasant to be led by a pretty woman.

'The DCM has hired a new cook and he is really good. The spread today may not be as sumptuous as what you are used to in Delhi but it's not bad – his paranthas rival anything I have had in the Paranthe-wali-gali in Old Delhi. I'm sure you have been there,' she said as she led Amit to the buffet tables.

'Yes, I have been there a long time ago. Paranthe-wali-gali has always meant excellent food and execrable hygiene. But today the paranthas at the Khyber restaurant at the Taj Palace Hotel are just as good and the hygiene is certainly better... er... I'm very sorry but I think I can't remember your name. I have an awful memory.'

'It's Rita. You've met too many people today and the names and faces must all be one blur but it's also clear that I have not made an unforgettable impression,' replied Rita with a dimpled smile.

'It's your smile that is to blame. It was unforgettable. It smothered the name,' replied Amit gallantly.

'It's nice to be told such lies. Your memory is forgiven.'

They reached the buffet tables behind which Moti Ram was standing, looking decidedly uncomfortable in dark trousers, a white shirt and a white apron. Amit helped himself with Rita fussing around him and instructing Moti Ram to give him a particularly juicy portion of lamb in the Nawabi Gosht.

Plates loaded, Rita manoeuvred Amit to a quiet corner away from most of the crowd. She wanted a few minutes with him. An idea had formed in her head – a heady idea which she found difficult to carry – she needed to speak to Amit and let him either quash it or help it take concrete shape.

Rita was a Bombay girl. Her father, Akash Nerurkar, was

a wealthy solicitor and her parents were a part of Bombay's westernised, English speaking, liberal elite. Rita had studied in a 'convent' school and then had gone on to complete her Bachelor's in Mass Communication Studies at Sophia's. She graduated with honours. An uncle had known Pradeep's father and he had suggested to Akash that perhaps Pradeep, who had then just joined the foreign service, might make Rita a good husband. Rita's parents, already apprehensive about Rita's stream of restless, feckless Bombay boyfriends had readily agreed. The Nerurkars, like many Indian families of that city and class thought arranged marriages to be old-fashioned but at the same time were reluctant and unwilling to let their children make their decisions entirely by themselves. They coaxed Rita into meeting Pradeep. Rita laughed at the idea of an arranged marriage but let herself be persuaded into meeting Pradeep. Secretly, the thought of being a diplomat's wife, travelling across the world, attending and hosting elegant soirees, did appeal to her. And the thought that a Foreign Service officer was coming all the way from Delhi to Bombay to take her out for dinner flattered. She found Pradeep to be boyish, intelligent, well read and so very different from her slick Bombay friends. In spite of herself, she fell a little in love with him. They were married six months later.

Six years later, things had changed as they mostly do. The diplomatic world still appealed to Rita but she found Pradeep stolid and predictable. His boyishness grated. She was irritated by his habit of lacing his English sentences with 'Arrey' and 'Bhai' and 'Achcha.' Often, she found herself dreaming about her previous existence – her friends, Sophia's, the discos, the Gateway of India at four in the morning, and the parties they called corkscrew parties for a variety of reasons. She was restless. She wanted to work but a peripatetic existence as a diplomat's wife did not give her many options. Now with Amit she saw a glimmer of a possibility.

'Amit, you were mentioning earlier that you were looking to grow your exports to Europe. Would you possibly be looking for a bright, well travelled, persuasive, pleasant but very tough person located here in Brussels to work for you and ensure that you met the export targets you have in mind? And am I being obvious enough?' asked Rita flashing another of those ones.

Amit was taken by surprise – pleasant surprise.

Amit smiled. An indulgent smile. He took a forkful of Nawabi Gosht into his mouth, giving him time to think. There was his father to consider. But with Ratnesh and Harish's help he should be able to find a little money in the saffron deal to pay Rita a salary without troubling his father. He had a vision of travelling to Paris with Rita (Air France – adjacent seats in first class) to make a presentation to the senior management of Carrefour. She was wearing a business suit. Dark blue. She looked very good. And she was very forceful and effective. Carrefour placed a big order with them. His father was pleased.

'The answer is yes to both questions,' replied Amit. 'I will be delighted, Rita, if you worked for us. I can see that you are persuasive and I feel too that you have the tenacity and drive we require in this job. There are of course a number of details to work out but I think I can ask the question – when can you start?'

'Wow. I can't believe this. I need to pinch myself to believe it.' Rita pinched the back of her left hand with her right. It left a tiny red crescent. 'I too have to work out a number of details. Not just details. Macros too. I haven't even discussed this with my husband. I haven't considered the children. But I'm sure I can work things out. The answer to your question is tomorrow!'

'Why not tonight?' asked Amit, 'I'm busy tomorrow and will probably have to leave for London in the evening. Do you think we could go somewhere quiet after this party and discuss your responsibilities in greater detail? You see, I'm currently working on a deal with a couple of Indians here in Brussels and I would like you to handle it once I return to India. Before that you need to have some understanding of Trehan Foods and the way we work.'

Rita considered the options. She could take him home after this party but Pradeep would be hovering around with gratuitous suggestions on the best way to communicate between Europe and India and needless advice on the most effective negotiating tactics to use with Germans. This was going to be her project and hers alone. There was a little bistro

– taverne was what they called it – La Tourelle, on Boulevard General Jacques. It was quiet and stayed open until 2am. That would be the right place.

'Sure. As the Americans say, there is no time like now. I believe they also say that there is no place like here but we can ignore that part of their advice. I would suggest we talk at a little bistro I know. It's quiet. They also have a wide selection of the quainter Belgian beers. And thankfully I have my own car with me today.' Rita's eyes were bright with excitement. Excitement after six years of abstinence.

'Sounds like a plan. I believe Americans also say that. Well, I guess we could leave this party in another half an hour without being guilty of any impropriety,' said Amit, thinking that this was turning out to be some day.

'Absolutely. Well, let me introduce you to that group of ladies near the dessert table. They have been eyeing you since you came and I am sure they will be delighted to meet you. Don't forget to try the chocolate mousse. I was told that it is yum. The regulation in Indian embassies in Europe is that the main course is always Indian but the desserts are European. God knows why. In the mean time I will go and meet my husband and tell him the good news. I hope he sees it that way.'

For a split second Rita wondered about the girl who had come with Amit. Was Amit planning to bring her along? No, that was very improbable. God knew who she was and how close she was to him. Apparently not very. She was probably just a political groupie whose pedantic pretensions Amit was now obviously escaping from. Rita was certainly not going to remind Amit about her.

Amit, on his part, had completely forgotten about Seetha.

Chapter 23

Half an hour later, Amit and Rita were in her red Opel Corsa, travelling up Boulevard Waterloo back towards the city centre.

Rita had needed just five minutes with Pradeep. He had seen the determination in her eyes and knew better than to be uncooperative. In point of fact he had been very encouraging. Rita sensed that he was almost happy to get her out of his hair. She had been increasingly difficult over the last one year.

Next Rita had gone over to talk to the DCM. He proved to be far more difficult. Amit was virtually the official guest that evening and how could she simply abduct him. He wanted to know where she was taking Amit and why. How exactly did she imagine she was going to help Amit in his business – and that too at midnight? Could she not meet him tomorrow? The DCM's eyebrows were arched in seeming incomprehension. Rita had been patient but skimped on details. In the end the DCM relented because the plan appeared to be Amit's and who was the DCM to further question or investigate the motives of the foreign minister's nephew.

But the DCM did have another question. Why did she want to take Amit in her own car – a Corsa at that – when the embassy Mercedes was waiting outside? But Rita did not want a chauffeur around even if he was Belgian. She sensed that the embassy car and driver might cramp their style that evening. Again, Rita invoked Amit's name. Amit had not wanted to trouble the embassy any more than needed. It was he who had actually suggested her car. The DCM pursed his lips sceptically. Rita took the DCM's silence to be agreement.

The DCM wondered about Seetha. Had she not come with Amit? Was she going to be left behind or was she going to accompany Amit and Rita. He almost asked Rita but decided in the end that it was none of his official business. Later, after the guests had left, when he and his wife had their customary after-party going-over, they would speculate at leisure over glasses of Bailey's – while the Filipina maids cleaned up and

Moti Ram deep froze the leftovers.

In the red Opel Corsa, Rita and Amit were giggling. They were like schoolchildren who had managed to cook up a story to convince the headmaster to let them out of school.

'The DCM is a nice chap but he is very proper and careful. The Ambassador had placed you under his care and that being so, the DCM would have liked to personally be in control of every waking moment of yours and then have one of his flunkeys like that Promod Khera tuck you into bed. I'm afraid we have upset his plans. I'm sure that he thinks that I have put ideas into your head and behaved very badly.'

'Thank you for putting ideas into my head,' said Amit smilingly.

Rita turned on the stereo. It was Whitney Houston. Amit hummed along.

There was little traffic on the road on that cold, foggy night. Rita slowed down as she approached a set of traffic lights. The light was a bright red, but Rita nevertheless went through, her only concession to the lights being to look to the left and the right and slow down before proceeding.

'I can see that some Indian habits die hard,' said Amit.

'Why on earth should I slavishly stop at a red light when there is no traffic for miles around? The West is sometimes obsessive about rules. Blind observance of rules is not for me. It is a waste of intelligence.'

'I thought that Indians in the West went out of their way to be good, law-abiding, traffic-rules-observing citizens.'

'There are those kinds too but I think they are hypocritical, ingratiating clods. The DCM is a prime example. I have taken a ride in his car in Delhi and there he drives like a maniac, even in areas like Paharganj, shocking even hardened Delhi taxi drivers – but here – here he is ever so correct. If he sees a hint of amber a mile away he will slow down. And when the lights turn green and he starts again it is ever so slowly, like a cruise liner pulling away from its berth.'

Amit laughed. 'I know. When I was coming to Europe, my father who has nothing but disdain for those who follow rules in India, exhorted me to be careful in observing all the white man's rules. In Punjabi English he put it succinctly – in East might is right. In West, white is right,' added Amit complicitly.

'I love our Indian pragmatism, um... realism, acceptance – what you will. Philosophically and ethically I don't think there is anything wrong with it,' said Rita with some finality.

The word 'philosophically' acted as an unpleasant trigger in Amit's mind. 'Holy shit!' he exclaimed and brought both his hands up to cover his face. How could he have forgotten?

'What happened?' asked Rita, braking and veering on to the shoulder with some alarm.

Amit slowly brought his hands down. He sighed deeply and then blew out his breath slowly between his teeth. Anyway, if he had had to drop Seetha back he could not have driven off with Rita. His memory lapse had obviated the need to make a difficult choice. And surely, the DCM or someone at the party would take care of Seetha. Right now, she may be having a good time for all he knew. And he had not promised her anything. He had just invited her to the party. In point of fact he had not said anything about dropping her back. She lived in Brussels and knew her way around. He barely knew her and she should not expect too much. It was not such an unpardonable action.

'There was this girl who came to the DCM's party along with me. She was someone I happened to meet in the waiting hall at the British embassy and well, I just invited her to come along to the party. She came along and then I clean forgot about her. I should perhaps at least have made sure that she got dropped back,' said Amit.

'Not to worry. I'm sure the DCM will take care of her. She's not a baby anyway,' soothed Rita, relieved to know that Seetha was only a pick-up at the British embassy.

Gratefully accepting Rita's justification, Amit did not allow his thoughts to linger long on Seetha. The night was still young – and very promising.

Amit had had more than a few drinks. He had not anticipated this late-night rendezvous. If he had, he would have kept himself more sober. Now, he was floating along, excited and happy, yet knowing that his faculties were a little less sharp than he might have liked. He was reluctant to start a conversation as he wasn't sure that his thoughts and words would all be coherent. He felt safe enough to confide in Rita before he said something silly.

'You know, Rita, I normally plan my drinking. If I'm just with friends and know I'm going straight home after the party – and I know I am not driving, I allow myself occasionally to get just a little drunk. We all need these little escapes from the handcuffs of life – you know what I mean – family expectations, need to achieve, need to outdo, all the iron.'

Rita listened silently, understandingly. She looked straight ahead but nodded slowly. He continued.

'Today, I let myself relax at this party. The last week has been tough – meetings, cutting deals, sizing up a new market. And the DCM has a good liquor cabinet. Nor did I ever anticipate that we would be making business plans past midnight – so do forgive me if I show some signs of very mild inebriation.'

A surge of understanding welled up in Rita. She wanted to muss his hair and tell him not to worry. Of course all business leaders needed to relax. That was why they all had reliable seconds-in-command.

'You don't need to apologize. I can imagine the kind of week you have had. And if you hadn't told me that you had one too many, I would have thought that you were as sober as Mother Teresa.'

'You may know something about Mother Teresa that I do not,' said Amit laughing, relieved and thinking that Rita was going to make a dream lieutenant.

They turned into Boulevard General Jacques and Rita expertly manoeuvred into a vacant parallel parking slot which was just a little longer than the car itself.

They stepped out of the car and Amit was stung by the cold. He wore no gloves and it numbed his hands. Amit shook his head briskly and jogged a few steps hoping to warm himself and at the same time clear his head.

They walked over to La Tourelle. It was rather dimly lit, and like most Belgian pubs, bars, bistros, taverns and restaurants except those in the touristy areas, deemed it improper to be flagrantly inviting. Rita led the way towards it, but as they neared the taverne door, Amit overtook her, gallantly opened the door and let her enter. Rita couldn't help thinking about Pradeep who persevered with his perfect Ujjain manners even after eight years in the diplomatic world. If Pradeep reached a door before her, he opened it and entered first. If she reached the door first she was of course expected to open it and enter first. If they reached a door together, the person whose side the door handle was on, was expected to open the door and enter without ceremony. Perfectly simple.

Inside, Amit helped Rita out of her white overcoat. Her red sari made the few heads in the taverne at that late hour turn. The waiter came over. Rita appeared to be a regular and the waiter made a great show of welcoming her, kissing her thrice, right, left and right again. He led them to a corner table, close to a window and a radiator, handed them the menu cards and withdrew.

La Tourelle was a collage of a number of contradictory half-hearted attempts to give the taverne some character – any character. There was a surfeit of large potted plants, the chairs were of cane, the tables were wrought iron and the table tops were marble. The bar was mahogany – long, very Belgian and stolid. The soft music in the background was always American Country and Western. The prints on the wall were Margarita and James Ensor. The waiters wore dark green trousers and white dress shirts but did not bother with aprons. Amit and Rita fitted right in. They too added character.

Amit looked at the long list of beers in the menu. Should he risk another drink? Rita decided that he should. After all, he was with her and safe.

'I think you really should try the Kwak. It is just another Belgian beer but it is always drunk in its own special glass which needs its own special holder and the whole contraption looks like a piece of apparatus I last saw in my chemistry lab in school. It's not one of the stronger Belgian beers so don't worry. I'm going to have one myself. I like an occasional beer but I hate to drink when I'm with the embassy crowd. That lot, especially the women – they can be bitchy pavitra naris.'

Amit nodded but added, 'Sure, but let me begin with a cup of espresso. That should get my mind in good working order.' He did not want inebriation to arrest his enjoyment of this eventful evening.

The waiter was near the bar but he was keeping an eye on their table. Rita attracted that eye. He hurried over and Rita ordered.

'I must confess that I have never bothered to learn French or any other European language for that matter. To learn any of those languages properly takes too much time and effort which I don't want to spend and I don't want to just learn a smattering and toss off the occasional "Je voudrais" or "Pas mal" or "Bien sur" which is all that most expatriates in Belgium can manage anyway. Besides, in Brussels, while the butcher, the baker, the candlestick maker and the girl at the supermarket check-out counter will all make a great show of knowing only French and refuse to understand any English – pas de Anglais is their battle cry – it changes dramatically in the upper reaches of society – diplomatic, social and, I suspect, business too. There I find that it actually helps if you bluntly declare your ignorance of French and start off in rapid English. Your Belgian interlocutor will switch to English too and cringingly ask you to excuse his lack of fluency. That of course you will do graciously. It's a continental inferiority complex. I suspect it has something to do with Waterloo, the two world wars and Hollywood. But as usual I'm off on a tangential rant as my dear husband so often declares. All I wanted to say to you was that I hope my lack of fluency in European languages is not a major impediment in my ability to handle the tasks you outline for me.'

'I don't need to say anything. You have very effectively answered your own question,' said Amit, smilingly.

Their eyes met and they laughed together.

The waiter arrived with the drinks. An espresso and a Kwak along with its elaborate glass and holder.

'Let's drink to the success of Trehan Foods in Europe,' said Rita, soft brown eyes smiling, raising her glass.

Amit raised his espresso cup and clinked it against the Kwak apparatus.

'Remember the date – the tenth of December. And remember the place – La Tourelle. Ten years from today when management schools try to analyze the phenomenal growth of the Trehan Food empire in Europe they will note that it all began when the CEO sat down with the newly recruited European head one dark and wintery night at La Tourelle and sketched out their plans for growth on paper napkins,' said Amit, dramatically lowering his voice and ending with a flourish of a napkin.

Their eyes met again and lingered as they laughed.

'Okay. Let's get down to business,' said Amit, draining his espresso and pushing aside the tiny cup.

'I'm raring to go,' said Rita, drawing her chair a little closer, taking out a Mont Blanc from her handbag and drawing up a paper napkin. She put her elbows on the table and settled her face in her hands.

For the next ten minutes, Amit told Rita about Trehan foods in India – the range of products, the modern factories, the extensive network of distributors and dealers, the steady growth. He painted a picture of his father as a legend – the benevolent, old-school dictator of the Trehan empire. He spoke of his own education, his dreams, his zeal to modernize and professionalize the Trehan conglomerate. He told Rita of the unsuccessful attempts Trehan Foods had made over the last few years to get a foothold in the European market. Now his father had put Amit in charge of the Trehan Foods' foray into Europe.

Amit told her about his week in Europe, the lack of real progress, the ineffectual Promod Khera, the difficulties of language and the reams of EU and national regulations governing food imports.

Rita listened intently. She had begun by enthusiastically noting down specifics (wasn't that what a good employee did when the boss expounded?) – sales turnovers, product profiles and competition. Gradually her note-taking become more half-hearted. She was never a great one for details. Instead, she kept her eyes on Amit and intently absorbed his tone, his gestures and his eyes. Never mind the fine print – she clearly understood the bottom line. He, Amit, was the promising son, the Harvard-educated boy who was being groomed to succeed. Europe was his first assignment. His father had given him the continent. He needed to deliver. And she was to help him do just that.

'You know, Rita, I think we will make a great team... and we will succeed. I feel it in my bones.'

'Of course, we will,' said Rita instinctively reaching out and putting her hand on his. She let it rest there for a few seconds and then withdrew it, just a little surprised at her boldness. His hand was warm but bony and his fingers were long. Artistic. Must ask him if he is a Piscean, thought Rita. She wanted to caress his fingers and feel the bones in them but now knew there would be other occasions for that.

Amit looked up and into her eyes. The unexpected touch of her hand had felt like static, charging him though in an infinitely more pleasant way. In that heightened state, he wondered if the word ecstatic was derived from static. In another corner of his mind, he noticed that her touch had done more to sober him than the coffee. Sober, though not like a monk. More like a tennis player in the tiebreaker of the fifth set.

After such a moment Amit found it very difficult to find the right words. And Rita was happy for now to let the silence be. They looked deep into each other's eyes for a long time. Amit was excited, a little unsure, not wanting to sink the moment with a banality but also not knowing how to take it to an even higher plane.

It was Rita who was controlling the silence and she decided to break it. She spoke slowly, continuing to look gently into Amit's eyes.

'You know, Amit, you must have read of kindred souls. I know it sounds really wonky and mushy and nineteenth-centuryish. But that's the phrase that comes to my mind. You want to achieve, to create, to live fully and I want to do exactly the same. The last few years I seemed to have manoeuvred my life into a bland, blind alley with high, grey walls all around and today it looks as if I can see a breach in the wall and you on the other side and of course I am going to sprint towards the breach. I am going to seize this opportunity with both hands.'

'Thanks, Rita, I know I will be able to depend on you. Together we are going to breach Fortress Europe,' said Amit, lightly bringing his fist down on the table.

'And have fun doing it,' added Rita, once again stretching out her hand and taking Amit's loose fist in it.

This time Amit brought his other hand and caressed Rita's hand in both his own. She continued to look gently into his eyes. He was kneading her index finger intensely and it mildly hurt but she didn't mind. It was such a long time since she had received this kind of attention.

'Let's go to my hotel. My room has a clear view of Central Brussels. I can see a number of tall boxes of light and a few gloomy domes. You can tell me what is what.'

Rita squeezed his hand and looked for the waiter.

Chapter 24

Having spent nearly half an hour animatedly conversing with Seetha, Gopalakrishnan began to get just a little uncomfortable. Were people thinking that he was monopolizing, haranguing or boring Seetha? He had no idea how Seetha was related to the foreign minister's nephew or why she had been invited to the party and he did not want to be committing any faux pas. He also had the traditional Tamil male's innate reluctance to hold a prolonged tête-à-tête with a woman in public, (Aiyaiyo, what will people think we were talking about?) a reluctance which twelve years in the foreign service had not done much to mitigate.

Gopalakrishnan was surprised that Seetha had so far not showed any signs of wanting to meet other guests or join Amit. He decided to make the first move.

'Well, I suppose we could talk bandwidths and blogs all day but I'm sure that you want to meet more attractive company,' said Gopal with a self-deprecating sniffle.

Before Seetha could reply, he added, 'Vango, let me introduce you to our fairer and better halves.' Again he ended with a sniffle.

Gopal shepherded Seetha to a knot of women near the old marble fireplace where a fire was roaring and crackling. The women did not notice their approach, absorbed as they were in something one of them was relating.

Gopal and Seetha waited patiently for the storyteller to end. They heard the last few sentences.

'And then, bang in the middle of the frozen foods section, as I am standing with a bag of frozen peas in one hand and a box of chicken legs in another, this man, this sicko, who I have never set eyes on before that day – he looked Greek or Spanish or Moroccan or someone Mediterranean at any rate – God knows – comes up to me again and says in a conspiratorial tone, "Vous ete belle. Trop belle. Une houri Indien." The first time he said it, I couldn't follow what he said – you know my French – and I was getting ready to

scream and had decided that if I had to run it should be to
the right towards the fruit and vegetable section where there
is a crowd even in the afternoons, if only of old women and
gay men. And then he slowly smiled and repeated the words
– and I understood the gist this time but was still terrified,
wondering what was to come next. I brought both my hands
up in front of me, hoping that the chicken legs and frozen peas
would serve as some kind of shield. He did nothing but just
continued to sort of savour me – you know the way some men
do – and me dressed in a shapeless salwar kameez. I don't
know what he saw. I just blurted out a "Merci" and walked
quickly backwards away from him the way courtiers walk out
of Dasharath's court in the filmi Ramayana.'

The uproarious laughter and hoots would have continued
longer had not Gopal interrupted the group with: 'Ladies,
pardon, pardon, but it my pleasure to introduce to you Seetha,
who I don't know too much about but who I do know is a
computer whiz – one of those who is helping India improve
its foreign exchange reserves.'

Seetha squirmed but smiled.

'This is my wife Renuka, next to her is Jyotsna, then Jyoti,
Rachel, Prakriti and Anamika. The tres belle houri you just
heard describing her experiences is Ritika,' continued Gopal.

There were polite hellos and smiles. The women all seemed
to know each other and Seetha felt that they were mildly
resentful of her, and not simply because she had interrupted
the good time that they had been having.

'I will leave you in this enchanting company (sniffle), I have
to have a word with the DCM,' said Gopal, leaving the group.
He was well satisfied with the handover.

There were a few moments of awkward silence before
Rachel took the effort to make Seetha feel at home.

'Pradeep was talking to me a few moments ago and – I
believe you were talking to him about the Upanishads – he
told me that you were a philosopher and writer. And now
Gopal introduces you as a computer whiz. You must be a real
polymath.'

Rachel appeared to be genuinely interested in knowing
more about Seetha. Her eyes had crinkled into a smile as
she enunciated the word polymath. She had a faint but

unmistakable Malayali accent. The 'o' in polymath constituted two syllables all by itself.

Seetha fleetingly tried to recollect the last time she had last heard anyone use the word polymath. She wondered what Rachel had studied and where. B.A. in English Literature at St. Mary's Degree College in Quilon?

'No, not really. I'm now working as a software designer but have read some philosophy and have written a little. And what do you all do?' said Seetha politely, flinching at being the focus of the conversation.

There was a moment's silence. Enough for Seetha to wonder if she had asked the wrong question.

It was Jyoti who answered, 'We are what is described rather appropriately as trailing spouses. We trail behind our beloved, incredibly talented spouses from city to city, country to country. We wash and clean and look after the children and make the chapattis every night.'

'And when asked to, we wear our silks and grace occasions,' added Ritika smilingly.

Seetha wondered what to make of these replies, particularly as Jyoti had delivered hers in a flat monotone. She smiled hesitantly. Once again she felt the familiar feeling of disquiet. She could not see Amit anywhere. Where on earth was he?

'Don't pity us too much. Our world has its compensations. Most women in India would give their... their all to be in our high-heeled Guccis as we catch the 8am Thalys for a day trip to Paris because we had read that Versace had redecorated its shop window on the Champs Elysee and we simply had to have a look,' added Jyoti. The flat monotone now had an edge.

'And some of us have besotted Latin admirers who follow us into supermarkets,' added Anamika, winking at Ritika.

Jyoti pursed her lips. She was not amused by this introduction of frivolity which softened and blurred the hard edge she was working herself towards.

Seetha smiled uncertainly. She looked around the hall for signs of Amit. She saw him a mile away, holding court. The girl in the red sari was by his side. He certainly did not seem to be looking around for Seetha. Had he had invited her solely to add colour to his retinue when he made his entrance? Or was she being presumptuous in expecting his attention? Was she simply expected to take care of herself and have a good time and then be led off on Amit's arm when the curtains fell? Or did his inconsiderate behaviour have something to do with the girl in the red sari who was standing by his side, apparently drinking in his every word? Seetha wished she knew. Her usual confidence had evaporated.

Again it was Rachel who came to her rescue.

'I'm a Christian, a Marthomite actually, and I don't really know too much about the Upanishads. You know how it is. Growing up in small-town Kerala, you are actively discouraged from learning too much about any other faith. And I am afraid that in India we Christians are more closed than Hindus. Something about being a small minority perhaps. My parents would never let me visit temples or learn anything about Hinduism. I don't think they knew very much about it either. On the other hand, my Hindu friends would be perfectly willing to come with me to the school chapel – it was a Catholic school – and pray to Jesus...'

It was Ritika who put a hand on Rachel's arm and interrupted, 'When I was in school, come examination time, I used to be in my school chapel – I was studying in Loreto's, Delhi – every morning at eight before class to pray to Jesus to help me do well in my English language and English literature exams. A friend had told me that she had read that our Hindu gods did not know English and so it was no use praying to them for help in the English exams. She said that Ganapati was the God to pray to succeed in arithmetic and Vishnu could ensure success in science but for English, it had to be Jesus!'

Everybody laughed. Even Jyoti smiled.

'Most Hindus I knew – at least when I was growing up – were perfectly willing to give Jesus a place in heaven beside Shiva and Vishnu and Brahma. But Christians never wanted to return the favour. My mother once told me that the Christian God was a jealous God. I initially thought that she was being critical but she said she was quoting from the Bible and that He had a right to be,' added Rachel animatedly. It looked like she had long wanted to make this point. The others were silent. A little uncomfortable. But Rachel did not notice this squeamishness and continued.

'A few years back – do you remember, Jyoti? – a swamiji had come to your home and I asked him about the reason for Hindu eclecticism and tolerance and he said that the form and way in which we worship God should be the least of our concerns and that what was important was to grasp the eternal truths. He asked me to read the Upanishads. Ever since I have meant to but haven't got around to it. So now that you are with us, I see a far better way to get to know the Upanishads. Can you not give us a quick five-minute summary?' ended Rachel with another crinkled smile, looking expectantly at Seetha.

The others persevered in their silence.

Jyotsna murmured quietly to Anamika that she thought that the samosas were a little too oily.

'Girls, quiet!' hushed Ritika, 'Listen, here's a chance for all of us to redeem ourselves and let Seetha know that even we, trailing tarnished trophies, do think beyond samosas and have an interest in the higher truths and mysteries. Seetha, please do begin.'

Seetha could see that not everyone was interested. Jyotsna was looking at her watch. Anamika was using her fork to scoop out the potato filling from the samosa in her plate. She seemed to be examining it intently. But Rachel was encouraging and Ritika was flippant but friendly – and at least explaining the Upanishads would give her a role in this unsettling milieu.

Seetha smiled as a prelude to beginning but was interrupted quickly by Jyoti.

'Rachel, I have a lovely book on the Upanishads. It has the text and a commentary. The commentary is very lucid. It was written for an American audience so it's all simple sentences. I'll send you the book tomorrow through Rahul – and Anamika, that poem you wrote that won the first prize last week in that contest for expats. Didn't the blurb in the *Bulletin* call it Upanishadic? Please recite it. It's short and I'm sure Seetha and all of us would like to hear it.'

'Yes, please let's hear it,' added Seetha almost too hurriedly.

Anamika looked up from her dissected samosa and smiled. 'I'm always ready to recite. It's an audience I find difficult to gather. Since I have actually received a request, let me begin before anyone changes their mind – but I must warn you,' she continued, turning to Seetha, 'I certainly don't think the poem is particularly Upanishadic. For one, I am the author and I know next to nothing about the Upanishads. The *Bulletin*, like most people here, assumes that anything which is not about sex or war or cats and other feelable things and is written by someone with a name like Anamika Harshvardhan must be Upanishadic. Anyway, here goes. In case any of you are into titles, this poem is called "Worry".'

The women in the group composed themselves into a half circle around Anamika. Some looked directly at her with appreciative smiles as she recited. Seetha was in that number. Some others looked at their feet. All were respectfully still. Anamika recited.

Whoever worries,
Can't be happy or even sad,
Can't be good or even bad.
Can only worry.

The heart can't be large
With joy or sorrow.
Can't give or take;
Can only lend or borrow.

The furtive mind
In mindless hurry,
Can only scurry
From worry to worry.

Can't love.
Can't hate.
Can only worry
About being late.

Anamika ended with a big smile. The audience burst into applause, causing heads to turn right around the room.

'That was wonderful!' said Rachel.

'Cute,' said Ritika, 'Mika, I never guessed that such talent lay hidden amongst us. And what do you know about worry, you princess?'

Anamika laughed. 'I have a big worrier in my life – Harsh. He worries enough for the two of us. He worries about his work. He worries about me and the kids. He worries about the increased hum in our washing machine. He worries about India. He worries about global warming. So you can say that I have come to know worry very intimately.'

But Rachel had not forgotten her request. In a determined voice, softened by her ready smile she said, 'After poetry what should naturally follow is philosophy. Seetha, it's your turn now. The Upanishads, please.'

'Ladies, dinner is served. And it smells good. Let's go,' said Jyoti, intervening without looking directly at either Seetha or Rachel. Jyoti guided Jyotsna and Anamika who were on either side of her towards the buffet table.

The others followed Jyoti a little hesitantly. Ritika gave Seetha an apologetic smile. Only Rachel stayed to talk to Seetha.

'Sorry, Seetha. I guess I should have realized that a party like this is not the ideal setting for a discourse on the Upanishads. Give me your phone number. Jyoti is a nice person but she is sometimes a little rude. I'm going to call you soon and invite you home for a meal. We can then have a nice discussion and some good appams and stew. Are you a vegetarian?'

Seetha nodded.

'I'll make it a rich vegetable stew then. Come, let's go and sample the delights the DCM and his cook have laid out for us.'

Rachel's a darling. But I don't like to be where I am not wanted. I think I want this party to end. I want to be back in my little studio. I've had enough excitement for a day. Now I only want to get back.

As they walked towards the buffet tables, Seetha looked around for signs of Amit. It was difficult to spot Amit among all the men in similar dark suits but it was easy to spot the red sari – and sure enough – Amit was standing next to it. He was speaking and must have been spouting a witticism because everyone laughed. The tinkling laughter of the girl in the red sari carried across the room. Seetha noticed that she had a glass of red wine in her hand.

Sophisticated, aren't we. And we do want to make an impression on the foreign minister's nephew, don't we. I don't care. I just want the party to end. He is a fool and she a floozy. I just want to get home.

The rich Indian food would normally have made Seetha's mouth water but today her mind was distracted, wary, on edge. She did not have an appetite.

The ladies filled their plates and went back to the lounge chairs where they all sat down in a large circle. Seetha was quiet through most of her meal, speaking little and then only when directly addressed. She was waiting for the evening to end. She glanced at her watch. Ten.

Another half hour for dessert and goodbyes. Then surely the guests should begin to leave. Hope Amit does not think he should be the last to leave. By rights he should be the first. He's the chief guest. But look at him with that tart in red. Looks as if he's oblivious to the passing of time. A half hour drive home – even a cad like Amit will surely drop me home and not expect me to take a taxi from his hotel. Fifteen minutes to change and flop into bed, snuggle under my quilt and review this day. I can't wait for it to be eleven-fifteen. My studio is where I belong. My dismal, cheap studio. I don't belong in diplomatic salons. I might some day. But for now I am happy with my studio.

Happy seeing Seetha put in her place and order in the universe restored, Jyoti was moved to be charitable. She came with her plate and sat next to Seetha and explained to her in horrible detail the relative advantages and disadvantages of shopping for clothes at Marks and Spencer, INNO and Hema. She goaded Seetha into describing her apartment. She explained why, for an expatriate on a short-term contract, a used BMW was a better bargain than a new, small Japanese car. Seetha refrained from telling Jyoti that her salary ruled out buying a car of any size, shape or age. Seetha was exhausted and intimidated enough by the evening to play along docilely as Jyoti ground her fine in the mills of Indian expatriate trivia. Victory complete, Jyoti was magnanimous and took great pains to get the kitchen to prepare a special, eggless dessert for orthodoxly vegetarian Seetha.

Dessert over, Seetha looked at her watch. Liberation was

near. She looked around for Amit. No sign of him – or the red sari for that matter.

Has that hussy in red silk dragged him to an upstairs bedroom? Though I don't think she would have needed to drag him. He'd have gone willingly enough.

She saw Gopalakrishnan helping himself to a chapeau de curé at the dessert table and decided to ask him.

'Gopal, I need to have a word with Amit. I can't see him anywhere. Can you please help me find him?'

'Sure,' said Gopal, looking around.

Not finding Amit, Gopal suggested that they ask the DCM. They went over to the DCM who was expounding to a meek audience the true nature of Indo-Pakistan relations.

'Basically it is three parts love and one part hate. But the hate, when it surfaces, is pure visceral hate – ancient and bloody – in the sense of it being in the blood,' they heard the DCM say as they neared him.

The DCM turned towards them, a little peeved at being interrupted when he was in spate.

'Sir, Seetha here has been looking for Amit. Do you possibly know where he is?'

'He has left with Rita. I assumed Seetha knew,' the DCM blurted out before Seetha's stunned look made him slowly realize that perhaps the situation was more complex than he had imagined and called for some tact and more elaboration. It was irritating being called upon to exercise his faculties after he had sufficiently blunted them with an inordinate amount of Scotland's finest. He surreptitiously pinched the back of his right hand very hard with his left. The pain whistled through him, clearing his head to an extent. It was an old trick he had been taught by the first Ambassador he had worked under.

Turning to Seetha, he said, 'You see, Seetha beti, Amit, as I am sure you know, is leaving for London tomorrow and before leaving he needed to work out some business details with Rita. They had to leave the party in a hurry to complete that work today.'

'But why in such a hurry without telling me? After all he invited me here today?' asked Seetha slowly, beyond niceties now. The anger rose deliberately and overtook her uncertainty. Her voice had risen just a fraction.

Gopalakrishnan murmured something about having to have a word with Promod and sidled away from a potential complication. The rest of the DCM's audience stood rooted in interested silence. A little real life drama was not a bad way to round off a pleasant evening. And liquor always made images a little sharper. It was a highlight pen. They were a little disappointed when the DCM guided Seetha a little way apart with an avuncular hand on her arm.

He chose his words carefully. It was difficult to know what to say when one did not know who one was speaking to. He decided that his duty and safety lay in defending Amit.

'Beti, I believe Amit needed to plan something related to his work in London and Rita was helping him with some contacts there. Since Amit was leaving tomorrow, they needed to leave this party to make a few calls and complete some paperwork.'

'Is Amit coming back?'

'I don't rightly know. I think Amit is a glutton for work. I think he gives it priority. I guess he will return only if he and Rita have completed what they need to get done.'

'Thank you. I think I'll be leaving now. I enjoyed the evening very much. Thank you again.' said Seetha, poker faced but not being able to help her eyes welling with tears.

'Beti, it was a pleasure meeting you. I'm sure we will meet again. I will put you on our embassy list here. And, how are you going home? Can I arrange something? I will have you dropped home in the embassy car. Promod will see to that... Promod,' the DCM turned around and called loudly to Promod across the room.

Voices around the room were becoming more muted and more eyes were closely following the unexpected drama.

Promod immediately left Gopal who he had been talking to and was beginning to hurry across the room, when Seetha called out in a voice that carried, 'No thanks, Promod, don't bother. I think I can manage without any help from either Amit or his embassy.'

Seetha strode to the door, tossing her hair and looking straight ahead. She opened the door and stepped into the hallway, collected her overcoat from a surprised attendant, went through the front door which he held open for her, and stepped into the cold, dark, foggy, windy Brussels night.

Seetha walked up the long driveway in her uncomfortable heels. As she had stormed out from the DCM's residence she had shivered with outrage but now she shivered with cold. She needed to get home quickly. She could go over the day's hurt and pain later. Now she needed to focus on getting home. The street outside was deserted. Almost eerie. She knew that she was somewhere in the commune of Sint Genesius Rode. She walked to the end of the completely empty road, dimly lit by street lamps whose light was lost in the tree tops and the winter fog. Her clicking heels seemed dangerously loud. She read the name of the street from the small sign mounted high up on the wall of the corner house – Zevengaten Laan. Now she had an address and could call a taxi. A taxi was expensive and normally she regarded it an extravagance but today she had no choice. She hoped she had the number in her cell phone. She got out her cell phone and flipped it open. She looked up her number list for Taxi Bleu. P,Q,R,S,T... Tariq, Thangiah, Thomas, Tracy... no Taxi... no Taxi Bleu. She had a moment of panic. Surely she had stored the number. Then it struck her. She must have stored it under B. Balu, Bindu, Boris... no Bleu.

What was she to do? She could call Luc or Tracy, both colleagues at Expobel. Either would give her the phone number of Taxi Bleu.

Luc might even offer to drive over and pick me up. He will certainly do that. He is a gentleman unlike the pretentious, sari-chasing minister's nephew.

She called Luc. His phone was switched off. She called Tracy. Ditto.

Don't panic. Just think clearly. This is Brussels. This is a safe town and this is a particularly safe commune. This is not a back lane in Errukancheri.

She squeezed her mind for options. She could ask. But who? Most of the houses were set back from the road with private driveways. This was an affluent neighbourhood. In this country she could not simply march up to a front door, ring the bell, smile sweetly and ask for help. She could do that in Madras – without a second thought! But here she would be a brown girl at the door near midnight. The police may be called and she with her broken French and nonexistent Flemish... and this was a Flemish commune. Or she may set off some burglar alarm or there may be a dog. The person opening the door may be a lecherous, single, fifty-year-old spending the evening drinking heavily and watching porn. Seeing her, he would assume that he had just stepped into the next episode in a 3D, TripleX-rated reality movie where the local whore comes a calling. No, she had to think of something else.

She simply had to wait till somebody – somebody decent – came along. She waited, stepping back and half hiding herself in the shadow of the corner house. A car came along, its lights piercing the fog eerily. Seetha took her courage in her hands and walked to the edge of the pavement and put out her hand. The car slowed a little and then sailed past. Dimly she could make out a grim, middle-aged couple in the car. The man was in a suit and the woman wore a hat. They stared suspiciously at her.

Seetha stepped back into the half shadow and considered her next step. She looked across the road and saw a sign with the Belgian railways logo and an arrow pointing to the road on the left. So there was a train station nearby. That was where she needed to go. There would be a skeletal service even at night. Some of her colleagues who worked late at Expobel had told her that they used that service. Seetha's spirits cautiously rose and she turned the corner. She looked at the street sign. Confirmation: the road was called Stationstraat. She began walking towards the station.

As she walked, she heard a car behind her travelling in the same direction she was. As it neared, she was not sure whether to wish that it stopped or did not. She walked on, not looking back. She heard the car slow down and come to a stop near her. She turned around slowly, body and mind alert, prepared for any eventuality – skinheads, robbers, drunks, the police. But it turned out to be Pradeep in his beat-up Renault.

Pradeep reached across and opened the passenger door.

'Hello, Seetha. Get in. It must be freezing outside, haan naan? What on earth are you doing walking at this hour of the night? Any of us would have dropped you back.'

Seetha got in, shut the car door and burst into tears.

Pradeep let her cry. He let the engine idle and remained parked with his hazard lights on. He wanted to put an arm around her shoulders but touching a woman, even if it was only to comfort her, did not come naturally to him. He did not know what to say either. He had noticed the incident in the DCM's house and seen Seetha leave in what seemed to be a huff. Although he could see that there was much discussion of the incident in hushed whispers, no one had spoken to him about it and he had not asked. He shied away from talk about relationships or personal problems – anybody's personal problems – because he had always been vulnerable himself. He did think a lot though about that side of life. He guessed that in some way Amit had humiliated Seetha. And perhaps his wife too did have something to do with it too. He liked Seetha.

Seetha quieted herself in a couple of minutes. Gradually her sobs died down. Pradeep pulled out a few tissues from the box in the car and gave them to her. His unspoken friendliness and the warmth of the car were comforting. She wiped her eyes and blew her nose and finally looked up at Pradeep and gave him a weak smile. But her eyes were still red and she held the tissues tightly clenched in her hand.

'We all have our bad days when life gives us a beating. Just leave it at that, yaar. A smart girl like you with the world at your feet will shake it off in a few hours. Now just relax. Let me play you some music.'

Pradeep fiddled with the knobs and an old Kundan Lal Saigal song began to play. It was a quintessentially Saigal song – of lost love. Quickly Pradeep changed CDs. This time it was Hari Kumar Chaurasia on the flute.

Seetha listened in silence. She was glad the music was playing even if her mind noted without comment that the music was Hindustani, not Carnatic.

'Seetha, tell me where you live. I'm going to drive you home.'

Seetha told him without demur and Pradeep put the car into gear and slowly moved away from the shoulder. They drove on for a few minutes and the silence was comforting.

'It is hard to be serene and detached and Upanishadic through all the twists and turns that life serves up, isn't it? I don't even try,' said Pradeep.

Pradeep's a good man. The witch in red doesn't deserve him.

After more than a minute of silence she found herself replying with an impish smile, 'I'm afraid you are using the word Upanishadic very loosely.' She could be professorial with Pradeep. She continued.

'And you're not alone. To most people, Upanishadic simply means serene or detached or Buddha-like but in reality the Upanishads are so much more. They explain why we do have a basis for serenity in the face of all the slings and arrows of outrageous fortune. It is the basis that is important. The serenity is a corollary.'

'Then please to explain, O Guruji.'

Seetha was happy to once again take refuge in philosophy. Asylum.

'Well. Here goes. But remember that this is my interpretation of the Upanishads. There are many sages and schoolmen who have spent their lives trying to understand and interpret the Upanishads and they have variously arrived at differing conclusions. Another thing. What I am about to give is a corporate executive overview which means that it will be brief, free of nuances, shorn of abstract nouns and have just the big ideas. '

Pradeep laughed. 'Indian Foreign Office briefings are rather different – they are full of nuances and abstract nouns, fill reams of pages and don't contain any big ideas. But back to the Upanishads please.'

'Okay. Slide One. Point One. Reality is enormous. Man, the earth, this age, all sink without a trace. Little pebbles into the vast placid lake of eternal reality. The Upanishads believe that the entire material world is but as a hair on the tail of the majestic elephant of reality. It is impossible to maintain that man is God's chosen creation.

'Conceptually too, reality is vast. Indescribable. It isn't just material and it isn't just idea. It can only be described in terms of negatives. Any description of reality is false because it is incomplete. "Neti, neti", "not this, not this", is the way the Upanishads put it.'

Pradeep switched off the car stereo. He was happy to be

comforting a troubled little girl – and perhaps learning a little about the Upanishads.

'Slide One. Point Two. There is a unity in all that exists. The Upanishads like to call it Brahmin. It is this truth that we must discover behind the diversity of the material world. We all have occasional intuitive glimpses of this reality. Being one with nature is more than a cliché. The pantheism of old was an intuitive formulation of this essential oneness. Some other religions put it differently, they refer to the sacredness of all God's creations.'

The headlights laid silver pipelines through the thickening fog.

'Slide One. Point Three. The Upanishads feel that the three links of the chain that enslaves us, bruises us and hurts us are desire, attachment and pain. Of these, desire is primal. It results in attachment whose consequence is pain. Desire is what drives us. Its seamier side is a wanting to possess, to control, a lusting after. Its more acceptable face is the force of will. Desire results in attachment to the object of desire. The object of desire can be a skill, a person or a thing. In all cases, desire binds the desirer as much as the desired. Attachment limits and reduces.'

'And all too often, it results in pain,' added Pradeep ruefully. His eyes were on the road as he negotiated the junction at the end of Avenue Roosevelt.

They were now cruising down Boulevard General Jacques and Seetha had to tell Pradeep to take the next right into Rue Couroune. They arrived at the glum apartment block where Seetha lived and Pradeep stopped at the side of the road.

'Seetha, thanks for that little tour of the Upanishads although you didn't get time to go beyond Slide One. We'll complete the rest of that PowerPoint presentation some day. And in the mean time I promise to use the word Upanishadic more appropriately in future,' said Pradeep with a broad smile.

'I am only an expounder, such as I am, of the Upanishads. As you saw today, I am far from being a practitioner. I hope to be some day. And till then I will need the support of friends like you. You have been a friend in need.'

Seetha stepped out of the car, shut the door, then bent

down, looked at Pradeep through the window and added, 'If you had not come by when you did, I'd probably still be sitting on a bench at the Sint Genesius Rode train station – if I had managed to get that far – waiting for the next train, on edge. I'd be nervously watching the shifty-eyed hulk slouching on the bench opposite, the drunk vomiting in the corner and the pervert playing with himself by the turnstile. I'd be wishing to God a police patrol would come by. Most likely though, if a police patrol did come by, the police would ignore the three good Belgians: the drunk, the pervert and the shifty-eyed hulk. Instead, they'd look at me suspiciously and ask to see my ID. I'm a brownish shade of black, you see.'

'I also see that you are back to being your combative self. I'm sure we will meet again.'

Chapter 25

The persistent ringing of the phone woke Amit. He groggily sat up and picked up the bedside phone. The caller was Promod.

'Good morning, sir, I'm Promod. I'm in the hotel lobby. I have brought the faxes from London inviting you for business meetings, sir. Shall I come up and give them to you, sir?'

Promod looked at his watch. It was eight.

'Promod. Can you please just leave the faxes for me at the reception? I'll collect them on my way out. I was working late and am still quite unpresentable.'

'No problem, Amit, sir. I'll do that. Since you don't know the senders very well, I have also attached a small background note for you of each of the companies sending the faxes. I thought that may come in useful if you are interviewed. I have also enclosed your First Class ticket on the 5pm Eurostar. I think you will have your visa by then. Good luck, sir. Please call me if there is anything I can do to help.'

'Thanks, Promod. I'll call later. Bye.'

Amit let himself collapse back into bed. What a day yesterday had been. And what a night. Rita had left at four in the morning. He thought of her and her body. The good times were just beginning to roll.

Well, he better be rising and getting ready. He intended to be among the first to arrive at the embassy. If he got his visa by noon, he would have just enough time to squeeze in a lunch with Rita before rushing back to the hotel, checking out and then catching the Eurostar.

The room had an electric kettle but Amit preferred to call room service and order some freshly brewed coffee. Till it came, he lay in bed, hands locked behind his head, smiling slightly, reliving the last twenty-four hours.

When he had returned to his room with Rita yesterday, the little red message light on the phone had been flashing. He had pressed the message button and the phone crackled with his father's voice.

'Beta, my secretary showed me your email. Keep up the good work.'

That had been the icing on yesterday's cake. Rita had been with him, holding his hand, when he had pressed the message button. They had listened together, his heart beating. When the message ended she saw the thrill on his face and pumped a little fist into the air and hissed a happy 'Yes'. Then she had kissed him deeply. He broke the long kiss to let his lips and hands move over her body as he gently backed her into bed.

The coffee arrived. The waiter mumbled a surly 'Bonjour' and set the coffee tray down a little too hard on the table, spilling a little of the coffee. He wiped the spilt coffee gracelessly, unapologetically. With newfound confidence, Amit told him to be more careful and refused to tip him when he signed the bill.

Amit reached the door of the British embassy visa section at 8:55am. A small queue had formed by then and he joined it.

He looked at the queue in front of him. It was the usual ragged, jagged rainbow of Third Worlders. Amit looked at them with quiet superiority, raising his chin just a little. Could any of them even imagine his life and times?

He looked behind him and saw that three others had joined the queue. The last was Seetha. She was looking away – deliberately?

Amit froze. The joys of the last evening and night had erased Seetha from his mind. But there she was – and she appeared grim and foreboding.

Chapter 26

Seetha had not slept at all. Entering her studio, she had kicked off her heels and simply flopped into bed without changing, drained of all energy. Switching off the lights, she had pulled the quilt over her and curled up in a foetal ball. And then she had sobbed. Amit, Rita and Jyoti filled her thoughts by turn. All three had gratuitously insulted her when she had only tried to be friendly. She played and replayed in her mind the hurtful scenes – putting out her hand to shake Rita's and being rebuffed with a namaste. The way Jyoti effectively prevented her from speaking about the Upanishads and instead bogged her in consumer prattle.

Try as she could there was no way in which one could charitably explain Amit's abhorrent behaviour. Rita was a poisonous snake and Amit a lustful fop. That was it. Seetha kept trying to drag her thoughts away but she couldn't help thinking about what Rita and Amit might be doing now. The DCM had said that they had some work to complete. The DCM may choose to be a credulous old fool but she knew just what kind of work they would be doing. And Rita was married. That too to a gentleman.

Seetha told herself she didn't really care what they were doing. She was angry only because Amit had thoughtlessly and callously put her in an embarrassing and difficult situation. When she had stormed out of the DCM's drawing room, she could feel the many eyes following her – some pitying, others censuring, grimly satisfied. Pitying because Amit had left her to hang on a forgotten clothesline. Censuring because she was a political groupie, a hanger-on, a moll. Grimly satisfied because the upstart had been shown just where she got off. Even under the quilt she could feel her ears tingle and redden. And this Jyoti – just a frustrated, frigid, bloomers-wearing bitch who could not bear to see a pretty, younger woman with a career, a vocation, a face, a head and a future. With photographic clarity she could see herself standing at the corner of a dark and deserted Zevengaten Laan close on midnight, shivering and frightened. She burst into tears again.

At two in the morning she gave up all attempts to sleep. She went to the kitchenette and put some strong Ethiopian coffee powder in her South Indian coffee filter and poured in boiling water. She went back to her bed and waited for the decoction to filter through. She had never cried so much. She might occasionally have tears in her eyes but she had never sobbed loudly since the time when she was six and her uncle Ramu – come to think of it, he was as jealous as Jyoti – had gleefully crushed in public her pretensions to being an arithmetic whiz kid.

She had been particularly good at the kind of sums they made kids in school do – if three men can lay ten feet of paving in six days, how many feet of paving can nine men lay in twelve days. Her mother was very proud of her and she would often call Seetha to do such sums – perform them – for the benefit of indulgent aunts and uncles. Now Uncle Ramu had a son of six who was as slow as Seetha was quick and Uncle Ramu was waiting for a chance to see Seetha trip and fall on her smug little face... He got his chance one Deepavali day when the whole extended family was sprawled around the drawing room after a very full lunch.

'Can I ask you to do another sum for me, little Seetha?' said Uncle Ramu.

'Sure,' her mother answered and pulled Seetha to her feet and set her in front of the family.

'Now Seetha, if a goat has four legs when it is a year old, how many legs will it have when it is three years old?'

In a flash, Seetha replied, 'Twelve.' The roar of laughter had left Seetha stunned and confused.

'It is not fair to ask a six-year-old trick questions,' said her mother, springing to Seetha's defence but the laughter still continued. Seetha still had not understood the joke. Three times four made twelve, did it not? And then her cousin Geetha had gleefully whispered into her ear. Seetha had reddened and dissolving in tears had run to the children's room and remained there for more than an hour sobbing furiously.

And that was more than twenty years ago. Yesterday was

just as bad.

Seetha got up, mixed her coffee and took it to the sofa. She was still thinking about yesterday but more calmly now – dispassionately, clinically. She sat crosslegged on the sofa, hands cradling the warm mug of coffee.

Yesterday was all about a young girl from a middle-class family being shown her place by three card-holding members of India's elite. Yes, that really was what had happened yesterday. Amit had only wanted her as a prop and as light entertainment and once her usefulness was over, she could be ignored and forgotten. Jyoti had wanted Seetha to clearly understand that she could meet her betters only on their terms. Rita had wanted Seetha to learn that while Seetha might be a star in her own class, she was quite out of her depth in a higher class and stars in that class could and would run rings around her...

Maybe it had been her fault in going to the DCM's house uninvited. She did not belong there and that had been made clear to her in a rather unpleasant manner. She should have known better than to assume that she could be a full member of India's charmed circles. She remembered an old, rustic Tamil proverb her grandmother was fond of using: If a goat tried to shit like an elephant, it would only tear its butt. And yes, she had got her butt mauled yesterday.

But be that as it may, thought Seetha, Amit's behaviour is unpardonable and has nothing to do with stations in life. He's just a cheap cad with an eye for a skirt – actually for a red sari – and a willingness to milk his uncle's status for all it is worth. No morality. No values. No decency. That word does have meaning. Amit dropped me like a brick as soon as he had found a more available woman. And look at his pathetic willingness to wheel and deal with the likes of Ratnesh. It is people like Ratnesh and Amit who are the bane of India. One speaks better English and has a sliver, a thin sliver of education – that's all the difference. That poor Harish, he doesn't know what he's getting himself into by dealing with the likes of these two. Should I warn him?

Should I warn him? Maybe I should. Just maybe I should. I will warn him. I'll go early to the British embassy, meet Harish before he steps into the visa section and warn him against dealing with the two. I'll tell Harish all that Ratnesh blabbered drunkenly at lunch. I'll tell him about the money-laundering. Just you wait, Amit Trehan, just you wait.

She now had a plan and that helped clear her mind.

She was excited. She wasn't trying to get even. She was doing her bit to ensure that a poor unsuspecting honest small-time trader did not unwittingly get drawn into a swindle. She made herself another cup of coffee. Fresh decoction once again. Came back and sat down crosslegged again. Nursed her coffee for a long time. She looked straight in front of her, eyes steely with determination. It was now five in the morning. Seetha set the alarm for seven and got back into bed. She fell asleep almost immediately.

Chapter 27

As soon as Amit saw Seetha, his mind went into overdrive, working furiously.

He could simply ignore her. She was just an IT professional, one of the droves that India produced. He had picked her up from her humdrum world and given her a taste of the high life. He might have been a little inconsiderate in abandoning her yesterday but someone must have dropped her back. If she had had to face a little inconvenience – too bad. That was how life was. If now she planned to put on a 'hurt and wronged' act, the best thing to do would be to simply ignore her. He had too many good things going for him and was not going to waste his time coddling and consoling an ambitious climber.

On the other hand, she had been good fun and pleasant company. And maybe she was not particularly upset. Maybe she had had a wonderful evening and had not really missed him. And if she was a little miffed, he would certainly apologize and she would most likely be very glad to have him as a friend again. She was very unlikely to have any friends at all in the circles he moved in. He was on a roll and he was confident he could handle a little feminine sulking.

He tapped the shoulder of the elderly gentleman (North African? Middle Eastern?) in front of him and told him that he would be stepping out for a minute and could he please keep his place in the queue. The gentleman nodded vigorously but it was uncertain what he had understood.

Amit went up to Seetha and put out his hand.

'Hi, Seetha. I guess we lost each other yesterday at the party.'

Seetha couldn't resist the opportunity. She ignored Amit's outstretched hand. She folded her own hands in a coldly formal namaste.

'I just learned yesterday that that is the way to greet those who aren't really your friends.'

Amit was puzzled. What did she mean? This was not how

he had intended the meeting to begin. He tried to gain control again.

'Not sure what you mean but I hope you had a good time. Did you try the Nawabi Gosht? It was lipsmacking good,' and Amit brought the fingers of his right hand to his mouth and gave them a loud kiss.

'I am a vegetarian. I don't like killing animals, cutting them up into little pieces and eating them. I guess you do.'

'Look, you seem to be upset. What happened? Didn't you have a good time? Did I do anything wrong? I'm sorry if I did,' said Amit, putting a hand lightly on Seetha's arm.

Seetha recoiled with a start, pulling away her arm. 'Oh, I had a wonderful time. And I learned so much. I learned that the embassy can arrange invitation faxes for some of our country's favoured sons. I learned that it is not polite to speak about anything faintly intellectual at such exalted gatherings. I also saw that eleven in the night is the best time for some people to begin working on business plans.'

Amit gave up all attempts to appease Seetha. He let it rip. He let the bitch have it.

'I think you are jealous, dolly. Jealous of Rita, jealous of me, jealous of the whole world I let you peek into yesterday. Creep right back into the world you're familiar with, drudge for sixteen hours a day, grovel for your next pay rise and finally go marry a bank officer in Madurai chosen by your father and raise three little monsters in your grim, tight-assed image.'

'Don't worry about me. I'll manage very well. Thank you. But before I creep back into my world, I am going to do all I can to thwart your slimy, thieving plans which, unfortunately for you, you and Ratnesh let me have a glimpse of yesterday. And I'll make sure honest men like Harish don't get mixed up in your swindles. I'll be talking to him. And I may find it necessary to talk to the Visa Officer too about Ratnesh and also perhaps about all the unusual faxes of invitation you have got from people who don't know you.'

They had both raised their voices and many heads were turning their way. Seetha turned away from Amit and looked straight ahead down the queue. Amit, at a loss for words, slowly went back and regained his place in the queue. The old gentleman welcomed him with another series of nods.

It was now exactly nine and the ritual of the opening of the door to the visa section was under way. The queue shuffled forward slowly. Amit was thinking about Seetha's words. How much of his plans with Ratnesh had Seetha had she been privy to. He could remember that both he and Ratnesh had been expansive at lunch. But the bitch wouldn't really have the guts to try and disrupt his plans. And what could she do? But maybe she would try. She did have a terrifyingly determined look on her face and her eyes were popping out with rage. She was a weird one. An unpredictable witch. He would warn Ratnesh. And what did she say about talking to the Visa Officer? The Visa Officer would not take cognizance of what one applicant said about another. He should not. And anyway there was nothing wrong in the embassy helping Indian citizens promote their business interests.

Amit got past the security guard with a minimum exchange of words, passed through the metal detector (which failed to beep even though he had a large metal buckle on his belt, and was carrying a metal pen and a leather briefcase with metal fasteners), climbed the single flight of stairs, joined the queue in front of the counter in the Visa Hall and finally submitted his application along with his faxes of invitation. He was asked to wait.

He saw Seetha in her turn talk to the man behind the counter. He saw her smile and look at her watch. It looked as if he she had been asked to come back later. Amit saw Seetha leave the room and go down the stairs. Was she really going to stand outside to stop Harish and talk to him?

Amit sat in a chair at the back of the Visa Hall lost in thought. Rita, his father's message, the DCM and his crew fawning at him, Ratnesh and the distinct possibility of having found a way to siphon money back to India – all were pleasant recollections. Now and again though, his brow furrowed with worry about the explosive harridan who'd just descended the stairs. He should never have invited her to the party. How would the Visa Officer react if Seetha told him that all the faxes had been sent on demand last night, the senders not knowing Amit and having no great interest in meeting him? The Visa Officer would certainly give Amit a chance to explain. And Amit's explanation would be simple. Yes, the embassy arranged for the faxes. That was their job – to facilitate business meetings for Indian businessmen. The Visa Officer would surely not have the gall to reject a visa applicant vouched for by the country's ambassador. Not possible. Amit breathed a little easier.

What about Ratnesh's visa application? What could Seetha do to stop a visa for Ratnesh? Even if she repeated verbatim to the Visa Officer all that Ratnesh had blabbered at lunch yesterday, would the Officer listen? Should he? Of course not. And anyway Ratnesh's tale as told by him at lunch was too bizarre for the Visa Officer to think it plausible. The Visa Officer would only be left wondering about Seetha's motives. And even if Ratnesh's application was rejected, it may not be such a bad thing. Ratnesh was useful in Brussels. Amit did not need him to be in London. The thought of Ratnesh's company in London was not a pleasant one.

Suddenly a thought came into his mind. Two can play your game, little smarty pants.

Amit remembered that Seetha had told him that she had given the Visa Officer the phone number of a professor from JNU – Raghunath, if he remembered right – who had agreed to act as a reference. Well, now Amit would arrange for another letter of reference. The bitch would learn that when the cauldron begins to bubble, it can be the witch who's pushed in.

Amit rose and went to the counter and asked the officer for the fax number of the visa section. He wrote it down, went back to his seat and took out his cell phone. He was about to dial when he saw the large sign on the opposite wall informing him that the use of a mobile phone was strictly prohibited inside the Visa Hall. The Belgian officer behind the counter had also mysteriously sensed that Amit was going to use a mobile phone. For once he was looking up and glaring at Amit, daring him to make a call. Amit put the phone back in his pocket, rose, ran briskly down the stairs, went out of the building and took out his mobile phone.

He saw Seetha sitting at a cafe table on the opposite pavement. Ignoring her, he looked at his watch. Nine thirty. Two in the afternoon in Delhi. A good time to call. Amit called Mukesh, his uncle's personal assistant. Mukesh would know the best way to put it across to the vice chancellor of JNU. A minister's personal assistant was usually good at this sort of thing.

He got through to Mukesh on his third attempt. Mukesh asked a few questions and then said that he would do his best. Satisfied, Amit walked back into the visa section without another glance at Seetha who continued to sip her café au lait and watch the road.

Chapter 28

Ratnesh had spent the last evening and night at Hamid's. Hamid had been more expansive and welcoming than on the previous evening. Perhaps he was a little remorseful about the previous night - at having so unceremoniously turned Ratnesh out into the cold Brussels night. One again they had swapped yarns, first over sweet tea, then over sweet tea laced with vodka, then finally over neat vodka. They both knew that the other was exaggerating. It was simply a pleasant way to converse and spend the evening.

This time most of the conversation was about the difficulties people found in going legit. Hamid regretted that in Europe, governments and law enforcement agencies aided by all kinds of technology and databases, were increasingly unforgetting and unforgiving. That virtually made a criminal stay a criminal for life. Ratnesh told Hamid about India's underworld and the relative ease of moving to legitimate business there – the dons of Mumbai who now financed film-making, the old bandits of Uttar Pradesh who owned and farmed thousands of acres, the kidnapping kings of Bihar who now ran transportation companies and the corrupt politicians of Tamil Nadu who put their money into setting up large breweries or running television channels. Both Hamid and Ratnesh shared a world view in which crime was just another profession. Not a particularly attractive profession – the returns were uncertain and the risks were high. But it was one of the few professions open to people of all races, all backgrounds and any or no level of education.

Warmed by the similarity of their philosophies, Hamid was moved to offer Ratnesh a spare bed for a night. Past midnight, he took Ratnesh to a large room with three beds and a single radiator. Two of the beds were already occupied by Hamid's nephews. Hamid roused one of them from the bed nearest the radiator, gave that bed to Ratnesh and sent his grumbling nephew to the third bed near an uncurtained window.

Ratnesh had risen at eight, woken by one of Hamid's

nephews bringing him a piping cup of tea. Ratnesh drank the tea, washed, thanked Hamid, embraced him and left for the embassy. Not all the circumcised were bastards. Perhaps it was only those from Pakistan, figured Ratnesh. His day had begun well.

Outside the embassy, just as he was about to step inside the visa section, he saw Seetha sitting at a café table on the opposite pavement. Full of good cheer and ready for a little, harmless banter, he crossed the road and came up to Seetha.

He greeted her in English, 'Good morning, Seetha madam, today in Western clothes you look like very big executive in multinational company. But to tell you truth, yesterday you looked more better in sari. A woman looks beautiful and womanly only in sari, even ugly woman.'

Seetha continued to sip her coffee and look intently at an old maison de maitre across the road.

Ratnesh was surprised and wondered if he had said anything wrong. He thought he knew what. 'Sorry, Seetha madam, if I said wrong thing. My English not good like you. When I said ugly woman I was talking about other people like that one across the road in the green dress. You are beautiful in any dress. Only even more in sari.'

Seetha sat still, not showing any sign of noting Ratnesh's presence or his contrition.

Ratnesh gave up. God knew what the snooty cow was thinking about. He wondered if he should bring his hand in front of her face and make an internationally recognized sign of contempt involving two fingers. He decided against it. Amit liked the stuck-up book bag and he did not want to offend Amit, at least not now.

He entered the Visa Hall, went up to the counter, informed the officer there that he was ready to be interviewed and was told to wait. He saw Amit and went up to him with a big grin.

'Yaar Amit, your friend, the beautiful Seetha, seems to be in a rare mood today. I went up to her and she completely ignored me. She was looking at some stupid old building across the road and seemed to be counting the number of bricks in the facade.'

'Sit down, Ratnesh. The girl is mad. Let me tell you what

happened.'

Ratnesh sat down and Amit related the events of the last twenty-four hours. It focused on Seetha and was his version of course. Amit repeated verbatim Seetha's threat to talk to Harish and the Visa Officer.

Ratnesh was relieved. He had never liked Seetha but had suffered her because of Amit. Now, he was free to dislike her and treat her in a way that came naturally to him.

'This pussy is getting too big for its boots. She needs a whiff of the real world. I'll make sure she gets it. Give me your mobile phone. I need to make a call to Hamid, a friend of mine.

Ratnesh took Amit's phone and left the building. He was back in a few minutes.

'Hamid will take care of what needs to be taken care of,' said Ratnesh grimly to Amit.

Amit did not ask for details. When Seetha was taught her lesson, however that may be, he hoped that she would realize that he was the mastermind and Ratnesh just the tool.

Chapter 29

Seetha was on her third cup of coffee. It was cold on the sidewalk and she wondered if she should move to a table inside but decided against it. She needed to look for Harish. Besides her table caught what there was of the weak winter sun. The waiter presented her with a bill each time he brought another cup of coffee and expected her to pay immediately. Seetha was irritated and wondered if she was being singled out for this treatment but she looked around and found him to be impartial in his mistrust. The system had its advantages. It made it convenient for her to leave the moment she saw Harish. The Belgian officer at the visa counter had told her that she was likely to be interviewed after eleven so she still had lots of time.

She was happy with her icy response to Ratnesh's flippant greetings this morning. She saw him come out again and make a phone call. He looked at her, a little sinisterly she thought, and then went back into the building.

I've almost forgotten that I have a lunch date with Luc today. Hope they give me my visa before lunch. Then it can be a celebratory lunch. A celebration with Luc. Luc won't really understand the importance of the visa for me. He thinks it is only a tourist visa. That's what I have told him. But because I will be thrilled, he will share in my happiness even if he doesn't understand what all the fuss is about. That's Luc. These Europeans don't understand the importance of visas. They don't need visas to go anywhere. It's only we Third Worlders who need them. The whites just waltz past customs and immigration desks at airports, ports and any border crossings, waved on by smiling, friendly officers who compose their faces into menacing, distrusting snarls the moment they see a brown or black face.

Where do I take Luc for lunch? Has to be an Indian restaurant. That's the only kind of restaurant where I can understand the menu and make suggestions to Luc. I'll have to order something mild for Luc, mild yet flavourful.

Something like palak paneer. I wish there was an authentic South Indian restaurant in Brussels. Maybe I'll open one after I become a famous writer. Young poets will read their poetry every Friday at lunch time. Live Carnatic music on Saturday evenings. The waitresses will wear starched white aprons over silk Kanjeevaram saris worn the madisar way.

She waited another quarter of an hour and still there was no sign of Harish. She debated about a fourth coffee but decided against it.

Moderation maketh the Man.

It was the adage her father used most frequently when she was growing up. It was used both when she was picking up her third laddoo and when she pleaded with him to be allowed another hour of television. Her father spoke to them mostly in Tamil but admonitions, exhortations, adages and aphorisms were in English. However much her hackles had risen when her father used these droppings from the Raj, they now kept popping up unaided in her mind and gave it a sort of Victorian, imperial scaffolding.

The only Indian restaurant I've been to here in Brussels is Le Punjab. The food's not too bad and the woman who runs it, Sarita, is friendly but it's hardly a romantic place. The tables are too close together and assorted Indian men, presumably Sarita's relatives, are always walking in and out of the restaurant, talking loudly. You can also sometimes see fingerprint smudges on wine glasses. Luc might form the wrong impression – even if it is the right impression – about Indians. I better take him somewhere else.

I think I should take him to La Porte des Indes. I've only see it from the outside but it looks very swish. I have my credit card so I don't need to keep on worrying and doing sums in my head as I choose dishes and order. I'm sure the tables there will be well apart. They may even have booths.

What I'd really like to do is to pick up a takeaway lunch from somewhere – maybe the Porte des Indes – and take it to the Bois de la Cambre and eat, sitting on one of the park benches there. It's so beautiful there in winter, so quiet, only a few people around.

Don't be silly, girl. The Bois is only for lovers. Arms around waists or hands in each other's pockets. Kisses at every bend in the pathway. Not the place to take your colleague or manager. Not true. I have often seen officegoers and shopgirls at lunch time with their sandwiches and cans of Diet Coke. Having a takeaway lunch in a nearby park is not unusual. I know that Dirk and Nicole from Expobel often lunch in the Parc Royale.

Okay. Decision made. It's going to be a La Porte des Indes takeaway consumed in the beautiful Bois de La Cambre. But wait. Indian food does not lend itself to being taken away in brown paper bags. It's oily and saucy and gooey. Shut up. Don't endlessly vacillate. One can choose Indian dishes that can be packed safely and hygienically in polystyrene boxes.

As soon as she got her visa she must quickly return to her safe, if dismal world of Expobel, her studio... and Luc. She could not understand and did not fit into the world of Ratnesh or that of Amit. But first there was unfinished business. Some people needed to be taught a lesson.

She saw a tall, closely cropped man in jeans and a black jacket manoeuvre a small, beat-up Citroen into a parking slot across the road and get out. He looked across at her – almost stared, she thought – and then proceeded to stroll down the road. 'Small-time French-Algerian drug dealer waiting to pick up a small packet of heroin from a contact,' thought Seetha to herself smugly.

Legs stiffening in the cold, Seetha got up to stroll down the road up to the corner and back. She reached the corner and was walking back when she saw the putative drug dealer walk towards her. He seemed to be looking across the road as he walked. Definitely a drug dealer – look at his eyes – thought Seetha. When the man was only a couple of feet away he suddenly jumped in front of her and his left hand held open his leather jacket to reveal his right hand holding a gleaming twelve-inch knife. The knife was pointed straight at Seetha's stomach and its tip pushed lightly against a button on her shirt. To any uninterested passerby, it would appear that the two of them were just standing close together and talking. The knife would not be visible.

Seetha froze. The man's black eyes were unblinking and pinned her motionless.

'Non, non, no talk with Harish. No talk. No interfere with

Ratnesh – if talk, if interfere, I kill. Very slowly,' said the man softly but with a snarling smile, the tip of the knife now pressing a little more firmly into her shirt button. And then he was gone.

She watched frozen as he ran to the car, got in, tore down the road and disappeared. The whole incident would not have taken more than twenty seconds. It seemed unreal.

Seetha was shaking violently and her heart was hammering audibly. She leant against a lamp post and then walked over to the café table and sat down again. She could not think. She hadn't even remembered to note down the number of the car.

The waiter came and asked her if she wanted another coffee. She nodded dumbly. Au lait? She nodded again. The coffee came. She paid.

The shivering was slowly settling into a cold fear. She thought of simply running away – running home. From Amit and Ratnesh. Abandoning even her visa application. She couldn't. She had submitted her passport and she needed to get that back. Perhaps she could get that later.

She thought of calling the police but what would she tell them. What crime had been committed? How could she explain – particularly in Flemish or French?

She thought of calling Luc. Dependable Luc. Belgian Luc. He'll know what to do. She picked up her mobile phone, retrieved his number and called. His phone was switched off. Tears welled in her eyes. Why did he have to switch off his phone so often? The automated voice told her that she could leave a voice mail message if she wished to. She did.

'Luc, this is Seetha and this is an emergency. I am outside the visa section of the British embassy on Rue President near Place Stephanie. I am being physically threatened by two other visa seekers – Amit and Ratnesh and their hired hitman. Please call immediately or come here if you can, please.'

When he gets the message he won't call. He'll just rush down here because it's me.

She felt marginally safer. At least somewhere in the world her assailants' names were now recorded. If anything happened, somebody would know who was responsible.

Her mind was slowly beginning to function again and

slashes of anger were now ripping through her fear. She couldn't let them succeed with such blatant intimidation. She must be brave. She must be brave. She must not alter plans.

And she was in a city in the orderly, law-abiding West. How much could Ratnesh do? Threaten again but beyond that there was little that that he could really do to her.

Here for the first time in her life, she was in a position to fight evil and she could not possibly run away. She remembered reading about two kinds of courage – raw courage and deliberate courage. It was clear that she did not have raw courage. The fact that she was still shivering, ten minutes after seeing a knife pressing against her body, was testimony enough. But she could have deliberate courage. That meant reviewing one's options, deciding what the honourable thing to do was and then calmly going ahead and doing it regardless of consequences. Gandhi had deliberate courage. He had written about it.

I can't back off now. Mustn't. If I do I'll always feel guilty, gutless. I must go ahead as I planned and warn Harish and the Visa Officer. It's even more imperative now that I do so. Now there's no longer any shadow of doubt that Ratnesh is a criminal and Amit his financier and willing accomplice.

And if they want to up the ante I can too. I can talk to Sangeetha who works for the *Times of India* or to Suresh Periappa who used to work for the *Hindu* and expose this outrage in the Indian papers. They would love a scoop like this. I can see the headlines. Minister's nephew in visa fraud. Foreign minister's nephew in money-laundering scam. Indian embassy accused of abetting visa fraud.

She noticed Harish as soon as he turned the corner. She rose and walked up the sidewalk towards him.

'Good morning, Harish. I need to speak to you. Can I take a minute?'

'Namaste, Seetha mademoiselle, bien sur. But please permit me speak Hindi. I think Seetha Hindi better than Harish English.'

'Sure. Go ahead. You speak in Hindi. I can understand but can't speak Hindi. I will speak in English. Tell if there is something you don't understand.'

'Bien sur, mademoiselle.'

'Listen, Harish, you may think that this is none of my business but I feel I have to tell you. I was listening to all of you talking yesterday and I could gather that Amit and Ratnesh wanted you to join them in a project to import saffron into Europe. Please don't get involved with them. They are not legitimate importers of saffron. They are running some kind of a money-laundering racket.'

'You think so? That is exactly what Zulfikar too thought. He thought that they were trying to bring money into India by over-invoicing.'

'That is exactly right. I'm glad the two of you came to the same conclusion. When you tell Ratnesh, he is going to think that I led you to that conclusion but never mind. The important thing is that you have thought clearly and have avoided getting involved in an immoral, dangerous project.'

'No, mademoiselle, I don't think you have understood. Zulfikar and I did conclude that Amit and Ratnesh were laundering money but we still decided to tell Ratnesh that we were willing to go ahead with the project. The money will be useful for us.'

Seetha was dumbfounded. She took a few seconds to respond.

'How can you? When you know what they are really doing? Don't you have any ethics?'

'Madam, their karma is theirs. Zulfikar and I are just importers, importing for a margin. Amit and Ratnesh are the seller and the final buyer respectively. All we will be doing is handling the logistics in between for a fee. In the world we live in, governments make laws which make some actions legitimate and others not. The Indian government and European governments too. Each government has its reasons, mostly concerned with the welfare of their more influential citizens. Naturally, these influential citizens observe these laws punctiliously. Others are not so attached to these laws. Ethics does not come into all this. Ethics is all about seeking the eternal truths and avoiding hurting others. This is my humble opinion. I am not well read and I know I have not thought too deeply about these issues.'

'Don't give me convenient pop philosophy. I'm really disappointed in you. I thought you were an honest man. Now

I know that you are just a rationalizing petty crook.'

'Seetha mademoiselle, please don't be upset. I know that you have good intentions and good values. May you always be given a life which enables you to live them. I will live the life I have been given, as best as I can. And I will always think highly of you.'

Seetha turned on her heel and stormed away from him and into the visa section. She entered the Visa Hall and took a seat as far away from Amit and Ratnesh as possible. She found herself sitting next to a Chinese teenager, dressed in a tight pair of jeans and a tank top. Seetha's mind, blank with anger and frustration, escaped to familiar pursuits. 'Taiwanese. Visiting Europe, trying to decide where she should study,' thought Seetha. The girl spoke reasonable English and soon Seetha and she were deep in conversation about the new Taiwanese pop sensation Seetha had seen last week on TV Cinq. As they talked, Seetha smiled and laughed a lot, more than she was wont to. Amit and Ratnesh were staring at her and she did not want them to think that they had been able to intimidate her.

Chapter 30

Doug Evans pushed aside *The Times* and looked up as his Belgian colleague, the Assistant Visa Officer, walked into his room. It was the officer who manned the visa counter. The Belgian placed two sets of papers and passports on his table. One set were of those applications which were fairly straightforward. These had been perused by the experienced Assistant Visa Officer, found acceptable and only needed to be signed by Doug. The other set of papers were of those applications which were a little trickier, the Belgian assistant deciding that the Visa Officer needed to use his judgment.

Doug trusted his assistant's long experience and impartial indifference to all applicants. Doug signed off all the visas stamped in the passports in the first set without a second look. He then turned to the second set. There were four applications in that little pile. Looking at the four shabby blue passports, he could see that all the applicants were Indian.

Doug found Indian and Pakistani applications the hardest to judge. Fact and fiction, intent and actuality, the past and the future all blurred in the applications. There were also a fair number of cases of blatant forgery, downright impersonation and concealing of information. He normally found it necessary to interview the applicants. Often the interview left him no clearer or surer. Occasionally he would have to finally resort to statistical averaging – if he received ten plausible applications and the interviews had not been conclusive either way he would simply shrug, select and approve seven applications and reject three since that was the annual average ratio for interviewed applicants.

Doug picked up the first application – gingerly and with distaste, the way one picks up a handkerchief one might find on the road – and perused it.

Ratnesh's scruffy head stared at him from the photograph on the application. Doug remembered Ratnesh well. He was the insolent one. Doug needed to find a reason to reject this application. He looked at the attached papers. Sham's

(Ratnesh's sponsor in the UK) resident visa and work permit had been vetted and unfortunately were in order. Well, there was no alternative to interviewing Ratnesh again and looking searchingly for a chink in his armour.

The next application was Seetha's. Doug decided that Seetha looked prettier than her photograph allowed. An attached note from his assistant informed him that he had spoken to Dr Raghunath Singh, professor of philosophy at Jawaharlal Nehru University. Dr Raghunath Singh had described Seetha as '...being well-versed in Indian philosophy and a talented writer'. He had further said, 'I would definitely consider her to be one of India's more promising literary prospects in the coming years.'

Well, she could be given a visa, couldn't she? He could simply sign the application now and ask his assistant to stamp her passport with a British work visa. But he wanted to meet her again. God knew his job had few compensations and most applicants were not the kind Doug would ever consider spending five voluntary minutes with. He wrote 'Second Interview required' in a corner of the application and handed it back to his assistant.

Doug picked up the next application. It was Amit's. Four faxes of invitation were attached. So was a letter from the Indian Commercial Attaché vouching for Amit's bonafides and praying in the Indian Ambassador's name that Amit be allowed to enter Britain without let or hindrance. Doug's assistant pointed out to him that all four faxes were identical in wording. Obviously stage managed. God, why did they have to be so crude? There was no escaping an interview here too.

The last application was Harish's. The assistant pointed out that all Harish's papers were in order but he had a very small bank balance – €623 – not the kind you would expect from someone who planned to spend half of that money on a holiday in London, watching a cricket match. Doug had played cricket for his school. It would be interesting to find out how much this Harish really knew about cricket. Interview, wrote Doug on the application form.

Doug moved towards the interview room with all the papers and asked his Belgian assistant to send in the first of the applicants – or was it gladiators? If the applicants were the gladiators, what was he? Not the lion. No, he was the Emperor. His to sentence and his to reprieve. The lion was the system. Happy with this grimly satisfying metaphor, Doug opened the door of the interview room, placed the papers on the table, sat down and idly looked around, waiting for the first applicant to enter. As he waited, his left hand drummed a slow tattoo on the table. Maybe that is what the Caesars of old had done too.

Soon after he had come to Brussels he had written a note to the powers that be suggesting that the interview rooms be designed by someone less paranoid and be made brighter, friendlier and less intimidating. The note had elicited no reply and Doug had not bothered to pursue the matter. Now, having interviewed applicants for more than a year, he would be glad to retract his earlier note if anyone higher up bothered to ask. He liked and needed the safety of the bullet proof glass with the angled vents. On three occasions he had had applicants, seething with rage, attempting to smash the glass and get at him. One huge Serbian, his visa denied for the third time, had stood up on his chair and had attempted to squeeze his head and right hand through the six inches between the top of the glass and the false ceiling and hit him on the head. Doug had pulled his chair back just in time. The police had been called. They had let the Serbian off with a warning and had advised Doug to extend the bullet proof glass all the way to the ceiling.

Doug heard the door open on the other side. He saw Ratnesh come in and sit down. Ratnesh did not offer a greeting and Doug was equally polite.

'Mr Ratnesh, I need some convincing evidence that you do not intend to stay on in Britain after the expiry of your six-month visa. Can you offer any?'

'Not many Indians want to stay Britain one second longer than they must. Me too. I am going to London to meet my friend Sham who I have not seen long time. I think we both happy to spend one single week together. After that, Britain has no pull for me. The weather is cold and the people not friendly for Indians. Of course not you. You are warm and friendly man. Also, you can see that I have confirmed ticket back to India for the 28th, ten days future from today.'

All this was delivered in a flat monotone. Doug wondered why applicants could not simply be normal. They either grovelled or were insolent. Insolence came naturally to this one.

'Mr Ratnesh, if I reject your application, will you return to India or stay on in Europe?'

'Mr Officer, I don't think you will reject application. After all I have all papers and meet all requirements. If you reject my application, what I do, I say humbly, is none of your business. But also, if you reject my application, I will not take this lying down. I will fight against this injustice. I will first write to Home Office. Then I will contact honourable Members of European Parliament from Britain. Next I will contact many honourable organizations in your country – 'Immigrants are just like us', 'Britons Against Racism', 'Give Others a Chance'. Other names I have forgotten. There are many others forums I can go to but I will decide as situation unfolds.'

'Mr Ratnesh, how much money will you be carrying with you to London?'

'Mr Officer, I don't normally carry much cash with me. I will carry thirty-forty euros only. Why should I carry more? My ticket on Eurostar will be bought by your own countrywoman, Ms Margaret Whatmore – she is my very close friend – and Sham will meeting me at Waterloo station so I don't need any more money. If I need any much more I will ask my company in India to send through bank or Western Union.'

Doug winced at the name of Margaret Whatmore. He had met her on more than one occasion. She was the doyen of the liberals among the expatriate community in Brussels. She campaigned energetically in support of vegetarianism, wind power, vanishing whales, mistreated pets, deported Nigerians, Aboriginal culture, the right to wear headscarves, plainsong, the cancellation of Third World debt, organic farming, public radio, Finno-Ugric languages, the right of speech for radical Muslim clerics, the Dalai Lama and the legalization of marijuana. She opposed big chemical companies, big dams, big shopping malls, racism in football, cigarettes, nuclear power, nuclear weapons, logging companies, evangelical Christianity, SUVs, Coca Cola, the WTO, the World Bank and of course everything American. She was most often harmless but she had nuisance value and was the daughter of a peer. Doug did not want to see her leading a street protest outside the British embassy.

'Mr Ratnesh, what is the total value of your assets in India?'

'My assets are not financial only. I have love and admiration of thousands of dispossessed in India. I have secret respect of many political leaders in Bihar. Even if you want to know about financial assets I have lots. Only it is not all in my name. In India we have system called benaami system. We put money and houses and wealth in name of trusted friends or relatives or servants. That way, no one, not upper caste peoples, not Income Tax peoples, no one angry or jealous of you. Including benaami money I am mahacrorepati – multicroreman in English.'

Doug wrote down in the section for Official Use: 'Applicant is unable to offer any tangible evidence of assets.' A small skirmish had been won but was it sufficient to throw out the application? Doug needed to think a little more.

'Well, thank you, Mr Ratnesh, it has been such a pleasure talking to you. I will make up my mind, consult the rule books and let you know by around three in the afternoon today. You may leave.'

'Thank you very much, Mr Officer, Myself much honoured to talk to you. I hope to see you again – in London.'

Doug stared at the featureless wall for more than a minute after Ratnesh had left. The interview had left him with two opposing feelings. On the one hand he wanted to immediately throw out the visa application of this impudent, cold and calculating scoundrel. On the other hand he had a glimpse of the world Ratnesh came from, the world Ratnesh had fought through and Doug could not but have some sneaking admiration for the bold, cocky, cheeky street fighter. He did make a refreshing contrast to the crawlers, the kneelers and the cringers he had to interview most days.

Doug looked up at the ceiling and thought a while. He could justify a decision either way. He chose to make that decision after completing the other three interviews.

He picked up the phone and asked the assistant to send in Seetha.

Seetha knocked, entered and greeted Doug with a loud and cheery 'Good morning, sir.'

'Good morning, Miss Subramanium, er, Seetha. One of my colleagues has spoken to the reference you gave us, Professor Raghunath Singh of the Nehru University. He has some nice words to say for you.'

Seetha smiled prettily.

Doug knew that he had all he wanted to make a decision. Seetha might think so too. He felt obliged to give Seetha a reason for continuing the interview.

'Since you don't have a formal degree or any qualification in philosophical studies, I need to be completely convinced that you have the knowledge of philosophy required to write this book. Professor Singh's recommendation does help but I would like to ask you a few more questions too.'

'Sure. I'll answer them the best I can.'

'Yesterday, you talked about Indian thought. And the impression I got was that Indian thought was a single cohesive body of thought. On the other hand, a friend, just returned from India, told me that Indian, Hindu thought is very diverse and that you have your splinters, slivers and sects just as Christians do. '

'All Hindus accept the authority of the Vedas as also the texts up to and including the Upanishads. It is after the period of the Upanishads that the differences begin in the period of the schools. There were six major schools of interpretation and they were very diverse. All of them swore allegiance to the Vedas, the existing body of Hindu scripture, and hence were known as orthodox schools. All of them accepted the foundations of the Upanishads – the existence of Brahman and the need for liberation and they built on and around these truths.'

'You called the schools orthodox schools. Does that mean that there are other heterodox schools?' asked Doug. After Ratnesh, he felt he deserved a good half hour of Seetha. He stretched out his legs under the table. His eyes crinkled and his mouth pursed. His classmates at school would have recognized that look, not his colleagues in the visa section.

'Yes, Buddhism and Jainism are what are referred to as heterodox schools because they do not accept the authority of the Vedas. I'll come to them. Please let me begin with the orthodox schools.'

Doug waved her on with a very slight movement of his right hand.

As Seetha went on and explained the six schools of interpretation, one by one, Doug let his thoughts wander. He did not want to make the effort to follow the details. He was just enjoying the broad sweep and the chance of a little reverie.

As for Seetha, she was one of those teachers who could continue teaching a class, unmindful of the fact that all the students had left.

Doug regained interest when Seetha began speaking about the school of Yoga. Now that was a word he was familiar with.

'Another of the schools was the school of Yoga. It was based on the writings of the sage Patanjali. Yoga's a method to grasp the higher truths, to attain Brahman. Severe disciplining of the mind is Yoga's method. Yoga believes that the intuitive powers of the mind can be focused on the truth only when the mind is freed from wandering. Yoga has been defined as chitti-vritti-nirodha, which literally means "cessation of all modifications of the mind".'

Now Doug was a little confused. Wasn't Yoga really some kind of Eastern aerobics? Gymnastics in very slow motion?

'Of course, before one can even control one's mind one must learn to control one's body. This one does through mastering various aasanas or postures as also pranayama which means the control of one's breath. This part of Yoga is called Hatha Yoga and popularly this is what is regarded as Yoga itself.'

So that was it. What he had thought was Yoga was only a prerequisite for Yoga.

Doug had had enough of the six schools of interpretation. Before Seetha could launch into the Nyaaya school he interrupted with one last question which had been in his mind for some time now.

'Does Hinduism have its set of dos and don'ts? Are there a set of ten commandments that all Hindus obey?'

'In Hindu thought, ethics has never been highlighted or treated separately as in many other religions. Hindu thought looks for the truth. It assumes that the good will follow. Other religions seek the good. They assume that the truth will follow,' replied Seetha a little smugly.

Seetha paused and looked at Doug, uncertain if he wished her to continue.

He smiled at her and said, 'That was quite a tour de force as they say here. Educative. Well, come back at three. We should be ready by then.'

Doug had made up his mind to grant Seetha her visa. He did not want to tell her though. There was a small pleasure to be had in holding the aces as long as one could. Especially with a queen like Seetha.

It was only when Seetha had left the interview room, entered the Visa Hall and saw Ratnesh that she realized with a start that she had completely forgotten to tell the Visa Officer about Ratnesh's dark side. It was now too late.

Chapter 32

Doug rose and went to use the toilet. Not the locked toilet opening into the landing near the lift. There was a staff toilet, well inside the visa section, hidden from the prying eyes of visa seekers and safe from their disgusting personal habits. Flushing, zipping up, cursorily washing his hands, blow drying them, opening the door and stepping out, Doug walked over to the coffee machine and poured himself a cup of black coffee in a paper cup. Till as recently as ten years ago officers had used monogrammed china at the embassy but all that now seemed a distant dream.

He looked at his watch and saw that it was a quarter past twelve. Twelve thirty to one was lunch time at the visa section. He needed to finish his next two interviews in fifteen minutes. After walking up to his Belgian assistant and asking him to send in the next applicant, Doug want back to the interview room and sat down. He looked at Amit's papers. All clear. The NOIDA branch of the State Bank of India had sent a fax detailing the financial assets of Trehan Foods. They were very considerable indeed. Not benaami assets if that was the word the scoundrel Ratnesh had used. Amit was Director of Trehan Foods. The Indian embassy had also strongly supported his application.

The application should have been automatically accepted had it not been for the identical, obviously orchestrated faxes of invitation. Applicants were not expected to ask correspondents for letters of invitation with the express purpose of producing them in the course of their applications for visas. Business applicants must have correspondents in the UK who genuinely wanted to meet the visa seeker and explore business possibilities. In which case they would have indicated in some form – email, fax or letter – that they were looking forward to meeting the visa seeker in the UK. That correspondence was what Visa Officers wanted to see. And here were four faxes that had clearly been dictated by a single person – and judging by the floridity of the English, that person was likely to be an Indian bureaucrat. Doug read one of them.

> Dear Mr A. Trehan Esq.
> It has been our pleasure to have been in correspondence with you and your esteemed organization for the last few months. We would like to invite you to visit us at our headquarters in London in order to enable us to meet directly, strengthen our bonds of trust and friendship and formulate mutually beneficial plans to enter new fields of business endeavour.
> We are looking forward to your visit. It will be an honour for our organization and a pleasure for me.
>
> Rahul Premchandani
> Managing Director,
> Prestige Food Products

The other three letters were virtually identical bar the names. All four names were of Indian origin. Doug was looking forward to hearing Amit's explanation. He drummed his fingers on the table, impatiently waiting for Amit to come in.

As soon as Amit heard the Belgian officer call out his name, he had a last look at the background notes prepared by Promod and walked towards the interview room. Ratnesh and Harish both slapped his back and wished him luck.

Amit knocked and entered on being told to do so. He was wearing a natty business suit. The Rolex on his wrist caught the light from the lamp above Doug and winked.

'Good morning,' said Amit, still standing.

Doug wished him in turn and asked him to sit down. He picked up Amit's passport and turned the visa pages, looking for visa stamps.

'Mr Trehan, is this your first visit to Europe?'

'My second. I stopped over in Paris for a couple of days on my way back from Boston last year.'

'And have you ever been to Britain?'

'No. But I hope to be there this evening if I get my visa.'

'How long have you worked for Trehan Foods?'

'Little more than a year. I joined soon after completing my Master's in Business from Harvard.'

'And you are already a director, Mr. Trehan.'

'Yes. My father is the Managing Director of the company. It is a closely held company and our family owns most of the shares. My father would like to see me running the company in another five years. My current responsibility is our operations in Europe.'

'Mr Trehan, does your company enjoy business relations with any company in the U.K.?'

'Not as yet. We hope to soon.'

'Mr Trehan, how long have you know the four companies which have invited you to the United Kingdom?'

Now this was getting tricky. Promod had briefed Amit about the companies but a relationship had to be conjured out of thin air. Amit knew he had to carefully choose his words. He did not let his uncertainty show though.

'Varying periods. On an average, our company has been in correspondence with them for a few months.'

'Mr Trehan, have you or someone you know dictated these letters.'

'No. Why do you ask?'

'Is it not unusual that four different companies should send letters which are identical, word for florid word?'

Amit could feel the sweat break out. The wretched fool, Promod, must have been responsible for this crude orchestration. And more fool, he, for not noticing this obvious manipulation before.

'Let me be honest with you, sir. I know these companies well, have been in correspondence with them and can tell you what they do and exactly how we plan to work with them. But these letters – till I came to the visa section of the British embassy yesterday, I had no idea that such formal letters of invitation were needed. I don't have an office here and so could not arrange to speak with the companies directly. But the Indian embassy was helpful. Perhaps it was because my uncle is the minister for foreign affairs. I don't know. In any event, I gave them the names of the companies and told them that I needed these letters of invitation. The Commercial Attaché got to work. The faxes arrived at the embassy this morning. I think the Commercial Attaché, me and the senders of the faxes all assumed that this was just a formality.'

Good work, thought Doug. The clever devil had answered well. And he was the foreign minister's nephew. A fact he was not supposed to consider but could not ignore.

Doug could do one of two things. He could approve the visa, writing in the margin of the visa that the Indian embassy had arranged the whole business trip. Or else he could reject the visa and write in the margin that the invitation letters had been 'extracted'. In either case there was nothing more to be gained by further questioning of Amit.

'Well, that is all, Mr Trehan. You will know the status of your application at three today. Thank you.'

'Thank you, sir,' replied Amit rather dejectedly and left the room. The interview had not been the cakewalk he had thought it would be and all because of the fool, Promod, as well as his own thoughtlessness.

Chapter 33

It was twelve twenty-five when the Belgian Officer called out Harish's name. The crowd in the Visa Hall had thinned. Some applicants had left and others had stepped out for a sandwich lunch at the small Turkish sandwich and kebab stand at the corner of the road.

Harish patted down his hair, straightened his collar, and knocked on the door of the interview room.

'Come in,' boomed Doug's voice, slightly impatient.

Harish timidly entered, his shoulders slightly hunched in deference. He stood till Doug asked him to sit down.

'Merci.'

Doug flipped through Harish's passport. 'Looks like you've been a long time here but never stepped out of Belgium?'

Harish found it difficult to understand Doug's plummy accent or idiom.

'Pardon. I don't know well English. Translator possibility, please.'

'We don't have Hindi or Urdu or other Indian language interpreters on call. If you insist, I will have to postpone this interview, fix a later date, arrange for an interpreter and of course, you will have to pay costs,' said Doug with some irritation, shuffling together Harish's papers and preparing to terminate the interview.

'No, no, sir. Only French translation. Perhaps monsieur at visa guichet can do translation.'

Doug pursed his lips. The Belgian assistant did often serve as an interpreter but Doug did not like the idea of Harish making the suggestion.

'The monsieur at the visa counter has other responsibilities too. He is not always sitting on his hands, waiting to be called to interpret.'

Harish did not follow but could sense that Doug was irritated.

'Please, sir, you help me if there is a possibility. Find difficult to leave shop again again.'

May as well be done with it, thought Doug as he picked up the phone and called in the monsieur at the visa guichet.

Monsieur entered the room from the staff entrance, saw that a chair was needed, went back, fetched one and sat down at the table a couple of feet away from Doug. Monsieur had brought with him a small writing pad and a sharp pencil. He interpreted competently. His tone was completely devoid of any expression. Doug and Harish looked at each other as they conversed even if the words they were listening to were those of the Belgian assistant.

'Looks like you've been a long time here but never stepped out of Belgium?' Doug repeated his question.

'Yes, sir, I have been here twelve years but have been completely occupied by my work. In the coal mines, where I first worked I was paid an hourly rate and here in our Night Shop we cannot afford to close a single day or rather night. That is why I have not travelled anywhere.'

'Then why the sudden desire to travel to London?' asked Doug.

'Not sudden, sir. I have had this dream for a long time. To go to London, to Lord's, the home of cricket, and watch a match there. When I was younger, we used to listen to radio commentaries of cricket matches. I was listening too when India won the World cup in 1983 at Lord's. Since then I have wanted to watch a match at Lord's at least once.'

'But what about your shop? You just said that you cannot afford to close it for a single night.'

'I have a partner, Zulfikar. He will look after the shop when I am away.'

'When do you plan to watch a match at Lord's?'

'I plan to be at Lord's on May 17th. My neighbour has booked my match tickets over the internet.'

'You are applying for your visa a long while in advance.'

'Yes, sir. Wherever possible I like to finish what must be done as early as I can.'

'Who will be playing at Lord's on May 17th?'

Who would be playing that day? Harish tried to recollect.

'Two British countries – one is... I think... Glamorganshire and the other is... it begins with Su... maybe Sucks... I don't remember exactly.'

'It is counties, not countries. And you don't even seem to know who's playing whom. Why did you choose this particular match to watch?'

'I chose the day. The 17ᵗʰ of May is a Wednesday. I will travel by Eurostar on Tuesday the 16ᵗʰ. Tuesday and Wednesday are the days when customers are fewest. So I booked a ticket for Wednesday's match.'

'Which are the better teams in English county cricket?'

'I don't know. I don't know about British countries. I just want to watch cricket at Lord's. I want to watch the players in white coming on to the field. I want to watch an umpire slowly raise his finger and give a batsman out. I want to know what colour the stumps are. I hope to see lots of sixes and fours. I want to watch the players in the dressing room come out to cheer a batsman on his hundred. I want to see the statue of the God of Time on top of the pavilion. These are all the things the radio commentators used to talk about and I want to now see all these things. It does not matter to me who the two teams playing are,' replied Harish, a little agitated.

Doug sighed deeply. He did not know what to make of this variety of cricket fan.

'Mr Rawat, have you played cricket yourself?'

'Not much but yes, a little... near my home in Hissar. We even used to play matches sometimes between the different mohallas. But it wasn't a proper field. The boundaries were not marked. They were simply the trees or the houses around the maidan. We did not have pads or gloves and the umpire was the local policeman.'

Not a bad idea, thought Doug. Must suggest that to the ICC.

'Mr Rawat, do you know where silly mid on is?'

'I don't... No, I know. It is a fielding position. I have heard this also on the radio. I don't exactly know where it is because when we played we only talked about fielding near the bat or near the boundary. On the leg side or the bat side.'

Doug was warming to this unusual brand of cricket. Harish's enthusiasm was infectious. Doug smiled slightly.

'Mr Rawat, your net assets in the bank seem to be just 623 euros. Not a very large sum, you have to admit. How much will this trip to London cost you?'

'I think it will cost me around 150 Euros. I have bought a cheap return ticket on the Eurostar last week. That's one advantage of planning well in advance. I will be sitting in the most inexpensive stand at Lord's. I will be staying with my friend so I don't need to spend on a hotel bed. Within London I will be either taking the Tube or walking.'

'Have you a letter from your friend offering to put you up for the night and take care of any expenses?'

'No, I don't, Sir. I did not think that would be necessary.'

'Can you ask him to fax us such a letter in the next one hour?'

Harish shook his head slowly, 'I don't think that would be possible. Mukesh works in a small Asian grocery store and I don't know its name or number. I can only call him at home after eight in the evening. The earliest I can bring you such a fax is tomorrow by lunch. '

Doug pursed his lips. He wondered if it was worth Harish's trouble and his too. A fax would not necessarily confirm anything.

'You have been working for twelve years in Belgium and running a Night Shop for eight. Yet all you have in the bank is 623 Euros.'

'All my savings have gone into buying more stock for the shop. I think our shop today has stock worth more than ten thousand Euros.'

'Do you have an audited or certified stock statement to support that?'

'No, sir. We have kept our shop below the tax line. We have kept our stock evaluation correspondingly low – less than two thousand euros – but I will be happy to show you or any of your staff our shop. You will see that our stock is worth so much more.'

'Thank you, Mr Rawat. Please come back at three to know the status of your application.'

'Thank you, sir. I really want to watch this match. Please give me my visa.'

After Harish left the room, Doug and the Belgian Officer looked at each other. Doug smiled. The Belgian shrugged his shoulders in the usual, omnibus, Gallic expression of incomprehension and indifference and left the room.

Doug looked at the four applications on his table. He looked at his watch. It was five minutes to one.

He had to be at the Coq d'Or by one fifteen for lunch with Brenda. One of the things he had learnt in the month or so since he'd started seeing her was that she was a real stickler for time.

He had to make up his mind quickly and give his assistant the passports with the signed visas to hand over to the applicants. Only one application he could decide on. Seetha's. He would give her a visa – the work visa she wanted. The other three cases could justifiably be accepted or rejected.

There was a tap on the Staff door and the Belgian officer came in again holding a fax in his hand.

'This has just come in, Doug, and I don't know what to make of it.'

Doug looked at the fax. It was from the vice chancellor of Jawaharlal Nehru University in New Delhi. It read:

To the Visa Officer,
The British embassy in Brussels, Belgium

Dear Sir,

It has come to my knowledge that you have been making enquiries with some of our faculty about the advisability of granting visas to some of our students and associates. We would like to inform you that we have not authorized any faculty member to recommend any cases for the granting of visas without the approval of this office in writing. This has been done as a matter of abundant caution as many incidents of misrepresentation of facts have taken place in the past.

If you do need information about any of our students or research associates or an evaluation of their abilities please contact this office directly.

Yours truly,

Rudra Pratap Bhosale, PhD
Vice Chancellor, Jawaharlal Nehru University

Doug reread the letter. Now what the devil was going on? This had to refer to Raghunath's recommendation of Seetha. How on earth had the vice chancellor got to know? Neither Seetha nor Raghunath were likely to have told the vice chancellor to send a fax planting doubts about their integrity. Then who could have instigated this? And were Seetha and Raghunath really in cahoots? No, Seetha was too nice a person... or was she? He really needed to think. And decide quickly. Brenda was not one to suffer being made to wait. Lunch would be miserable.

Doug looked at all four applications. Should he apply the law of averages? That would mean approving three and rejecting one. Which one should he reject? He would love to reject Ratnesh's but that would lead Ratnesh to be most unpleasant – with God knows what consequences.

Should he apply the likeability test which his colleague Beth had told him was an acceptable and accurate way to help one decide? The likeability test was simple. It required you, irrespective of the category of visa a person was applying for, to assume that the applicant was going to eventually become a British citizen. In truth, that was what happened anyway. Then ask yourself whether you would like to see the applicant as a British citizen living in your town.

Doug applied the likeability test to the four. He would like, even love to have Seetha immigrating and living in Southampton, hopefully in the same street. He would not mind having Harish in Southampton too. Harish could run a grocery shop in some other part of town. Doug would like to pop in there once in a while and talk cricket. Amit was not his kind of bloke. But so what? Ninety percent of the British today were not his kind anyway. He could not ask them all to leave Britain. Amit, were he to immigrate, might do some good. He might set up a food processing factory of some kind – canned mackerel makhani perhaps. That would create a few local jobs.

Ratnesh would of course fail the likeability test hands down.

Doug tried to look at the applications from a purely technical point of view – the written evidence in hand. Seen that way, only Ratnesh's application was flawless. Harish had insufficient funds. Amit had orchestrated invitations. Seetha's application now had stapled to it the bombshell from the vice chancellor.

He thought a little longer and then, with a tiny shrug, picked up the phone and called in his Belgian colleague. He had made up his mind.

He made notes in the four applications and handed them over to his Belgian colleague. Deed done, he wondered wryly if he should wash his hands. He hurried to his room. He picked up his car keys, ran down the grand front staircase and left the office through the ornate front door. It was exactly one and the Coq d'Or was in Terveuren on the far side of town.

Chapter 34

The mental alertness required during the interview had left Seetha a little exhausted. She looked at her watch. Twelve ten. Had Luc got her message? In any event, even if he had not read the message he should be here in another fifty minutes for lunch as planned. She found a seat well away from her three fellow countrymen. She could do with some coffee. Was there a coffee machine for applicants in the visa section? She looked around. She could see a water fountain but there did not seem to be a coffee machine.

Maybe I can go to the sidewalk cafe just opposite and get myself a coffee. Oh God, what if that thug with the knife is around? Ratnesh may have phoned again and told him that I had spoken to Harish in spite of the warning. God, the knife point on my shirt button. I don't think he was pushing but I could feel the pressure. I can feel it still. The scene could have fitted right into a Bollywood film – except that a Bollywood hero should have dropped from the skies, disarmed the thug with a deft one-two and led me off to the Parc Royale where I would have danced a raunchy, breast heaving, thigh jiggling, butt wiggling, thanksgiving dance with the Belgian Royal Palace as backdrop. I'm still scared.

Can't imagine that this happened on a quiet street in the heart of Brussels. What are the police in this city doing? Hunting down and spearing immigrants. That's what they enjoy doing – are measured on, rewarded for.

Luc must have got my message. Why hasn't he called? Your phone is switched off, stupid. I must step out and check for messages. He may be waiting outside. Panting. Dishevelled. Anxious. They wouldn't have let him in. He must be desperately worried. How can you be so thoughtless? Run. Go see.

Seetha tripped quickly down the stairs. The security guard was reassuringly behind his desk at the reception. She opened the door gingerly and looked around. No Luc. Disappointed, she stood just outside the glass doors and switched on her mobile phone. No messages. Very disappointed. Let down.

He must be at a meeting with his phone switched off. Sometimes these meetings go on forever. Today's Friday. He may be at the weekly Senior Leadership Team meeting. Sometimes he forgets to switch on his phone again when the meeting ends. That's happened at least twice to my knowledge.

Perhaps he saw my message but couldn't believe it. Thought it a prank. Or believed it but decided that it wasn't really his business. I'm just a colleague. Not even a colleague. Just a contractor. A foreign contractor. May have thought me a little presumptuous to ask him to drop everything and come running to rescue me. That's the job of the police and I have their number – 199. No, he won't think that way. Not Luc. I know Luc. I know my Luc. It must be the meeting. I'll just go back upstairs and wait till one. He will certainly be here at one.

She went back to her seat, took out the latest copy of the *Bulletin* from her handbag, opened it, then put it down. Her mind was too full. She saw Amit go in for his interview. She saw him emerge, a little harried, she thought. Hope Doug gave him hell. Wish she had remembered to spill the beans.

Luc may want to take a can of beer along for lunch. I'll stick to orange juice. There are some things I cannot change, even for Luc. And he'll respect me for that.

At one, she put the *Bulletin* back into her handbag, got up and walked down the stairs. Halfway down the stairs she saw Luc. He was in the little reception area, arguing with the security guard. He did look dishevelled and anxious. Seetha's heart leapt like a little lamb.

'Luc,' she called out.

When she reached him he put an arm around her. 'Are you all right? I was at a meeting all morning and saw your message only at twelve thirty. I tried to call you but your phone was switched off. I rushed here but they would not let me in.'

Tears welled in her eyes but she held them back. She smiled and they stepped out of the embassy.

Standing on the sidewalk, she told him all that had happened. He asked her to take him to the exact spot where the man had accosted her. He wanted to know where the man had parked his car. He asked her if she could identify the man. His car. Did she remember its number? He asked about Ratnesh and Amit. Luc smiled when she told him that she had intended to tell the Visa Officer about Ratnesh and Amit's dishonest scheming but had forgotten. She told Luc all she knew. Mechanically, almost in third person.

Luc told her that an option was to call the police. The police would arrive in a couple of minutes. If she lodged a complaint, the police would probably take Ratnesh and Amit away for questioning. But then, later, they would be let off in the absence of hard evidence. It might, though, serve the purpose of warning them to keep off.

The other option was to forget the incident. Ratnesh and Amit were unlikely to cross her path again. They were also unlikely to bother to trouble her again, especially if they got their visas and were out of the country.

Luc said that Seetha should choose but that he personally would think the second option to be the better choice. Seetha agreed with him. She would have agreed with anything he suggested. She trusted him.

They crossed the street and got into Luc's car – a maroon Volvo sedan with beige leather upholstery. Inside it felt very safe.

'Luc, I have a suggestion for lunch. I hope you like it. Since the Bois de la Cambre is beautiful in winter, we can pick up a nice Indian lunch from La Porte des Indes on Avenue Louise and then drive down to the Bois, park, walk down to the lake and eat, sitting on one of the park benches by the side of the path which runs around the lake. It is a still, sunny morning and it's always very pleasant in the Bois.'

Luc agreed instantly.

Luc manoeuvred the car out of its parking space. Seetha noticed a white envelope in the recess under the glove compartment. She couldn't help noticing the single word written on the cover in Luc's bold hand – Anna.

Anna may be a sister, an acquaintance, a colleague. The envelope may have a cheque in it and Anna may be the concierge.

Don't fool yourself. This is the way the cookie crumbles...

Glad it happened so soon without more hurt. Stupid girl.

Acting like a love-sick teenager. Building castles in the air. My sandcastle knocked down by Anna as she walks down Knokke beach with Luc, fair hair flying in the Channel breeze. His arm around her slim waist. Joking in Flemish about the French. In the end we all prefer our own. I'm just an interesting, amusing, exotic friend. Not even a friend. Just a colleague.

What cookie? What castle? They don't exist. Never did. I'm just Luc's office colleague and friend. Always thought so. Always was so. I enjoy Luc's friendship. The concern of a good man for someone come from a distant land. Good, stable, long-term, limited-expectation friendship. Shared interests. Laughter. Makes work enjoyable. A dependable and decent friend – eesh. I know nothing about his personal life and it's no business of mine. I'm not curious either.

I think Anna must be the concierge. I don't think she is anybody special in his life.

They went into La Porte des Indes. When Seetha told the waiter that they wanted to order 'au partir', they were shown a table, handed menus and offered complimentary glasses of the house wine. Seetha demurred but Luc accepted. Luc took one look at the elaborate menu and asked Seetha if she could please choose and order for him an appropriate small lunch. Seetha said she would be happy to help but did he mind sharing dishes as Indian food was not really served in individual portions. Luc replied that he didn't mind at all and that he'd love to leave the ordering entirely in Seetha's hands. Seetha frowned in concentration over the menu and finally chose a small meal for the two of them, remembering to tell the waiter to make every dish as mild as possible. For once, she did not let the cost of a dish be a factor in its selection or rejection. This was a lunch with Luc.

Seetha was glad that she had brought Luc to the Porte des Indes. It was certainly very nice and the waiter was helpful and polite. The walls had large photographs, prints and paintings showing slices of India as it had been two hundred years ago. There was a hookah in a corner. One wall sported a collection of swords. The chairs had velvet upholstery. Luc said that he felt like a maharaja.

Their lunch arrived, neatly packed in brown paper bags. They walked down to Luc's car. She felt secure with him around. He was very solicitous of her. He walked close behind her. Seemed to be shielding her. Like a big bodyguard. She felt like a maharani.

Luc parked by the side of the road running around the Bois. They got down and walked slowly down the tiled path leading to the lake. It was a beautiful, clear, winter morning. A blue sky with just a few puffy white clouds. A still, sunny day. The lake was frozen white. Luc took off his overcoat and tossed it over his shoulder, holding the collar with his thumb and index finger. Seetha kept her overcoat on. She had her gloves on too.

On this working day, there were very few people around. A few lunchtime joggers. A grandfather come with his granddaughter to feed the pigeons near the lake. A man in a suit – Seetha decided that he was an investment banker – sat on a bench, reading a financial paper and eating a sandwich lunch. A young couple, so absorbed in each other, they missed a small step in the path. The girl tripped. She giggled as the boy held her from falling. He continued to hold her by the waist as they laughed and walked on in a meandering love-drunk path of their own, partly on the frost covered grass and partly on the tiled walkway. An artist in a red sweater stood in front of an easel, sketching. As they passed him, Seetha peeped at his sketch. The artist had painted a fantastic monster, slouching at the edge of the lake.

They reached the lake and took the path which went all the way around it. A sign in French and Flemish warned them and everyone else that it was both dangerous and forbidden to either walk or skate on the ice-covered lake. They came to a small bench by the side of the path. An empty, crushed can of Pepsi had been left inconsiderately on the bench. Luc picked it up and put it in the garbage bin nearby. They sat down and took out their brown paper bags.

She helped him with the food. Telling him the name of each dish and explaining the ingredients. They had ordered palak paneer, kadai gosht and kulchas. Luc pronounced the food 'awesome' but Seetha could see that the spices had brought tears to his eyes. She opened a can of Pepsi for him.

'Do you remember, I told you that there was something I wanted to speak to you about?' asked Luc.

In the excitement of the morning, Seetha had forgotten but now remembered. 'Yes, I do,' she replied.

'Yesterday morning I was speaking to your manager at Datasophy, Ohrie – our usual weekly status call, and he asked me if the application design would be signed off by the end of next month. I told him that that was what I expected. He then told me that if that were so, you should be able to return to Chennai early in February to lead the development team there. You would probably need to make just one more visit here and that should be during the application testing and implementation phase, perhaps around November. I suppose he has already given you an indication of this.'

Seetha wondered what was coming. Was Luc unhappy with the pace of work?

'Now I have been thinking, and I have discussed this with Timmerman, the IT manager too and we feel that this being an important application for us, perhaps our core application, we need to do all we can to ensure a smooth implementation. The implementation phase may itself take more than a year. After that, it is very likely that each year we will have to make a few design changes to keep up with changing business needs.'

Was Luc about to suggest an extension of Datasophy's contract? That would be good news. Ohrie would be happy and she might get a raise or at least a bonus.

Luc got up and stood in front of the bench, the better to look at her while speaking. He took a bite from the kulcha rolled up in his left hand and continued. Seetha remained seated.

'That being so, we feel that Expobel needs a knowledgeable Business Analyst on its rolls to liaise with the analysts from Datasophy as well as other contractors. The person will effectively be responsible for the smooth implementation, the running, the maintenance and the periodic updation of our core application.'

Seetha thought she could see what Luc was driving towards. A thrilling tingling slowly spread through her.

'I think that you should be that person. We would like to hire you in Expobel, as an employee. You will work for me. Expobel pays reasonably well and I'll make sure that you get a fair deal – on par with our European employees here.'

God. I can't believe this, God. Now girl, you don't be in an indecent hurry to accept. And there are some moral issues to be sorted out too.

'Thanks, Luc. I'm honoured. What comes to my mind immediately is that this would be a little unfair to Datasophy. After all, I work for them. They deputed me here. They have treated me decently. I can't leave their little steamer simply because I'm offered a job with a cruise liner at our first port of call.'

'You're right. I appreciate your concern. Naturally I will speak to Datasophy – to Ohrie. Only if they agree to let you go will we be making you a formal offer. I would think that Ohrie may not be too disinclined. Your being at Expobel will, in all likelihood, mean a long-term partnership between Datasophy and Expobel. A smooth working relationship. He can expect a fair amount of steady billing for a few years. That is finally the bottom line for any business organization.

'We will arrange for a fresh work permit for you. You will be taken as a permanent employee. "Dureé indeterminé" as we say here. You will get a new residence permit. If you stay with us for five years you can become a permanent resident. If you stay here for seven years you can become a Belgian citizen – if you choose to. I'm not sure you will,' added Luc smilingly.

This is what I want. This is what I think I want. Even if I do want to write philosophy, I can do it here. While keeping a steady job. With Luc as my manager. Luc must think well of me. I know he likes me. Pinch yourself, girl. The good times are beginning to roll. You don't need the British visa now. The stupid, snotty, snooty British with their absurd visa rules, their locked toilets, their rear entrances and their pompous Visa Officers. 'Does Hindu philosophy have its ten commandments?' Stuff your question, you know where, dear Mr Visa Officer of once-great Britain.

Give a calm, considerate, reasoned answer. Don't act like a sans papier from Gautemala who's just been shown a gap in the Mexico-US border fence.

'Luc, I'm really flattered that you think well enough of me to make me this offer. I can't thank you enough. For me, this is a big decision to make. One of life's big forks. I need to think it through. Talk to my father. Give me the weekend. I'll let you know on Monday.'

'Monday will be fine. On Monday morning I should also have talked to the people in HR and be in a position to give you an idea of your remuneration. I don't think it will be less than three thousand five hundred euros a month.'

Three thousand five hundred euros! I live on a thousand now. The first thing I'll do is move out of the black hole of Brussels where I now live. There are some beautiful studios in the Des Etang area. We're moving up in life, girl.

'I think we should be going. Didn't they ask you to come back at three?'

Luc stretched out hand to help Seetha up from the bench. She took his hand. He pulled her up, effortlessly. Her hand did completely fit into his.

Luc drove his Volvo up to the rear entrance of the embassy. It was two forty-five.

'Good luck with the tourist visa. If you feel unsafe for any reason when you step out of the embassy, give me a call and I'll come and pick you up. Don't take a chance.'

'Thanks so much, Luc. I know you found the food a little too spicy. I'll invite you home soon and initiate you into Indian food, good home-cooked South Indian food. Good Indian food is not all chillies and pepper. What about this Sunday evening?'

'Thanks for the invitation. I need to check with Anna and see if she's planned anything. Anna's my girlfriend. She loves all things Indian. You'll like her. Can I bring her along?'

'Of course, Luc. Do call and confirm. Bye and thanks again.'

Seetha switched off her mind. Before it could blow up.

She climbed the steps of the visa section mechanically and sat down in a chair. She took out the *Bulletin*, opened it at random and stared fixedly at it, not reading a word.

The Indian men were in the far corner. She could see Ratnesh sniggering at something Amit had said.

Five minutes later, she slowly powered her mind on again.

So he's got a steady girlfriend. You always half suspected he had. Why then, are you so devastated? He hasn't lied or betrayed you in any way. Deceived you. Two-timed you. You're acting as if he's your husband. All along he was just being friendly and you fool, you couldn't read that. You haven't learnt to read Western men. You're such a pathetic fool. You think you're a level headed systems analyst. That's a job which requires reason. Rationality. It's a job he is willing to pay you three thousand five hundred euros a month to do. He does not know what an irrational fool you are. When he offered you a job, you thought that was proof that he had strong feelings for you. Was afraid to lose you. Wanted you to stay close to him. Can anyone be more stupid? He was just making a business decision in the interests of Expobel.

Anyway, nothing's lost except some innocence. Don't dignify it by calling it innocence. Naiveté. Stupidity. Those are the right words. And the job offer still stands. A wonderful job offer with Belgian citizenship at the end of the rainbow. And he'll be your boss. A good manager, a good friend. You'll work together, laugh together, occasionally have lunch together.

But after work each day he will go home to Anna.

The job offer proves another thing. I'm good at my work and there is a demand in the West for the skills I possess. I'm sure I can get a similar job if I applied to other companies. Here or even in Britain. Britain is English-speaking and so there it should be even easier. Once I get my visa, I can move to London and work there. Simultaneously, I can begin work on my book. Maybe that is the right thing to do.

I don't think I'll have a problem in getting the visa. Doug's been quite sympathetic and I suspect he quite likes talking to me – interviewing me.

If I stay at Expobel it might all get a little complicated. I know myself. And anyway Belgium is a prim, unfriendly, racist country. I don't think I will ever fit in. London's so big. A giant human Noah's ark. With a hundred thousand of each kind. By definition you can't be racist on Noah's ark. And it's an English-speaking Noah's Ark. Nominally at any rate.

That's what I should do. Once I get my British visa I should talk to him and decline his offer politely. I should then resign from Datasophy, hand over my project properly and leave for London. I will find a job there that will pay me more than what he offered. And I will write that book. I may even find a colleague called Luke.

She looked at her watch. It was two minutes to three.

Chapter 35

At exactly three the Belgian Officer came to the Visa counter, withdrew the small catch and pushed open the small voice window in the bullet proof glass partition. He had with him a sheaf of papers and four blue passports.

In the Visa Hall the four Indians were waiting. The three men together in the far corner. Seetha alone in the near corner. All of them were silent, looking at the officer. The hour of judgment had come.

'Mr Ratnesh Kumar,' the Belgian officer called out. His voice gave nothing away.

Ratnesh went up to the counter. His strut and his swagger were obvious. He needed them to be ready for any decision. The other three Indians had their eyes glued on him.

They saw him converse briefly with the officer, they saw him take his wallet from his hip pocket and draw out same notes. He handed them to the officer. The officer counted the money and tapped a few keys on a computer keyboard. A small printer began printing. The officer pulled out the receipt and handed it to Ratnesh along with his passport.

Seetha watched as Ratnesh stepped back and studied his passport, flipping the pages till he saw the visa. There it was, shining with its lamination and holograms. She saw him turn and begin to walk back towards his friends, a large grin on his face. He made a thumbs-up sign. Noticing Seetha watching, he turned slightly towards her, lowered the thumb, raised two adjacent fingers instead and scowled in hateful triumph. Seetha looked away. Her heart now thumping loudly with anxiety and some fear.

'Mr Amit Trehan,' the officer called out. Amit went up, his heart almost stopped and his hands trembling. If he were to have his visa application rejected by an embassy which accepted Ratnesh's that would be impossible to live down. He reached the counter.

'Mr Trehan, you application has been accepted. Please pay fifty euros which is the business visa fee.'

Amit felt his knees go weak with relief. He fished out the money and paid. He took his passport and returned to his friends smiling. It was just another day at the office for this suave international businessman. He did not look at Seetha.

Seetha saw him receive his visa and that only served to make her more nervous and angry. They could not be accepting all applications. Maybe it was hers they had decide to reject. She rubbed her palms on her trousers to wipe the gathering sweat. Her right hand went up to just below her neck to hold and rub the little medallion of Lord Ganesha that her mother had made her wear on a thin gold chain.

She looked up when she heard Harish's name being called. She hoped he would get his visa too. His ethics were questionable but why shouldn't the little man get his when the big fish had got theirs. Also, as far as she could tell, he was perhaps the only one whose visa application told the entire truth.

She saw the Belgian officer talking at length with Harish. She saw him trying to make a point but the officer was shaking his head. Finally Harish turned away. As he passed Seetha to go to the far corner, Seetha stood up, put a hand on his arm and said, 'I'm really sorry, Harish.'

'I don't know why they rejected mine. I think it must be my bank balance.' Harish seemed more confused than upset. 'Now I will have to cancel my train and match tickets also. I hope I get a refund. They told me I could apply again after a couple of months but I don't know if I will.'

Harish went over to the far corner to talk to Amit and Ratnesh.

'Miss Seetha Subramanium,' the voice intoned. Seetha rose swiftly, knocking down her hand bag. She picked it up awkwardly, put it on the next seat and hurried to the counter, her right hand remaining near her neck, holding the medallion.

'Miss Subramanium, your application has not been accepted.'

Seetha's face froze in anger and disbelief.

'But why? I have given you all the details you wanted. You have spoken to my referee. You have interviewed me twice.'

'The Visa Officer has reviewed your case in detail and has

concluded that he is not in a position to recommend that you be allowed to live and work in Britain"

'I think he is making an error of judgment. Can I speak to his superior? Appeal to anyone further up?' Seetha spoke with an angry urgency.

'You may write to the Home Office to review your case. It is only in very, very exceptional cases that the decision of the Visa Officer is overturned.' The Belgian officer was expressionless.

He pushed Seetha's passport back into the bowl like window. He closed the voice gate. Seetha picked up her passport.

She walked quickly to her seat, looking straight ahead, the incomprehension and disappointment burning her ears and numbing her mind. She picked up her handbag from the yellow plastic chair she was now so familiar with. She stuffed her passport into it and ran towards the stairs.

Behind her, she could hear Ratnesh say loudly in Hindi, 'Looks as if Teacher didi has not got her visa. Maybe they found her degree in philosophy to be a forgery.'

Ratnesh's comment was met with loud laughter from Amit. Their laughter hooted her down the stairs.

She stormed out of the reception without a glance at the security guard. Outside the glass doors she hesitated for one brief moment, thinking about the thug with the knife. Let him come. She didn't care any longer.

Luc had promised her that he would come if she needed him to. She spewed him out of her mind.

She walked to Place Louise and took a tram home.

She changed into her pyjamas. She made herself some coffee. She was silent. Beyond even haranguing herself. She was in full retreat.

She sat down cross-legged on the sofa. Shell-shocked. Shattered. For many minutes – it could even have been an hour – she sat absolutely still. Then she rubbed her eyes, seeming to come to some kind of decision. Stretching, she picked up her laptop, opened it and powered it on. In a few minutes she was on the internet. She wrote an email to her manager, Ohrie: 'Hi Ohrie. I have a personal request. I find it difficult to cope with the weather and the food here in Brussels. I would like to come back to Chennai asap. Preferably next week.

The application design is almost complete. I can complete it in Chennai. Confident of getting Expobels's sign off. No further on site work required. If you agree, please confirm and I will make my travel bookings. I would also like my next assignment not to require me to travel. Would like to stay in Chennai for a year at least. Rgds, Seetha.'

Seetha needed to be among her own for a while. She needed time to lick her wounds. To overcome desire, attachment and pain. To become a practitioner of the Upanishads.